The Finkelstein Legacy

A novel by
Hugh Grant

© Hugh Grant

First published in 2013 by
For The Right Reasons
(Charity no. SC037781)
Printers & Publishers
60 Grant Street, Inverness,
IV3 8BS

British Library Cataloguing in Publication Data.
A catalogue record of this book is available
from the British Library.

ISBN
978-1-905787-29-6

Cover design by Hugh Grant

Frontispiece: By Kind permission of Willie Morrison, a fellow
market trader.
Art Work by Margaret Maclennan B.A Edin

In memory of our beloved son Paul, who loved good books.

By the same author:

A Game of Soldiers 1957-1960

Contents:

CHAPTER 1   The Croft

"Denzil!" Jean called out. No response.

She sighed, went to the foot of the stairs and called out again raising her voice, "Denzil!"

"Yes, just coming," came the reply.

"Get a move on or we will miss the bus and no mistake."

Denzil was in the upstairs bedroom admiring himself in the large full-length mirror attached to the wardrobe door. His first pair of long trousers. How strange they felt. This rite of passage from boy to young man would certainly take a bit of getting used to.

Jean, down in the living room, was checking on the fire as well as fussing over other household things with one eye on the old clock ticking noisily on the mantelpiece above the fire. Denzil eventually clattered down the stairs. Jean cast an appraising eye over him and clearly he met with her approval as she made no comment.

"Will you put Ruby in the field before you go? Don't forget to leave the top half of the byre door open as well. Best put on your wellies so as not to get your shoes dirty." The black shoes in question lay by the fire grate highly polished.

"Aye, right," replied Denzil quickly donning his well scuffed wellington boots before making for the door.

Once outside the croft house he raced across the hard packed yard ground scattering the hens that were pecking away at the corn that Jean had dished out to the birds earlier. As the hens squawked in alarm, fluttering out of his path, the large white cockerel strutted as if indignant at this unwarranted disturbance of his harem.

Denzil entered the byre allowing his eyes to become accustomed to the dim interior after the bright sunshine outside. The old familiar musky smell of stale milk, hay and manure assailed his nostrils. Ruby, the large roan cow, happily chewing her cud, turned her head at his sudden entrance with the jangling of her chain round her neck securing her to the wall of her stall.

Denzil went first to the pen at the side of the byre. He looked over the wooden barrier. The three day-old calf with its matted black coat took fright at his sudden appearance. It pranced away unsteadily on stiff legs across its straw bedding to the far side of the pen to look with large dark eyes at this strange human figure.

Turning back to Ruby's stall Denzil undid her neck chain. He gave the cow an affectionate slap on her rump and at this Ruby wheeled in her stall making for the open byre door. Once out she made for the field with her steady gait and large pendulous udder swinging from side to side. Denzil secured the bottom half of the byre door; then with Ruby now grazing in the field he secured that gate as well. Back in the house an anxious Jean was ready for the off, with a last minute check of her shopping bag as well as fixing her head scarf.

Denzil squatted down to slip on the polished shoes before accepting the clean handkerchief that Jean handed to him.

They left the croft house simply by closing the door behind them. The door was never locked. In fact like most croft houses no such key existed. They set off down the path that sloped from the house to the main road that led through the Cabrach crofting community. They had hardly gone fifty yards when Moss, their collie dog raced past them with his tail in the air clearly intent on going with them.

"Moss, here then," called Denzil. The dog ran obediently back to him. "Away, then!" Denzil said in a loud voice with a hand gesture indicating back to the croft house. Moss lowered his tail but ran back to the house as directed. Once there Moss lay on a grassy bank with his pink tongue lolling out. His amber eyes followed the two figures as they continued on their way until they met a turn in the path and disappeared from view. At this the dog lowered his head to rest between his paws and continue his silent vigil.

Just where the path joined the road stood a whitewashed croft house with a red corrugated tin roof. At this point Jean disengaged a small milk can that she was carrying in the same hand as her shopping bag. She handed it to Denzil. "Here, slip this inside Jessie's door. Don't disturb her as I doubt she will be up and about at this hour."

Denzil took hold of the can still warm from Ruby's early morning milking. Jessie MacLeod was their immediate neighbour. Widowed for some twenty years and now well into her eighties she lived alone. The crofting community had an age old way of looking after their own. Her croft fields had been taken over by Jack Munro, another crofter who took over her croft rent. He also ensured that she received a regular supply of potatoes and turnips. Jean, for her part, supplied her with eggs, milk and crowdie, while yet another neighbour popped into see her on a weekly basis with oatcakes and other baking produce. When Jessie had been an active crofter's wife she had in her turn, had helped elderly and infirm neighbours so she was simply in a sense being repaid in kind.

Jessie's only son had emigrated to New Zealand during the depression in the 1930s. He had settled there, married and had four of a family with very little likelihood of ever returning home to Scotland. Jessie's only contact with her grandchildren was occasional letters along with a framed photograph that took pride of place above her fireside.

When Denzil had rejoined her they walked for some distance in companionable silence. Jean was satisfied that they were in good time to catch the bus with Denzil still trying to get used to walking in his long trousers. The springtime sunshine made for pleasant walking. It was a time of year that Jean loved as the countryside seemed to be coming back to life throwing off the long dreary days of winter. Silver birch trees fringed the road with birdsong ringing out on all sides. Ahead of them a rabbit broke cover, scuttled across the road, hesitated for a moment before disappearing into the long grass on the other side.

In the far distance they could detect the dark blue waters of the Firth while beyond lay the high mountains to the west still speckled with late winter snow that clung to the deep corries.

Eventually they reached the old General Wade arched bridge that spanned the waters of the Rulick Burn as it flowed on to reach the Firth. At this point their secondary road merged with the main road that led onto the far north. Over the bridge a rusting metal post indicated the bus stop. Several people were already gathered there waiting. They were greeted warmly exchanging small talk with one and another. An elderly gentleman, very dapper in his business suit with a raincoat draped over his arm, lifted his hat in a smiling welcome. Mr Forrest was a retired accountant who lived with his wife in a small cottage with a well attended garden close by the bridge. Twice a week he caught the bus making the ten mile journey into the town of Inverdeen to do the books for a family bakery firm.

It was not long before the red double-decker bus swung over the bridge coming to rest at the bus stop. The bus was crowded with a lot of service personnel still in uniform returning from leave. Two young RAF servicemen gave up their seats to Jean and Mr Forrest who gratefully accepted them. Once seated and underway Mr Forrest took out his pipe and when it was lit to his satisfaction he turned to give his attention to Jean.

"Well, Mrs MacGillivray, and what takes you both into town on this fine spring day?"

Jean responded, "Quite an important day in fact. Denzil has left school at the Easter term, so he is now looking for a job. Well, I spotted an advert in the last week's Courier that the Royal Hotel was looking for a junior porter. So I got Denzil to write and apply. We got a letter back from the manager himself inviting him to attend for an interview today." At this point Jean patted her handbag as if to reassure herself that the letter was safe.

"Well done for you," exclaimed Mr Forrest removing his pipe. "Jobs will be hard to come by now that the war is over and this lot get demobbed and hit the job market." At this he gestured with his pipe stem in the general direction of the noisy servicemen that filled the bus. They fell silent while the red faced conductress with her ticket machine strapped to the front of her uniform, fought her way through the strap hanging passengers to take their tickets.

Forrest resumed, "So your lad left school at Easter. Where have the years gone to I often wonder. Mind you in only four years time when he is eighteen he will be liable for military service. Here's hoping that Prime Minister Attlee and his Labour lot steer clear of any more armed conflicts. Surely by now we have learned our lesson. When the Great War ended it was generally thought that would be the end of warfare so the soldiers came home with the promise of a land for heroes. Some bloody hope, if you'll pardon my language! They handled the peace just as badly as they had conducted the war. What did we get? Some twenty years later we are plunged into yet another bloody conflict with the same enemy. An enemy we are supposed to have conquered! Honestly, it defies belief!"

He paused at this point to relight his pipe. Jean sat back relaxed, enjoying his conversation as it helped to take her mind off the coming interview. The aromatic pipe smoke that wafted over her brought back bitter sweet memories of when such smoke had filled her own living room.

Mr Forrest picked up where he had left off.

'We all pay a price for war as we both know to our cost. You had your own sad loss whilst I am left with a permanent limp along with memories that quite often cause me sleepless nights. I suppose I was lucky in a sense as I copped my wound at Ypres after having survived the bloodbath that was the Somme.'

He fell silent for a moment before emitting a quiet chuckle.

'I was taken off the front line before ending up in a field hospital some distance behind the trenches. I mind I came round to find a Catholic padre giving me the last rites. I don't know who got the bigger surprise when I told him in no uncertain manner that I was of the Presbyterian persuasion. A few days later I was moved to some impressive chateau some miles back from the front before they decided to ship me back to Blighty.

I can tell you it was at that chateau that I saw the war in a very different light. High ranking officers were billeted there in some comfort with the best of food and wines. There they were in some style planning the conduct of the war while a few miles away men were fighting and dying in the living hell that was trench warfare! I remember after the war attending a regimental reunion. I was chatting away with an old comrade Jimmy MacPhee who had been a rifleman in my platoon. An elderly Brigadier with an impressive array of medals on his chest spotted us – well he saw our campaign medals and boomed in a loud voice, "I say, were you men with me on the Somme?" Quick as a flash Jimmy, who was always a bit bolshie, replied, "Never saw you there, sir!" I can tell you that the Brigadier didn't hang around to talk to us. Och, I packed up going to these reunions after that as I only tended to come away depressed as memories were roused that were best left in the past.'

He fell silent for a time.

'Mrs MacGillivray, I must apologise for talking so much about the war, that is what happens when you get to a certain age in life. Now young Denzil here has grown into a fine young man I must say. A real credit to you. How did he do in school?'

Jean stirred herself. 'Oh, average I suppose. But the headmaster told me that he possessed a very fine natural singing voice. If he had been lucky enough to get voice training he might even have had a professional career as a singer.'

'Well fancy that!' Forrest exclaimed, 'Coming from D.J. Donald that is praise indeed, after all he himself won the Gold medal at the Mod in Oban in 1937.'

The bus by now had reached the outskirts of Inverdeen, stopping at one or two halts to unload some passengers. Soon they swept into the busy bus depot. Several buses were coming and going while two MacBrayne buses in their distinctive livery were loading up prior to setting off on the long run to the west coast.

Denzil was the first to alight before Jean and Mr Forrest joined him. They said their goodbyes. Forrest tipped his hat to Jean in farewell.

'Well Mrs MacGillivray, I must say I enjoyed your company and Denzil, my boy, every success in your interview.'

CHAPTER 2   The Royal Hotel

On their own at last, Jean had a quick check on the large clock set above the entrance to the booking office. Time she noted was on their side. Twenty minutes to spare before the time to report to the Royal Hotel. Leaving the busy bus depot they walked up the side street that led to Hunter Street one of the main shopping areas in the heart of the town.

Inverdeen was widely regarded as the unofficial "Capital of the Highlands". The town had grown round its natural harbour. A harbour that for centuries had seen the harvest of the Caledonian Forest shipped out to foreign parts. Over the years it had slowly developed as the administrative centre for the area and now boasted a population of close on fifty thousand citizens. Naturally it provided an attractive shopping centre for not only the townsfolk but also for the many villages and farming area that lay to the west and north. The river Deen that drained the high mountains to the west flowed through the centre of the town before decanting into the Firth that led to the open sea.

The ruins of a sandstone built castle stood on a high hill dominating the town centre. The castle with its weather beaten tower still standing had been sacked during the 1745 rebellion and now stood as a mute reminder of the area's turbulent history.

The town's development had been fairly gradual until the coming of the railway in the mid nineteenth century. This permanent link with the rest of the country changed things forever. Prior to the rail link contact with the central belt of Scotland could only be made by slow horse-drawn transport over the rough Highland roads. These roads had been the handiwork of a certain military engineer called General Wade in the aftermath of the 1745 uprising. Contact with London and the south of England had been largely done by sailing from Inverdeen Harbour with the slow progress that that entailed.

Now all at once it seemed that the great wilderness of the Highlands was easily accessible. The nouveau riche spawned by the Industrial Revolution could scarcely believe their luck. They were able to quit the grimy, smoky towns where towering chimney stacks belched out their fortunes and escape to this veritable paradise on their own doorstep. Estates were bought over from grateful clan chiefs for sporting purposes. Lodges were built in remote glens while crofters found welcome employment as ghillies and gamekeepers.

This welcome development was not confined to the wealthy elite as general tourism followed quickly. Accommodation became a priority to handle this influx of visitors. The need for a quality hotel became apparent and Inverdeen rose to the challenge.

A group of local businessmen formed a company to purchase the Chisholm Arms, an old coaching inn. The inn in the town centre had started life as a halt for drovers as they herded their cattle on foot to the distant market in the south before becoming the coaching centre for the town. Horse drawn coaches used to set off on a daily basis from its yard to endure the long journey south along dusty, rutted roads.

The old inn was razed to the ground while in its place a substantial architect designed building rose in its place. It was a bold move by the far sighted directors who ensured that every feature of a luxury hotel was incorporated in their project.

On completion they decided that such a fine building should have a name that reflected its standing. One of the directors, son of a local clan chief, had been educated at Oxford and as a result had acquired a formidable old school tie.

One of his college friends had secured a post of some importance in the Government so this connection was put to good purpose.

It was eventually decided that Queen Victoria no less would conduct the opening ceremony. The Royal party were in the habit each summer of sailing up the west coast in the Royal Yacht before disembarking at Oban. They would then travel by horse drawn coach across country to holiday at their newly purchased Balmoral Estate. A break of their journey to open the new hotel would demonstrate royal approval of the enterprising tourist business now opening in the Highlands.

The hotel directors could not believe their luck and at a director's meeting it was resolved that the new hotel's name would be the Royal Hotel.

All was set for the big day. Bright sunshine set the scene with the town arrayed in colourful bunting while a huge crowd had assembled to witness the historic event. The Queen was due to arrive in her coach to be received formally by the Provost and town councillors at the Town House. From there the Royal Party would walk the short distance along High Street to the Royal Hotel to perform the opening ceremony.

However in the immortal words of Robert Burns the national Bard - "the best laid schemes of mice and men gang aft agley!"

A serious problem arose in some far flung part of the empire. It was regarded so serious that Prime Minister Disraeli along with the Foreign Secretary came north in haste to seek an audience with the Queen at Balmoral. Words to this effect were relayed to the Royal Party in transit and the upshot was to proceed to Balmoral without further delay. This would mean effectively that the hotel opening ceremony would not now take place.

Communications in those days was difficult so notice of this sudden change in plan was unfortunately not passed on to the Inverdeen Town Clerk in time.

So imagine the scene outside Inverdeen Town House. On a specially built tartan-draped platform outside the imposing building stood Provost Hector MacDonald, a magnificent figure with his bushy beard almost obscuring the gold chain of office suspended on his chest and glinting in the sunshine. Beside him stood a motley collection of councillors resplendent in their ermine finery and cocked hats. The street was thronged on both sides with expectant Inverdeen citizens and from time to time snatches of patriotic songs could be heard.

A lone horseman rode up over the bridge that spanned the Deen. He pulled up in front of the dais to inform the welcoming party that the Royal coach was close at hand. At this information a loud cheer went up from the crowded street.

Not long after the Royal coach came into view, trundled over the bridge and then to everybody's amazement carried on at some pace past the dais on down the High Street heading for the east.

The crowds cheering died away as they became aware of what was happening while consternation reigned supreme on the dais. Some spectators observed a languid wave of the Royal hand from within the Royal coach but to his eternal credit the town piper continued to play lustily on his pipes.

The sense of anti-climax that ensued was palpable. The Provost decided to make the best of the situation so with the piper in front he led the dais party down the somewhat subdued street to the new hotel. Once there flanked by the rather deflated directors he unveiled the marble engraved tablet set into the plinth of one of the columns in the hotel entrance. This ceremony completed everybody withdrew into the ballroom of the hotel to enjoy the magnificent official lunch prepared for the occasion.

The lunch started off understandably in subdued fashion but as the fine wines and drams flowed the general mood soon lifted. Stirring speeches were made and various toasts drunk to the new hotel's bright future. The Provost even proposed a loyal toast to Her Majesty so as to show no ill will.

Of course in true Highland fashion many muttered darkly that this bungled opening was a bad omen for the hotel and that no good would come of it. This was to be confounded as the Royal Hotel soon proved to be an invaluable asset to the town attracting a class of tourists that would not otherwise have been possible.

The hotel always strived to maintain its standing as the leading hotel in the Highlands. Any innovation to keep up with modern trends was actively pursued. The Royal was the first public building to have electricity installed in the town, the first to boast central heating, the first to have a passenger lift and in later years, when en suite bathrooms were all the rage, it was well to the fore.

This then was the background to the hotel that Jean and Denzil were heading to along a busy, bustling Hunter Street. It dawned on Jean that this was market day with many farmers' wives out and about doing their weekly shopping while their menfolk attended the mart. They paused for a moment by the pavement as a horse-drawn cart loaded with sacks of coal lumbered past with the begrimed coalman sat on top flicking the reins. A couple of grocery message boys on their distinctive bikes with the square grid in front to hold the box of groceries sped past shouting to one another.

Jean spotted the large Royal Hotel building at the end of the street and their pace quickened. The hotel seemed to dominate the street by its sheer size. The sandstone construction seemed to glow in the sunshine. A slated tower topped off the building where a white flagpole sported a Union Jack flag fluttering gently in the mild breeze coming in from the Firth. They were now on the pavement directly across from the Royal preparing to cross when a cycle bell tinkled and a telegraph boy on his bike whistling loudly shot past them down a side street heading towards the main Post Office.

Jean decided to take this opportunity to have a last minute chat with Denzil. She brushed his jacket and straightened his tie before addressing him.

"Look Denzil – it's almost time to report. I'm not sure if I will get a chance to talk to you before the interview. Don't worry about getting the job as there will be sure to be a lot of boys applying for the position. Just look on it as good experience and there will be other job opportunities."

This said they crossed the road towards the hotel with Jean warning Denzil to avoid the horse droppings that might soil his gleaming shoes. Jean dug deep into her shopping bag to take out the letter. Clutching it firmly they entered the imposing front door of the Royal Hotel.

CHAPTER 3   The Interview

The front door of the hotel took the form of a stone built porch that jutted out from the main building and above this portico stood two huge carved stone eagles with wings half-spread. Inside the porch was the marble tablet that proclaimed the building was opened by Queen Victoria in 1878. A tiled floor led to a large revolving door set into the main hotel building with brass fittings that glistened from years of polishing.

Jean entered first and then Denzil enjoyed his first spin through the revolving door. They found themselves in a large entrance hall and took time to get their bearings. The carpeted area seemed to go on forever with large easy chairs and tables scattered informally throughout. Impressive oil paintings depicting Highland sporting activity adorned the walls whilst a stag's head with antlers gazed mournfully down from a prominent place. The number of tines on the antlers denoted that it had been a "Royal" which seemed quite appropriate. To one side a large sweeping staircase led off to a landing before splitting as two separate staircases then set off on either side to the upper floor of the building. The broad staircase was the highlight of this impressive hallway and the landing provided a no less colourful backdrop.

Set amidst beautifully carved stonework was a stained glass window with the heraldic crests of the local clans preserved for all time.

Jean saw at the far end of the hall the reception desk with a striking floral display and a girl attired in a tartan uniform attending to a guest. They headed in that direction when suddenly they were stopped in their tracks.

"Aye and what are youse two after?" came in a loud voice.

They both turned. Just to their right was an unmanned desk with behind a wooden board set with pigeon holes and numbered keys hanging in neat array sporting a sign that read –

PORTERS LODGE. Behind the desk was a door and from this emerged the owner of the voice that had halted their progress. A burly red faced man came towards them in an unwelcoming fashion clad in a uniform that was topped by a tailcoat and a bow tie. The coat was picked out in gold braid with epaulettes and piping that led to crossed keys on both forearms denoting that he was the Head Porter.

Jean somewhat flustered brandished the letter that she was clutching and tried to explain their mission. The Head Porter rudely snatched the letter from her hand, opened it and perused the contents. He thrust the letter back into her hands.

"So you're here for the interview are you? Well let me tell you this entrance is strictly reserved for hotel guests and don't you forget it. You go out the door you came in and go round the hotel building until you see the side street and there you'll find the staff entrance – that's where you belong".

Having said that he turned on his heel and went back to the desk only stopping to ensure that Jean and Denzil were heading in the direction he had stated before disappearing through the lodge door.

Jean and Denzil were both glad to retreat the way they had come from this hostile reception and get back outside the hotel. They walked as directed round the building and found the side street where they could see a cart delivering provisions. A weathered sign read Staff Entrance. Once inside a polished lino covered corridor led them to an office staffed by several female staff. A young girl rose from her desk with a welcoming smile to attend to them. Jean's spirits rose as she reacted to the girl's welcome. She handed the letter over and explained who they were and immediately the girl left the office and conducted them to a room further into the building.

"Just wait here" she said "Miss MacLean will be with you shortly" and left them.

At the far end of the room were four boys about Denzil's age and Jean gathered that they were possibly waiting for the interview as well. They sat down in the seats provided and waited. The boys who had looked up at their entrance seemed to know each other and after looking the new arrivals over returned to whispering and sniggering among themselves.

After about five minutes had elapsed a door opened and a tall lady emerged bearing in her hand a mill board with papers attached.

"Ah – and who do we have here?" she enquired approaching Jean and Denzil.

They stood up and Jean gestured towards Denzil "This is Denzil and he has come for an interview"

Miss MacLean nodded approval and ticked off his name on the sheet attached to her mill board.

Miss MacLean's job title was personal assistant to the General Manager but in reality she was the powerhouse that virtually ran the hotel. A New Zealander she had thrown up a good secretarial job in Auckland after an unfortunate love affair and decided to take a year out and head to Scotland to check out her family roots. She ended up in Inverdeen and running short of funds had taken a position as temporary receptionist in the Royal. The position was temporary in the sense that it was supposed just to provide additional cover over the busy summer months. Her sterling abilities were soon detected and after two years she found herself promoted to her present position.

"Well Mrs Morrison – that's fine and now –"

Jean butted in – "Oh no! – my name is MacGillivray and Denzil's is Morrison. You see I'm his foster mother."

"Right oh" replied Miss MacLean "I was going to say that we are waiting for one more applicant to show up before we start interviewing. You are quite welcome to wait here but the process might take the best part of an hour."

Jean took the hint – "I have some shopping to attend to if that's alright"

"Certainly" said Miss MacLean briskly "It is now almost 10am so if you were to come back say just after 11am that would be ideal then"

With that she turned to walk back into the office and closed the door behind her.

Jean whispered to Denzil that she would see him shortly and shopping bag in hand headed out down the corridor into the side street. She hated leaving Denzil alone in that room very detached from the other group of boys but she realised that he would have to stand on his own two feet.

Denzil sat on his own very conscious of the other boys whose conversation raised in volume now that they were on their own. After a few minutes a voice exclaimed "Hey!" and Denzil turned towards the group of boys hoping that this might be a friendly overture. He could not have been more wrong. He caught the eye of the boy who had spoken and received a bold hard look before the voice came again – "Whose a Mammy's boy then?"

Denzil flushed but turned away and fixed his gaze on the wall to his front as the boys dissolved in fits of laughter. The group getting no reaction continued to speak among themselves while he sat in silence.

Suddenly the door leading to the hotel opened and a man strode in. He was tall, dressed in a business suit and carried himself with a military bearing holding in his hand a rolled up newspaper in the manner that an officer would carry his swagger stick. He did not break his stride, glanced at the boys and barked out "Good morning!" as he made for the same office into which Miss MacLean had emerged.

Taken by surprise the only one to react was Denzil. "Good morning, Sir" he replied.

The office door closed behind him. Silence ensued in his wake before the group of boys started chattering again. A few minutes later the door beside Denzil opened abruptly and another boy clearly the last applicant entered.

"Hi there Dezzy – what are you doing here? The new boy exclaimed plonking himself down on the vacant seat beside Denzil.

Denzil experienced a wave of relief at this totally unexpected warm greeting. He turned to see Alastair Gordon who had sat beside him in the Inchroy school classroom for the best part of three years and played with him in the school shinty team.

"Ally – what are you doing here? He enquired.

"Well – I would think same as you" responded Ally "this was not my idea but my old lady more or less put me under pressure to apply. My father said just to go along with it to keep her quiet."

Miss MacLean's reappearance cut short their conversation. She quickly established that Ally was in fact the final applicant and he was duly ticked off on her sheet.

Back in her office she put the millboard down on her desk. The manager John Drysdale sat at his larger desk nursing a black coffee while he signed letters that had been left by Miss MacLean for his signature. She noted wryly that he signed the letters without really checking its contents.

Major John Drysdale DSO was really a figurehead and had no real interest in hotel keeping as such. He had been invalided out of the army after injuries sustained at El Alamein in the North African campaign. Nursed back to health, he had endured an office job back at the regimental depot for about a year as the war ground to a finish, before making a decision to leave the Services. He secured the job as manager of the Royal Hotel almost right away. Life in the officer's mess had led to an appreciation of good food and fine wine along with the knowledge of how to pass the vintage port decanter. These qualities combined with certain man management skills seemed to satisfy the hotel directors.

He it was who had quickly recognised Miss Maclean's ability and had plucked her from the reception desk to be his assistant. She for her part relished the responsibility thrust upon her and very quickly her influence spread throughout the hotel departments. In time the staff came to realise that she was the power behind the throne. Any minor problem that would have normally surfaced to be dealt with by an harassed manager never reached Drysdale's desk as Miss Maclean handled it with with ruthless efficiency. She only ever told Drysdale what she felt he had a right to know.

As a result he had a gilded life – golfing three times a week with a coterie of local business men followed by a long and liquid lunch in the clubhouse and various other outside activities. Today was a golfing day so with his letter signing completed his mind was already on the first green.

"Anything fresh today – that needs our attention? He enquired rising from his desk.

"No, everything is in hand I think – so enjoy your golf." Miss Maclean responded.

He frowned for a moment before speaking – "That crowd of youngsters outside – what exactly are they here for?"

Miss Maclean looked up from her desk. "Oh them – they are the applicants for the junior porter's position. One of the porters has been called up for National Service and the boy Guthrie has gone to fill the gap leaving us short of a boots. I will interview them shortly."

"Good stuff but really that should not have to fall on your shoulders. If that head porter of ours was worth his salt he would be selecting his own staff but as we both know he would probably flog the job to whoever gave him a backhander!"

That said he headed for the door and then paused for a moment before turning once again towards Miss Maclean seated at the desk, checking stock sheets.

"I will make your job easy." He said, "Give the job to the coloured boy."

She checked her millboard - "The coloured boy? Why the sudden decision?"

Drysdale smiled – "As I came through the ante-room and he was the only one to respond and with a smile into the bargain. So he is the one for us and who knows? He might bring a splash of colour into our drab lives. Toodle-pip!" And with that he left the office.

As the office door closed behind him Miss Maclean smiled in a resigned fashion and said quietly to herself, "So be it."

She conducted the interviews almost right away giving each boy about five minutes and then informing them that she would be in touch in a day or so. When Alistair Gordon presented himself she was about to give him the same treatment.

Her opening question to each applicant had been, "Why have you applied for this job?

Alistair took her aback with his direct answer, "I really don't want the job and I'm only here to keep my mother happy."

Miss Maclean was forced to laugh, "Thank you for your honesty and this will be the quickest interview I have ever done. Best of luck to you when you find the job you want."

Denzil waiting alone outside was surprised when Alistair suddenly appeared – "OK Dezzy, I'm off the hook – best of luck and see you around" He gave a thumbs up and disappeared out of the corridor door as quickly as he had come.

Denzil was then summoned into the interview Office. Miss Maclean asked him a few questions about school and family life before putting her notepad down with some emphasis on the desk.

"Well Denzil, I am happy to inform you that you have been selected for the position. Here is a letter detailing everything you need to know such as uniform, wages, hours of duty, time off and the starting date. Please take it with you and discuss it with your guardian and then confirm your acceptance in writing to me. Congratulations and I look forward to you joining our staff. If you wait outside your guardian will collect you shortly."

Denzil withdrew from the office as directed. He kicked his heels for some time until at last the door opened and an anxious Jean with laden shopping bag in hand looked in.

"Ah. Here you are son" Denzil rose up to join her.

Once in the corridor Jean could contain herself no longer. She plucked at Denzil's arm, "How did it go? Tell me all about it."

"Oh fine," said Denzil in a matter of fact manner, "I got the job" and flourished the letter in her direction.

Jean stopped in her tracks at the totally unexpected news while a mixture of pride and relief swept over her. Denzil had carried on walking. Jean ran after him and caught his arm and together they walked out of the staff entrance into the sunlit street.

Chapter 4   Leaving Home

The morning dawned for Denzil to set off for Inverdeen to start his first job. He had difficulty in persuading Jean that it would be best for him to travel on his own. Jean had packed his case and was fussing over him as he got ready to leave.

"Here son, I've got something for you." She said.

Denzil turned and saw that she was handing him a brand new leather wallet.

"It's not much," Jean continued "Just a wee something to mark you starting your first job."

Denzil handled the wallet feeling the soft leather under his fingers and admiring the neat stitching. He opened the wallet and there nestling inside was a crisp ten shilling note.

"It's smashing!" He exclaimed gratefully "A great present but there was no need for the money as well."

"Och away with you,"Jean dismissed him, "You know that it is regarded as bad luck to give somebody an empty purse or wallet."

Denzil tucked the wallet carefully into his inside pocket before lifting his suitcase. Once outside the croft door he said goodbye to Jean and made his way down the path. In the other hand he carried the small milk can to be dropped at Jessie Macleod's door. When he reached the turn in the path he looked back to see Jean standing in her apron at the door with Moss beside giving her an enquiring look. He gave a final wave before being lost to view.

Jean stood at the door for quite a time trying to master her emotions. It was difficult to imagine that now she would be on her own for most of the time. She would miss Denzil for ever singing about the house along with the fact that she had someone else to cater and look after. She mentally resigned herself to getting used to the situation.

Her mind went back to the day when Denzil had first entered their lives. She and Duncan had married relatively late in life and, after a few years, decided to adopt a child. To this end they found themselves in an orphanage in Edinburgh after having been approved as foster parents. The matron took them on a guided tour of the baby wards. They entered a room with about six children in cots. Some were lying down, one or two crying and two were standing holding on to the bars of the cots. As they entered Jean made eye contact with the baby Denzil. He made a gurgling sound and opened his arms wide and gave what appeared to be a broad welcoming smile. This sudden action proved too much for his balance and he toppled backwards in his cot. They all laughed.

Something stirred in Jean at that moment – something she could never later quite explain. She went over to the cot and turned to the matron quickly before informing her that this was the child for them. Duncan at her side was silent before he made his feelings known. He asked her if that was the wise decision but Jean was adamant and that was that. The very next day the baby Denzil in a new carry cot was on the train bound for the Highlands. A coloured child in the Inverdeen area was quite a novelty but despite Duncan's initial misgivings Denzil was soon accepted into the community and later in the school yard.

Denzil meanwhile on his way to the bus stop left the path to put the milk can as usual into Jessie's porch. To his surprise the old lady with a shawl round her shoulders, leaning on her walking stick was waiting for him.

"Aye Denzil lad – so this is the big day then. Your Ma was just telling me the other day. Every best wish for the future and here is something for you for all you both do for me. Don't open the envelope until you get on the bus like a good lad."

Denzil thanked her and put the sealed envelope into his jacket pocket beside the new wallet. Leaving old Jessie with a final wave as he joined the road he walked on lost in his own thoughts.

He did not relish leaving Jean on her own although he knew he would be back in touch every week on his day off.

Jean for her part had assured him that he could handle the croft chores just fine. The life he had known he realised was to change for ever. Life of course for Jean and himself had changed abruptly in September 1944 in the closing stages of the war. Hard to believe that here in 1947 barely three years had elapsed since that fateful time.

Duncan MacGillivray had joined the local TA before the outbreak of war as storm clouds gathered over the European political scene. Then in 1941 as the conflict developed he decided to join for the duration of the war.

After basic training he volunteered to join the newly formed airborne forces and the Parachute Regiment in particular. Denzil remembered well running down the brae to meet him when he came home on leave. His father would sweep him up in his arms and the tobacco impregnated smell of the rough khaki battledress uniform. Duncan would stick his red beret with the silver winged cap badge on Denzil's head and together they would head for the croft house door where Jean waited with open arms.

They spent some anxious months when he was away fighting in the North Africa campaign. Nightly they listened to the war reports on the wireless and daily scoured the columns of the Daily Express newspaper.

It was with considerable relief that they welcomed him home on leave. Denzil had been intrigued that newspaper reports of the campaign referred to the fact that the German forces opposing the paratroopers called them the 'red devils'! His father explained that the paratroopers fought as infantry in their camouflaged parachute jumping smocks with a tail piece that hung down. During the battle they got covered in the distinctive red sand of that region and this allied to their fighting prowess had led the German forces to give them this nickname. Apart from that he was reluctant to go into any real detail on his experiences.

The war dragged on on as if it would never end. In September 1944 they were expecting him back on leave when

Jean received a letter. In the letter Duncan explained that some major operation was in the wind and if successful would mean a swifter end to the war than anybody predicted. All leave was cancelled but he would be back in touch when he could with more information.

One evening in mid September, whilst they were having supper with one ear on the wireless war report, a sudden announcement caught their attention. The presenter declared that on the morning of 17th September three airborne divisions – the American 101st and 82nd along with the British 1st Division had been dropped into Eindhoven, Nijmegen and Arnhem.

Supper forgotten they looked at each other in stunned silence. Denzil ran to get an atlas to see if he could identify the places named in the report. Was the Parachute Regiment part of the British 1st Division? They supposed it must be and if so then this was the 'big push' that Duncan had referred to and therefore he must be in the midst of it.

The next few days were fraught to say the least. At first everything seemed to be going well, then word filtered through the news reports that two SS Panzer divisions were offering more than stiff resistance to the lightly equipped paratroopers. To complicate matters the Allied armour had been held up for a variety of reasons and would not make it to Arnhem in time. The paratroopers held on doggedly and in the process wrote a glorious page in their early regimental history. In the end after taking heavy casualties they were forced to withdraw and the Arnhem Bridge that they had hoped to capture was destroyed from the air.

Jean and Denzil waited impatiently for news and a welcome letter from Duncan telling them that he was coming home on leave. Late in September it all came to a head. Denzil was up on the hillside behind the croft cutting bracken with a slightly blunted old scythe. Crofter never wasted valuable straw or hay on winter byre bedding for their animals when the russet brown bracken did the job more cheaply.

He saw the telegram boy from Inchroy cycle up to the Croft door and fish out the buff-coloured telegram from the belt pouch on his waist. He handed the telegram to Jean before cycling off down the path on his return journey.

Denzil threw down the scythe. This must be a message from Duncan informing them of his return. He ran as fast as he could and arrived through the door breathless only to stop short. Jean was seated at the kitchen at the kitchen table staring silently and blankly at the open telegram. Denzil somehow knew better than to speak. Suddenly Jean came to life with an angry gesture crunched up the telegram form, threw it under the table and walked out of the house.

Denzil waited then fished out the crumpled telegram, smoothed it out so that he could read it. It read "The War Office have to inform you with deep regret of the death in action in the recent Market Garden' Operation of your husband Sgt Duncan MacGillivray of the 1st Bn The Parachute Regiment..... Denzil could read no further as his eyes were blinded by tears.

Jean never broke down, as far as he could remember and they never really talked it out among themselves. It remained bottled up, although Jean would never listen to any further war reports and Denzil had to sneak the newspaper into his bedroom to follow the conclusion of the war. In due course, after the war, when the names of the fallen were added to the impressive World War 1 memorial, outside the church in Inchroy, although invited, Jean ignored it completely.

These then were the thoughts that occupied his mind as he stepped out, suitcase in hand, to catch the Inverdeen bus. Soon he was crossing the old bridge to find that only two others were waiting at the bus stop. His timing was good and shortly he was on his way with his suitcase lodged under his seat. He remembered the envelope in his pocket and fished it out. It was very thoughtful of the old lady to give him a good luck card was the thought in his mind as he tore open the envelope. Sure enough it was a card but a home-made one drawn by Jessie herself.

Jean had told him that the old lady had been an enthusiastic amateur painter in her youth and some of her own paintings adorned the walls of her house. Jessie had drawn a picture of a young man walking over a hill-top as a bright sun was breaking in front of him with the words '--Every best wish' below. He had to smile and opened the card to see if she had signed it. To his astonishment a ten shilling note nestled inside the card. He extracted it and placed it carefully in his wallet alongside the one he had received from Jean. He sat back well pleased with the financial boost this early in his first real working day. Hardly had he settled back when the bus drew into the bus stop at Inchroy. A considerable influx of passengers climbed aboard and Ally Gordon claimed the empty seat beside him. Denzil laughed "Hey you seem to keep popping up in some strange places!

"Aye so it seems" Ally replied "I have got a dental appointment this morning and that won't be a lot of fun. How about you - where are you heading for all dressed up?"

" You remember that hotel job we were both in for - well they gave it to me. I start work today." Denzil informed him. Ally slapped him on the thigh

"Good on you Dezzy. I felt sure one of those cocky town boys would have got the job didn't you? I've started an apprenticeship with my old man and that's exactly what I wanted. Things are going well as we got a contract to build a batch of new council houses in the village and the old man has had to take on a couple of workmen full time."

The two boys conversed all the way into Inverdeen. They parted company in the busy bus depot with Ally wishing him all the best. "See you around Dezzy" was his cheery final shout.

Denzil, suitcase in hand, set out from the depot to make his way up Hunter street to the Royal Hotel. Outside the imposing building he paused and took a deep breath before making for the side street that led to the Staff Entrance. Once inside, he approached the office. The same young girl who had attended to them the week or so before, spotted him and smiling rose from her desk to attend to him. Denzil told her that he had orders to report on arrival to Miss MacLean. The girl returned to the office and spoke briefly on the phone. "Miss Maclean will be with you shortly" she informed him. "Well Denzil, good to see you and welcome to the Royal. Come with me" came the greeting from Miss MacLean. Obediently Denzil hefted his suitcase and followed her as she led the way into the main hotel foyer that Jean and Denzil had ventured into on their first visit to the hotel. They crossed the foyer and made for the Porters Desk. Standing behind the desk attending to some paper work was the self same man who had rudely ejected them on that first visit. Denzil felt a sinking sensation in the pit of his stomach.

"Mr Scott" Miss MacLean spoke loudly " Here is your new boots - Denzil Morrison - can I leave him in your tender care?" The Head Porter barely looked up. He had always resented Miss MacLean's rapid promotion and never lost an opportunity to display his feelings towards her.

"Aye, I'll see to him in a minute, got more important things to attend to at the moment" he grunted. Miss MacLean just smiled never allowing the insolent rebuff to affect her in any way. She turned for a last time to Denzil "Right Denzil - Mr Scott will attend to you in due course. I hope you settle in okay. You will no doubt find first week a bit strange but don't worry I can assure you things will fall into place, they always do!"

With that assurance she strode away. Denzil stood suitcase in hand as the Head Porter deliberately ignored him. After some minutes the Head Porter raised his head and jerked with his hand in the direction of the Porters Lodge, "Away you go and wait in there. You're making the place look untidy." Denzil did as he was directed. Inside the lodge was a clutter of brushes and other cleaning materials while on hooks on the wall hung a variety of porters' uniforms in a range of sizes. A wooden notice board with a staff rota and other leaflets pinned to it adorned the other wall. Denzil's sinking stomach sensation at the first sight of Mr Scott would have gone a bit deeper if he had known the full story.

Apparently when the junior porter position had been advertised Scott had been approached in his favourite pub 'The '45 ' by a drinking companion looking for a first job for his son who had just left school. Fortified by a few drams, Scott had more or less insinuated that he was responsible for selecting his staff and to consider the matter done. A few more grateful drams were naturally slid in his direction at this insider dealing. Knowing full well that he would not be doing the interviewing he button-holed Major Drysdale one day and spoke highly of this particular boy. Drysdale was on his way at that time to deliver a talk to the Inverdeen Rotary Club who met weekly at the Station Hotel. His mind more or less occupied with this coming task he nodded approvingly and told Scott to get the job application in.

Scott failed to grasp that the one he should have spoken to was Miss MacLean. Scott thinking that Drysdale would go with his recommendation took the good news back to his pub companion. Yet more drams were consumed in a very convivial atmosphere. When he heard after the interviews that his favoured entrant had become an also-ran he was very put out. He felt very keenly the loss of face this brought about in the '45 Bar and had to invent an elaborate excuse to explain away the hotel decision.

Denzil sat on a chair in the lodge to await developments. A porter walked in to the lodge and slung his jacket on a hook while donning a porter's jacket. He glanced at Denzil, "Hello son. What are you all about?" Denzil explained the situation as best he could, aware that Scott was in earshot. The porter shook his head and pulled a wry face " So you're the new boots then. Well my name is Calum and I am second porter in this honourable establishment and lucky they are to have me!

What's your name son? Denzil told him. Calum turned on his heel and walked out of the lodge and Denzil could hear him speaking to Mr Scott. They both entered the lodge and Scott addressed Denzil. "Stand up when I speak to you boy. Calum will show you where to go. Remember one thing. I am your boss and any nonsense and you will be out. Got it! Right Calum take Sambo here with you. and get out of my sight". Denzil followed Calum out of the lodge across the foyer through another door that led down a flight of stone steps into a huge yard behind the hotel. En route Calum spoke to him "Denzil, don't let Scott get to you. He's a nasty piece of work and a real bully into the bargain if he is given the chance. Now this is the male staff quarters, used to be the stables of the old coaching inn." He opened a door and a lino covered corridor ran the length of the building with room doors at regular intervals. Calum continued in his cheery fashion "This will be home sweet home for you from now on." He stopped at a door and opened it with a flourish, "This is your abode, sharing with Montgomery the other boots. He is at work at the moment but will be with you shortly. He is expecting you and been told to show you the ropes. All the best and see you around!"

He departed and left Denzil once again on his own. He looked around. The floor was wooden with no covering and two single beds took up most of the room separated by two upright grey metal lockers One of the beds was clearly in use with blankets disarranged while the other bed by the window was made up. Clearly this was to be his and he sat down on it once again waiting to see what was going to happen leaving his suitcase unopened. The best part of an hour passed before the door burst open and a boy of about his own age entered slinging his uniform jacket on to the other bed. He was small and stocky with a round face that broke into a grin and somehow Denzil took an immediate liking to this newcomer.

The newcomer sat on his bed opposite Denzil and gave him a long hard appraising look before speaking, " Well, welcome to the hotel business. My name is Ian Montgomery but I'm known as Monty. What's yours?" Denzil told him. Monty nodded "Denzil, new one on me, is that an African name like?" Denzil laughed out loud at his honest direct question " I've no idea, it's just the name they gave me." Monty lay on his back on his unmade bed his head propped up by a none too clean a pillow. " Good to have you on board - work is getting a bit heavy with just me at the moment. One of the porters left to do his National Service and Peem Guthrie moved up to fill that vacancy. That used to be his bed you're sitting on. Do you smoke?" Denzil shook his head. Monty dug into his pocket and took out a crumpled packet Woodbine cigarette packet. Extracting a cigarette he straightened it before striking a match to light it then leaned back the picture of complete relaxation

Denzil suddenly thought of something that intrigued him. "Tell me something. They advertised the job as junior porter and yet everybody talks about us being boots? Monty laughed shortly "Junior porter, my arse! That's just the polite way of putting it. You will find that we are regarded as the lowest form of life among the hotel staff. Our main job, as I will show you tomorrow, is first thing in the morning to clean the shoes or boots that hotel guests leave outside their doors ready for them when they wake up. After that we are general dogsbodies as you will soon realise." They conversed on a wide variety of subjects and Denzil found himself enjoying the company of this engaging companion. He felt confident to mention to Monty his encounter with the Head Porter. Monty stubbed out his cigarette, "Oh Scotty, he's a right prick! Tried to give me a hard time when I first started the job but I told my Dad all about it. He met Scotty one night in the '45 Bar, let him know just who he was and offered to rearrange his face unless he laid off me. The result is that Scotty acts as if I don't exist and that suits me just fine." He suddenly swung his legs off the bed to face Denzil. "Lunch time old boy! I will take you down to the staff hall for scoff and introduce you around.

Cleano, that's Miss Maclean to you and me, asked me to show you around this afternoon but if you don't mind we will give that a miss. I have to go home to get some fresh shirts. Got a heavy date tonight for the pictures, back row and all that, know what I mean! There's nothing that can't wait until we are working tomorrow. Is that okay with you?" Denzil nodded agreement.

Monty opened the locker door and handed him the key with the warning to keep it locked at all times as, in his colourful language, he regarded some of the kitchen porters as thieving bastards. Denzil squeezed his suitcase in a standing up position into the locker and duly locked it. "Right then - we're off! " exclaimed Monty and the two boys left their room. They ended up in the staff hall where some members were already tucking into food at a huge well scrubbed wooden table in the centre of the room. Denzil at a rough guess saw that there were about 20 chairs round the table. They breezed into the room. "Right fellow citizens" Monty declaimed in a loud voice" Let me introduce you to Denzil my new assistant - and I hope you will always treat him with the respect my staff deserves!" There was some good natured banter directed back at Monty. Denzil was aware that the staff members had been told about the new boots and his ethnic origin. The first coloured person ever to work in the Royal Hotel had to be a happening of some interest.

Monty showed him how to obtain his food from a hot plate unit plugged into the wall of the room. They both sat down to eat with Monty talking non-stop to all and sundry. Denzil realised that he was really hungry and enjoyed his meal, happy that Monty was there to break the ice. Two young housemaids sat at one end of the table. They talked to themselves in Gaelic while giving Denzil sly looks and blushing if he ever glanced in their direction. Their meal finished they dashed off no doubt to regale their upstairs colleagues about the new boots. Their lunch finished Monty led the way back to the staff quarters. He roughly straightened his bed clothes out before removing an outdoor jacket from his locker. Slipping the jacket on, he had a final word with Denzil.

"Right Denzil, I'm offski! Just settle in and take it easy. Remember staff tea is between 5pm and 6pm. Just go the staff hall. I'll see you later and tomorrow is your big day. With that he was gone leaving Denzil alone and not for the first time that day.

He slowly unpacked his suitcase into the locker ensuring that his wallet was safely tucked away before securing it and putting the locker key in his pocket. He decided to spend the afternoon investigating the town so as to get his bearings. It proved to be a long and tiring afternoon trailing around the various streets. An easy decision was to skip the staff hall supper as he did not fancy dining among a sea of strange faces. He lay on his bed in early evening reading a book that Jean had thoughtfully put in his case.

About 9pm he found himself dozing off and decided on an early night. He located the bathroom with its cracked wash-hand basin and badly stained bath down the corridor. He cleaned his teeth. Once back in his room he pulled the rough blankets round him and reflected on the day's events. The one phrase that stuck in his mind was Miss MacLean's rejoinder not to worry, that things would fall into place. He fell into a deep, dreamless sleep and was only vaguely aware of Monty tip toeing into the room at some late hour giving off a whiff of stale cigarette smoke and cheap perfume. He turned over on his other side.

Chapter 5   First Week as "Boots"

Next day at 5.30 a.m. sharp Bert the night porter rapped sharply on their door to herald the start of their working day. Monty took some time to stir into life from his deep sleep. Denzil had been awake for some time. What awoke him was the sound of the town coming to life in the early morning. It was a feeling that was never to leave him. The alien sounds of workmen walking noisily to work, hailing each other combined with the horse drawn float clip-clopping on the cobbled street and the rattle of milk crates ensured his early arousal. It came as quite a contrast to the early morning sounds of his croft life, when birdsong and the full throated crowing of the cockerel were the only things likely to be heard. The two boys dressed hurriedly into their uniforms and headed out of the room with Monty trying to stifle a yawn

They were soon crossing the empty stillness of the main foyer to the Porter's lodge. Once there Monty foraged in a cupboard drawing out two wooden boxes each with a central handle. The boxes were filled with a variety of brushes, cleaning cloths, tins of black and brown polish and a packet with sticks of white chalk. Armed with their boxes they made for the lift and took it up to the first floor. Denzil enjoyed his first time in a lift with the smooth riding sensation. Out of the lift they looked along the carpeted corridor. It seemed to Denzil to go on for ever and outside most bedroom doors was neatly parked footwear awaiting their attention.

Monty explained to Denzil that the Head Housekeeper was very strict and would not allow shoes to be cleaned outside the bedroom doors. In case the polish stained the carpets or walls. Footwear had to have the room number marked in chalk on the upturned sole before being gathered and taken down the corridor to a housemaids pantry for them to do their work. The chalked room number ensured that the correct footwear went back to the right bedroom door.

They silently got down to work. Denzil quite enjoyed the process of cleaning shoes along with the feeling of satisfaction when he replaced them back outside a bedroom door returned to a high standard thanks to his efforts. Monty stopped for a fag break as he called it but soon they had finished the first floor. They moved up to the second floor knowing that a third floor awaited their attention. All in all it was 7.30 a.m. when the two boys completed the task heading back to the lodge to stow away their cleaning gear.

"Right Dezzy, let's grab an early breakfast before the rest of the staff get up and about!"

Denzil was always amused how quickly schoolmates had abbreviated his name and now here was Monty doing the same thing.

Back in the staff hall, one or two members of staff were seated at breakfast and viewed Denzil with some interest as he entered. Monty soon had everyone laughing as he described how his date for the pictures had stood him up but he managed to pick up another girl whose date had clearly taken cold feet. Denzil was so glad that Monty was there to lighten the atmosphere as otherwise if he had been on his own it would have been a bit of an ordeal. He was also aware that he had not eaten since lunchtime the previous day and a hearty breakfast soon restored his spirits. Monty finished his breakfast with a cigarette clutching his mug of tea.

He stood up as more members of staff filled the dining table and announced, "Okay me and my staff are ready for action as always!" A fair amount of cat-calling followed the two boys as they left the staff hall

"We'll report to Calum to see what he has got lined up for us. Scottie will be too busy looking after the departures hoping to collect any tips that are going. Did you know that Calum was a great footballer in his day? Aye he played for Inverdeen Athletic at centre half and my Dad says that the Celtic had come up to have a look at him with a view to signing him as a professional. Then in a cup-tie he broke his leg in two places.

They say that his operation was a botched job, but who knows? Anyway he never played again."

Monty chatted on and Denzil wondered if he ever stopped talking. The front Hall was busy with guests signing out at the reception desk and dropping keys off at the Porter's desk. The Porters for their part were occupied with carting guest luggage down by lift from the various floors. It was a scene of considerable activity as Denzil took it all in.

Monty nudged him, "See Scotty buzzing about, just like I told you."

The Head Porter was moving about the departing guests in an important manner like a crow hopping about a field looking for tasty morsels.

Calum took the boys in hand. He was attending to a considerable pile of newspapers that had obviously just been delivered to the lodge and from a sheet of paper was writing the room number in pencil on the appropriate newspaper. Their job was to deliver each newspaper to the room number inscribed on it. Although not every room ordered a paper it took the boys a good half hour to cover the three floors as quite often the lift would be engaged.

Their next job was to sweep out the corridor of the male staff quarters and perform some rough cleaning to the two bathroom areas, removing all rubbish to the bin area out in the yard. The seagulls up from the Firth were regular visitors to the rich pickings of the bins so that every morning fresh rubbish would be strewn about. A stable brush along with a large rusted shovel were used by the two boys to tidy up whilst large seagulls perched impassively on the roof of the staff quarters waiting patiently for their departure. The job completed Monty took the opportunity to enjoy another cigarette while keeping up a non-stop flow of conversation.

He pointed to a large building attached to the hotel that ran past the bin area.

"Know what that is?" Denzil somewhat puzzled shook his head. "Come on then I'll show you." They walked past the bin area out of the yard and into the street. Denzil was amazed to see that the river Deen flowed past on the other side of the road. Turning he could see that the rear of the hotel overlooked the river with striking views of the distant hills. A small car park with a few vehicles in it lay in front of them. Monty was intent on showing him the long building he had first indicated. The building was built on the land that sloped down to the river and was clearly at a lower level than the main hotel building.

Monty led the way up the car park until Denzil could see the entrance to the building. It had a sign that read, "Inverdeen Ballroom" with a smaller sign stating that dancing was held weekly every Wednesday and Saturday night to Harry Beach and his ballroom Orchestra.

"Come in, I'll show you around." said Monty as he led the way into the foyer stopping to speak to a woman busy mopping out the tiled area. Inside it took Denzil's breath away as a large carpeted area led to the sunken dance floor with a band area built into the far wall filled with music stands. He saw that a light fitting made up as a ball of hundreds of small mirrors hung from the ceiling.

He had only ever seen Inchroy Village Hall but this was definitely in a different league.

"Wow. It's enormous." He confided to Monty in a hushed voice.

Monty the fount of all knowledge imparted, "Aye it's big all right, they say they can get close on a thousand dancers in here on a good night. My father and mother met here at a dance you know. Apparently it went great guns during the war when a lot of the forces were stationed in the area. A lot of the company reps who stay in the hotel usually organise their rounds so that they end up here on a Wednesday so they can go dancing. I have heard my Dad say they call it, 'Grab a Granny' night! I'll give you a laugh!"

Denzil knew by now that Monty was heard to stop when he was in full flow.

"It was Calum who told me. About a year or so back a tobacco rep had a hot date for a Wednesday night but his company had organised things for him to be attending an important call in Bruaich. Now that's a hundred and ten miles due north of here as you know. That didn't deter the bold lad. He motored down that evening to attend the dancing and ended up kipping up with his fancy lady. His idea was to arise at 5a.m. and head back to Bruaich to start his work up there. Anyway his fancy lady didn't live in the best area in town so when he woke in the morning what did he find? Somebody had only broken into his company car and made off with all the tobacco stock that he was carrying – hundreds of pounds worth of stuff. He had no alternative but to head off north – couldn't report his loss as he would have had to explain to his company why he was in Inverdeen in the first place. Once he got back to Bruach he reported his loss as if it had happened there.

It was in all the papers. The local police spent weeks trying to track down the local thief without success. You have to laugh really!" Denzil had to agree.

Monty exclaimed, "Hey we had better get back or Calum will be having a pink fit."

They got back to the Lodge to be ignored by Scott for which Denzil felt a wave of relief.

"Where have you two jokers been to?" was the greeting from Calum inside the lodge. "I was on the point of putting out a search party."

"I was just showing Dezzy here the Ballroom." offered Monty by way of explanation.

"Listen Montgomery," responded Calum in mock severity "You can be a tourist guide in your own bloody time! The two of you had better high tail it off to see the Housekeeper as she was down here ten minutes ago looking for you."

They reported to Mrs MacBeth the Housekeeper in her living room cum office at the end of the first floor. She had been working at the hotel for some ten years and ran her department with a crisp authority that warmed Miss Maclean's heart. She had spent most of her married life out in Rhodesia where her husband had been a chief engineer on the railways. His sudden death at a relatively early age had turned her life upside down. She returned to Scotland with her two daughters almost right away and bought a small centrally situated cottage overlooking the River Deen.

With the girls safely settled into Inverdeen Academy she looked for gainful employment and the position of housekeeper at the Royal came as a godsend.

She was tall with slightly greying hair drawn to the back of her head in a fashionable bun and dressed in some style in a starched blue uniform rather like a hospital matron. She carried an air of natural authority and gave the boys a cool look as they reported to her.

"So there you both are!" She exclaimed, "Better late than never I suppose. Montgomery you know the ropes so you had better get to it as we have had a fairly major bedroom strip out today."

She turned to Denzil, "I take it you're the new boots that seems to be exciting a lot of curiosity at the moment? I hope you settle down well as you will find the first week more than a bit strange. If I can give you a word of advice, don't let this rogue you are with lead you astray. Now off with you both and let's see some action."

They left with Monty pleading his innocence but the housekeeper had turned her attention to other more important matters.

Their task was to take the soiled linen and towels stripped off the vacated beds now waiting their attention in the corridor outside the pantries on each floor. This had been helpfully put on to a single bedsheet and tied into a transportable bundle. Putting a bundle on their shoulder they took it down the fire-escape stairs to the enclosed yard where the main linen store was situated. The bundles were dumped there to be checked by the linen maid before being collected by a large van belonging to the Inverdeen Laundry Company. It took some time for the bundles to be collected from the three floors. That done Monty took the chance of a fag break. Denzil for his part took a look into the linen store where two women were hard at work sorting out the stacked linen. The room was clearly an old tack room going back to the coaching days. It had been gutted and wooden slatted shelving secured to the white washed walls holding in neat arrays all the linen items that a busy hotel would require.

At the end of this room was a workbench with two other ladies seated there checking linen suitable for repair. They were hunched over two Singer sewing machines and from time to time they whirred into action as some item of frayed linen was attended to.

Monty, his fag break over, appeared at his shoulder and soon engaged in noisy banter with the linen store staff. The operation was well organised. Mrs MacBeth had supplied the linen room ladies with exact requirements in sheets, pillow slips and towels that each floor would require. This is what the ladies were busy doing ready for the boys to transport up the floors for the staff there to deal with. In due course when the van appeared to fetch the bundles of soiled linen, they returned the linen from the previous day's collection. This freshly laundered supply was than stacked on to the shelves ready for the next day.

It took the boys quite a few trips with the fresh linen to the different floors where the housemaids were hard at work cleaning rooms and bathrooms before turning to make up beds. Denzil loved the fresh laundered smell coming from the crisp white bedsheets and towels that they carried.

Finished at last Denzil realised that this had taken most of the morning to accomplish. They reported back to Calum in the porters lodge. Another porter was present at this point. The portering staff numbered some six individuals in all. Headed by Mr Scott, with Calum as second in command there were four others, namely: Archie McColl, Andy Bremner, Roddy

MacRae and the night porter Bert Rattray. Archie recently demobbed from National Service with the Cameron Highlanders, Andy whose polio affected leg had made him avoid military service and Roddy a stocky man in his mid forties with slight learning difficulties. They worked a shift system so ensuring that the front hall was covered from 7-3Oam to 9pm daily.

"Right boys, there is a stock room client coming in on the noon train. Go with Archie and it will give Denzil a good chance to get some stock room experience." That said Calum sent them on their way. Outside the front door of the hotel was a large two-wheeled barrow with two long handles propped neatly against the side of the portico. It was painted dark green with the words "Royal Hotel" picked out in gold paint on both sides. Archie manhandled the barrow away from the wall and they set off for the railway station some 100 yards up Hunter Street. Monty took the chance to sit on the barrow and relight a half cigarette that he pulled from his uniform pocket. Denzil walked alongside Archie who was pulling the large barrow. He explained to Denzil that the stock rooms were an important part of the hotel business. Various companies sent an agent by rail to Inverdeen with samples of their produce whether it be fashion, jewellery, glass and china ware or tourist shop goods. The goods were displayed in the stock rooms and the designated local buyers or shop owners would be invited to attend to view and place their orders. Spring and autumn were the peak times for stock room activity. It was not confined to Inverdeen shops as buyers from smaller towns up north flocked in and even western island buyers would make a trip lasting some days. Apart from charging for the stock rooms the agents would entertain various favoured clients to anything ranging from drinks in the cocktail bar to expense account meals in the restaurant. The porters quite enjoyed this task as it often resulted in a generous tip from the agent.

Today's client would be a well known national jewellery company Paul Campbell and Son Ltd based in Edinburgh. The agent Frank Malone was a real character and a tipper of some renown. They hung about the station until the Edinburgh train steamed in and passengers alighted. Malone the agent made friendly contact with them before supervising his cases of samples being safely removed from the train to their barrow. That done he walked off leaving them to trundle the laden cart back to the hotel. It took the three of them to haul the barrow.

Once back at the hotel the cases were removed to just inside the front door entrance. The barrow was replaced against the outside wall. Archie worked on the revolving door to pin back one section so that the bulky locked cases could pass through before adjusting it back. Where to next? thought Denzil to himself. Archie turned sharp left and opened a door. At first glance the door looked like a section of the wall as it was covered in the same heavy duty wall paper and bore a shield with crossed claymores. It was like somebody performing a magic trick. The doorway led to several rooms on the ground floor while a flight of stone stairs ran up to more rooms, the larger of which was used by a Masonic lodge. They carried the cases into the largest room where the porters had laid out several trestle tables covered in white sheets ready for the sample display. The cases safely installed Archie locked the stockroom before taking the key back to the lodge for safe custody.

Lunch time called and they made their way back to the staff hall which was quite crowded with members coming and going. Monty again was soon in full flow with the other staff while Denzil was quite content to eat quietly at his side. Archie soon joined them and got chatting to Denzil about his army experiences and soon established that one of the Cabrach crofters Andrew MacLennan was an uncle on his mother's side. After lunch they returned to the housemaid pantries to take the black bags of rubbish down to the bin area. Once again they had to tidy up after the seagull activity. Monty grumbled, it was like "painting the bloody Forth Bridge!"At 2pm their working day officially ended. The two boys returned to their room in the staff quarters with a chance to relax for an hour or so. Monty then got ready to go out. "Hey Dezzy" He was searching his pockets, "Any chance of lending me a couple of bob?" Denzil had been half prepared for this request - "Sorry Monty but I'll have no money until I get paid."

"Och not to worry I'll just go and see my old lady. Mind you I haven't paid her back the last lot that I borrowed! See you later, I'll be back for tea time."

Left on his own, Denzil lay back on his bed and reflected on events. He had really enjoyed his first day working after the uncertainty and hanging about of the previous day. He had seen some of the hotel but realised that it would take some time to be familiar with all the nooks and crannies of the building. He had learned that Major Drysdale and his wife lived in a large suite on the third floor and was referred to by the staff as The Crows Nest. They had no children and Mrs Drysdale was in partnership with another lady in an upmarket shop in Caledonian road that sold prams and babywear. Miss MacLean on the other hand, who always appeared to be on duty, lived out.

She did have a guest room on the first floor when she was made personal assistant, until she had developed a close friendship with the housekeeper Mrs MacBeth. One night out socially, Mrs MacBeth had confided in her that she was contemplating letting out the single room in her house to help defray her mortgage costs. The upshot was that Miss MacLean moved in as the lodger which gave her a break from her fairly demanding hotel routine. Her guest room was released for letting purposes and so everybody was satisfied. The early morning start and the job activity soon took their toll. The book he was reading slipped from his grasp and he fell into a deep sleep. He was only awakened by Monty shaking him awake, saying that it was time for staff hall supper, exultant as his mother had given him a half crown. He did not bother to also tell Denzil that she had said no more money until he had squared her for the last two advances!

Chapter 6   Mr Finkelstein

Denzil would always remember that first week in the Royal Hotel. It was a stroke of luck having such an extrovert character as Monty to work with and show him around. The work may be fairly routine but every day somehow was different and he was quickly establishing friendly relationships with other staff. Nobody remarked to his face on his colour although Scott made a habit of referring to him as Sambo. He once heard Archie take him to task about this and Scott reminding him in colourful language about who was Head Porter in this hotel and he could say what he liked.

Towards the end of the first week an incident happened in the staff hall at lunchtime that strangely enough was to defuse any long standing problem with the colour question. Quite a number of staff were gathered round the table having lunch. It was a noisy session with a lot of banter and leg-pulling, conducted as always by the ebullient Monty The door leading to the kitchen corridor opened abruptly. An elderly man with a shock of white hair strode in and stood glaring at them. He was barefooted, dressed in canvas trousers rolled up the knee, topped by a white vest covering a scrawny chest. Almost immediately he was greeted by shouts from the seated table. "Hey Walter - how's it going -how was the holiday? Walter - old fruit - not often you grace us with your presence!" The old man ignored them and continued to glare around. "I heard tell there was a black boy joined the staff. Where is he?" he demanded. The room fell into an embarrassed silence. Denzil decided to meet it head on. He raised his hand and declared - "I think that might be me." The staff room dissolved in relieved laughter The old man looked at him - "You're no black boy! What are you talking about? I had some black soldiers in my unit in the War - part of an African unit attached to our battalion. Now they were black! Black as the Earl of Hell's waistcoat. I mind as corporal I had to take some of them out on night patrols in no-mans land trying to get close to the Jerry trenches for information purposes. I had to black up my face but these guys never had to."

At this point Monty interrupted, "Right everybody, tin helmets on." as Walter's war stories continued. Walter pointed at him, "Aye laddie you're so bloody smart - a winter in the trenches would fair sort your hash." He turned and left the way he had come slamming the door behind him.

"Who was that?" Denzil enquired of Monty as the staff noise resumed its normal level. "Oh him - old Walter - one of the kitchen porters - daft as a brush as you'll find out"

The incident naturally went round the hotel and in a strange way the colour problem, such as it was, seemed to have been put to bed! One day in that first week the two boots were at the Porters' Lodge waiting for Calum to organise the papers for delivery to the rooms. Denzil was engrossed with the general foyer activity with guests coming and going from the breakfast room, others checking out at a busy reception desk, while porters carried luggage to the front door. Mr Scott as always was out in the midst of it saying farewell to departing guests and ensuring the correct luggage was in the right hands. Denzil's gaze was suddenly switched to the main staircase. An elderly man was slowly descending down into the foyer. Denzil noted that he was middle-aged but it was his dress that caught his attention. He was dressed in a well-cut light grey business suit adorned with a small blue carnation in his button-hole while a Homburg hat of a slightly deeper shade of grey completed the ensemble. In his hand he carried a brown walking cane with a silver top. He walked slowly through the throng in the foyer and through the main door out into the street.

Just then Calum called them into action and the matter slipped from Denzil's mind. In the letter that Miss MacLean had supplied him with at his interview it had stated that pay was weekly but there would be a week's lying time. Jean did not quite understand this and told him to be sure and clarify that point with Miss MacLean when he started work. Denzil decided that he would not bother her and just see how things worked out. After all he had his own funds in his wallet.

It was the Thursday afternoon of that first week that the pay subject surfaced. It was after they had finished work and were back in their room with their day's work safely behind them. Monty was busy wreathed in Woodbine smoke pinning up a colour picture of Joe Louis, the American boxer, that he had cut out from a boxing magazine. He stepped back to admire his handiwork, "Hey Dez - you know he is the same colour as you. You might be related - how about taking up boxing and I could be your agent? I quite fancy exchanging the Woodbines for a big cigar and being in the big money. Talking about money thank God that tomorrow's pay day as the old ladies half dollar didn't last long!"

At the mention of pay, Denzil, who had been half listening to Monty's prattle, raised himself up on his bed. This seemed as good a chance as any to sort out the lying time situation. Monty was as usual the fount of all knowledge. Denzil was informed that he was not due a day off on his first week as the Monday arrival and induction day accounted for that. Pay for the week just worked was paid on the Friday of the second week - that is in arrears. However this set-up had led to problems with people starting work stretched for cash having to wait that length of time. Miss MacLean had solved the problem with her usual efficiency. She arranged that anybody who was in need of early payment could get half of their first week's pay as a signed for loan and the other half on the lying time pay day the following week. It would be the third week before the worker received a full weekly pay. "I told the pay office that you were short of funds - so tomorrow Dezzy my boy you will sign for the first slice of your ill-gotten gains. See how I look after my staff!" Denzil lay back smiling to himself thinking if Monty only knew about the two ten shilling notes in his wallet in the locker. So it was on Friday after work he reported with Monty to the self-same office in the corridor that he had reported to on his first day. The wage clerkess was seated at a desk with a wire tray in front of her bulging with a stack of brown pay packets. They both signed for their pays. While Monty, as usual, chatted up the clerkess Denzil thumbed open his packet to find the correct amount four shillings and sixpence. A sense of elation swept over him as he pocketed his first pay.

Saturday was Monty's day off. Denzil operated alone and, as the business week was over, the hotel was just about half full so he managed to cover all that was required on his own. By now he felt quite relaxed about using the staff hall for meals on his own without sheltering behind Monty's non-stop chatter. Scott was also on his day off so Denzil found himself assisting Archie once again with the newspaper round. Like a re-run of the other day Denzil spotted the man in grey descending the main staircase. This time the man crossed the foyer to the Porter's desk. Archie lifted his head at his arrival. "Good morning Mr Finkelstein - how are you today? I have got yesterday's Times here for you". The two men exchanged pleasantries and discussed the weather. It gave Denzil time to size him up properly. He was dressed exactly as on the previous occasion and Denzil noted that he wore an expensive looking pair of grey shoes that complemented his suit. His face had a sallow complexion that spoke of one who led an indoors existence while a pair of rimless gold glasses completed the picture. Eventually, his business with Archie concluded, he set off down the foyer out into the busy street. Denzil could contain his curiosity no longer, "Archie - who is that man?"

Archie lifted his head from the newspaper bundle "Who? Oh him that's Finkie our permanent resident. He owns the jewellers shop down in North Bridge street - Isaac Finkelsteins - been a resident at the Royal since before the war as far as I gather. His wife and himself occupy a suite of rooms on the second floor. Nice old guy and a real gentleman. We have a couple of other permanent guests - two old biddies the Misses Horne, two sisters both well into their eighties. Their old man had a good going engineering business but their only brother was killed in the Great War. He was supposed to take over the business but it was not to be. The old man carried on for a number of years before he sold out to some national company for big dollars. After the parents died the big house was sold and the two sisters moved in here. Apparently some family trust looks after their financial affairs. Hardly ever see them as they dine in their room and only come down into the hotel for an occasional lunch." That said Archie returned to his newspaper checking.

Later that morning Mrs MacBeth collared him, "Denzil, just the man I need, can you take a box of napkins to the Restaurant right away as they seem to have forgotten to collect them?" He took hold of the large wicker basket that contained a considerable number of white linen napkins neatly packed in a pristine laundered condition. The restaurant lay in a dog leg of the foyer well to the right of the reception desk. Denzil was in new territory as he had never ventured this far up the foyer before. He was astonished to see an area equally as big as the main foyer. There were signs indicating ladies and gents rest-rooms to one side discreetly tucked away. He observed the cocktail bar with staff preparing for opening for service. His eye was caught by a hand painted sign stating COCKTAIL BAR in gold lettering while sandwiched between the letters was a huge cockerel depicted in art deco style in coloured glass. The restaurant lay immediately to the right of the bar. He entered and stopped in his tracks. The restaurant was enormous with a veritable sea of white clothed tables stretching before him all set out for lunch service. At the far end of the room two waiters were busy setting up the last few tables with glassware and a girl florist was setting out fresh posy bowls. Denzil had never seen a room like this in his life. The predominant colour scheme was gold with two huge mirrors of tinted glass on one wall which seemed to make the room even bigger than it was. On one mirror was fixed an elongated gold encrusted clock with ornate embellishments. Recesses in the walls contained highly polished silver antiques. Where the walls met the ceiling an elaborate moulding was inset with beautifully painted figures from mythology depicted. The ceiling itself had a sunken circle in different colours with a large chandelier suspended as a centre-piece.

His reverie was soon interrupted, "Well young man, 1 hope you are suitably impressed"! said a voice to his right. The restaurant had so stopped Denzil in his tracks that he had failed to notice tucked to one side a man sitting at a table with papers and a coffee cup. A tail coat was draped over his chair as he relaxed in his black waistcoat with wing collar and black bow tie. Denzil held out the wicker basket and the man summoned one of the waiters to come and attend to it. "I understand you are the new boots that they are all speaking about. You have a great career in front of you if you handle it right - and who knows one day you might even be a waiter!" He smiled and turned back to his paper work and Denzil, task completed, returned to the Lodge. Once there he told Andy Bremner, the other porter, somewhat excitedly about his first impressions of the restaurant and the man who had spoken to him. Andy was only too happy to fill him in. He had just met Mr Mitchell the Maitre d'hotel who was a legendary figure in the Royal's history. He hailed from somewhere in Yorkshire and at an early age had gone into service with a local estate owner. Some years passed and a certain peer of the realm attending a shooting party enticed him away to his larger estate in Sussex. He soon became butler to the peer and his experience developed apace. The peer attended the House of Lords on a regular basis and members of the Royal family along with prominent political figures featured on his guest list. This privileged existence came to an unfortunate end when the peer suffered financial meltdown when unwise investments came home to roost in the major depression in the 1930s. The estate was broken up for sale and the staff dispersed. Mitchell had then gone to London where, with his impeccable qualifications, he joined the Savoy Hotel as one of the senior station waiters.

In 1938, like so many people, he sensed war was coming and London would not exactly be the ideal place to hang around with a growing family. He looked around for some months before applying for the position at the Royal. A standard for the restaurant was soon established that won many awards but his main forte was in training young people in the art of waiting.

Roddy finished by saying to Denzil that there were more characters running round the Royal than you could shake a stick at. He was just saying "if you want to meet a character just wait until you meet Paddy the cocktail barman…" when Scott bore down on them.

He directed his rage at Denzil. "What the hell are you doing here? My staff have more to do than have you chatting to them all day – Clear off!"

Denzil cleared off as Andy pulled a face behind the irate head porter's back.

When the next Monday dawned, he was awakened by the usual town noises as well as the seagulls making a determined attack on the bin area. He lay there for a while reflecting on the past week and that, as tomorrow was Tuesday, his day off, he would be heading back home to see Jean and tell her all the news. The night porter's rap came on the door as usual. He rose and dressed before shaking Monty's recumbent body into life.

"Hey Monty – wakey-wakey! It's another day, another dollar!"

CHAPTER 7   Settling In

The male staff quarters, Denzil soon found out, held about twenty staff from different departments. Three kitchen porters shared a triple room but Walter, the eccentric character that he had already encountered, had a room on his own as he proved too aggressive for his co-workers to live with. A mixture of kitchen employees, waiters, ballroom workers and porters occupied the remaining rooms. The week before Denzil started, the staff quarters had been the scene of a minor disturbance. Peter Smart, one of the waiting staff, had found a notice taped to his door which had upset him.

Peter was in his forties, very experienced at his job and popular with guests. His trouble was that he walked and talked in a very affected, effeminate manner that left him open to a lot of leg-pulling. The notice on his door that so upset Peter stated in bold letters,

' PLEASE KNOCK SOFTLY BUT FIRMLY - 'COS I LIKE SOFT, FIRM KNOCKERS!'

So upset was Peter that he took the matter directly to Miss MacLean declaring that obscene material had been placed on his door. Miss MacLean had a shrewd suspicion that this had been Monty's handiwork. She did her best to hide a smile as she did her best to placate Peter's outraged feelings. Monty when tackled was wide eyed with innocence as usual.

On the Tuesday afternoon, when his shift was over, Denzil prepared for heading back to Cabrach. He had spent some of his pay on a light holdall to transport his laundry items along with a box of Black Magic chocolates as a present for Jean. Not wishing to break into the money in his wallet he realised that he would have to conserve his spending to last out until payday. To this end instead of taking the service bus from the depot he walked the mile or so out of the town until he was on the outskirts. Here he paused and waited patiently. Soon a truck rumbled up and he jerked his thumb in time honoured fashion. The truck was bound on a regular run to the hydro-electric dam under construction some thirty miles away in the high mountains to the west in Glen Forrin.

He climbed aboard the truck with the driver quite glad of the company. Denzil chatted to the driver about bis new job as they sped along. Denzil had expected to be dropped off at the bus stop by the bridge but the driver when he learned where he stayed took the loop road so he disembarked close to the path by Jessie MacLeod's red roofed cottage. It was a lucky break. Waving to the driver he set off up the path whereas he rounded the bend. Moss came bounding down barking with delight. As he patted and made a fuss of the dog, Jessie roused by the barking appeared in her apron at the croft door. Once inside Jessie made tea. A plate of biscuits and homemade cakes were at the ready. She sat down holding her tea cup in her cupped hands before asking Denzil to tell all that had taken place. Denzil felt that he had talked for hours as he related his experiences and in fact the tea pot was replenished twice during that long afternoon. Jean was concerned about how he had got on with the rude man they had met on the day of the interview but Denzil played the matter down assuring her she had no need to worry on his account. Finished at last Jean bustled about getting his laundry into the wash. Denzil went out to the byre where the calf still stalked about in the pen and it too seemed to have grown in the past week. He took down from a peg a few rabbit snares that hung there. On the hillside behind the croft he looked out for the rabbit runs snaking through the long grass. Carefully he sank the wooden stake into the ground beside the run and then carefully looped the wire noose propped by a twig so that it hung over the run. He did this for about six different runs before heading back.

Jean was out on the drying green with pegs in her mouth hanging out his newly washed clothes on the line. She called to him to bring Ruby in from the field ready for the evening milking after they had supper. As he strolled down to the field he was back once more in the peace and solitude of the age old world of crofting. Quite a contrast to the working world into which he had been plunged.

That evening he stood at the byre door as Jean milked the cow. Hunched over on her milking stool with her scarved head pressed against Ruby's flank her strong hands worked on the teats sending spurts of milk into the foaming milk pail. Milking over Denzil chucked some hay into Ruby's manger as Jean fed the hungry calf in its pen. Jean then went through the ritual of passing the milk through a stainless steel sieve before decanting the milk into a couple of basins and placing in the outside larder. The larder, clearly the forerunner of the household refrigerator, was a sturdy erection raised off the ground containing wooden shelves with a felt roof to shelter the contents inside from the elements. It was covered in a heavy duty perforated wire gauze so that fresh air provided natural ventilation.

They talked some more that evening and Jean brought him up to date with the latest crofting gossip. Denzil slept well in his old bed but woke half expecting to hear sea gull bin activity, but instead he heard the distant sound of a cockerel from a neighbouring croft.

His first job on rising was to check the snares. He had done his job well as four rabbits had fallen victim. Two were already dead but two others he had to despatch with a sharp blow behind the head. He had done his tasks often in the old days with Duncan, as rabbits had always been on their weekly diet. He remembered some years ago going out one morning to check his snares to find a wild-cat had beaten him to it. It was sitting devouring the dead rabbit and, as he approached it, stood up hissing in a menacing fashion, so menacing that he very wisely left the animal to enjoy its repast.

Jean looked approvingly as he deposited his catch in the kitchen sink commenting, "Well done . I'll prepare one for old Jessie along with her milk this morning."

He cut logs and cleaned out the byre and calf pen along with fresh bracken bedding. Mid morning he took the milk can and freshly skinned rabbit down the path accompanied by an excitable Moss to the red tin roofed cottage. It gave him an opportunity to thank the old lady for her good wishes and financial contribution. The downside was that he had to tell her as well all about his new job so that by the time he returned to Jean it was time for a late lunch. The afternoon sped by and soon he found himself, hold-all in hand, heading along the road to catch the early evening bus.

He found his room empty as Monty was clearly out on the town.

The next few weeks slipped past as he settled into a routine, finding out more about the hotel and many of the people involved in running it. Major Drysdale was a shadowy figure who did not appear much in their lives whereas Miss MacLean seemed to be everywhere. She stopped Denzil one day in his second week to enquire how he was settling in. He assured her that he was happy with things and she in turn said if he ever had a problem her door was always open.

Most days he noticed the dapper figure of Mr Finkelstein leaving for his business always at the same time.

The Head Porter kept up with snide and wounding remarks but Denzil usually tried to steer clear of him at all times. Monty was permanently broke two days before pay day. Denzil soon realised that not only had he not repaid his mother but he had borrowed money from Archie. When Denzil was on his full pay of nine shillings a week Monty had tapped him for money but Denzil had used the excuse of having to support his widowed mother.

One day in the staff hall he got talking to one of the cornmis chefs, sixteen year old Brian MacGlennon, who hailed from Bruaich and roomed in the staff quarters. Brian invited him in to see the main kitchen. It was quite an experience to see the huge kitchen with its central stove and serving hotplate, the great array of stainless steel cooking pots and the display of copper pots of various sizes hanging on one wall. Brian showed him the various corners where the chefs worked at their particular skills. A staircase led up to a landing where stores were kept and the head chef had his office with a window that gave him an overall view of operations. Chef Bonnacorsi came down as he spotted the two boys moving round the kitchen and seemed quite interested in seeing Denzil as clearly his arrival had been the subject of much conversation.

Paulo Bonnacorsi, strangely enough, belonged to Inverdeen, born and raised in the town. His parents had emigrated from Italy and set up a business called the Merry Thought Cafe in Inglis Street, just off the High street. Paulo had gone south at an early age to London to train as a chef in the Savoy Hotel. By coincidence he had been working there in the kitchens when a certain Mr Jack Mitchell was deputy Maitre d'hotel there and now they worked together in senior roles in the Royal.

The Merry Thought Cafe was still run by Paulo's two brothers while Paulo himself was a sleeping partner in the business. The cafe had a great reputation for its ice cream while the restaurant section was always busy with its speciality fish and chip suppers and other staple British meals while introducing some novel Italian pasta dishes.

Now well into June the tourist season was in full swing. A war weary public seemed hell bent on taking a couple of weeks away from their working environment and rationing to recharge their batteries. Most people thought that rationing would finish when the war ended but it was not to be the case as Britain entered on another war of austerity.

Around the staff hall table Denzil listened to the grumbles of the married members of staff as they struggled to make ends meet. How lucky they were in their crofting community to be more or less self sufficient and rationing was a minor inconvenience. They had rabbits, hens, eggs, milk, potatoes, butter, crowdie, turnips backed up by home baking to hand. John MacLennan, a retired roadman, who lived along by the quarry was a keen fisherman. He ensured that salmon and sea trout were spread among his neighbours and when these fish were out of season he plundered the high hill lochs for brown trout. Venison was also freely available. Willie Allison whose croft was situated at the very top of Cabrach bordered the Forestry Commission woodlands that ranged far into the mountain. Red deer and roe deer would venture out of this woodland tempted by the better grazing and field crops in the croft.

Willie who had served as a ghillie took a steady toll of these interlopers. Denzil could remember as he and Jean worked on the croft hearing the spiteful crack of Willie's trusty .22 rifle carried down on the wind. Jean would laugh out loud remarking that they could depend upon a haunch of venison being dropped off at their door in a few days time. The Royal too had a restricted menu due to limited supplies. However Chef Bonnacorsi was not without his contacts. Shadowy figures slipped in and out of the kitchen, money changed hands and certain produce materialised. Bonnacorsi used to joke that his poached salmon was the real McCoy! The authorities were aware of this going on but unless it got really out of hand preferred to let sleeping dogs lie!

Denzil had been exactly four weeks at the Royal when an event happened that was to have a very profound effect on his life. It started in a very minor way. There was a Residents Lounge adjacent to the restaurant where guests would sometimes retire to finish a meal with a coffee or simply escape to read a paper well away from the main foyer activity. Mr Finkelstein had a routine that after lunch when his wife returned to open their shop he would slip into the lounge for his demi-tasse of coffee, look through the Times and fall asleep for a spell before going back to business. The restaurant staff mainly the commis waiters looked after this area normally. When the restaurant was busy Mr Mitchell ensured that either Monty or Denzil assisted in clearing away coffee cups and cleaning ashtrays. It was Monty's day off and Denzil was roped in to the lounge duty. The lounge was empty save for Mr

Finkelstein snoozing in his chair with the Times newspaper slipped from his grasp lying on the floor. Denzil had cleared the lounge and as a final touch thought that he would pick up the Times paper and replace it on the table in front of the elderly resident. It may well have been the rustling of the paper as he folded it carefully that awoke Finkelstein. He sat up sleepily and rubbed his eyes in a tired manner. "Thank you my boy. Now you are new here aren't you?"

Denzil confirmed that it was exactly four weeks since he had started work. Finkelstein asked him how he was enjoying his job, where he came from and whether he intended to make hotels his career. Suddenly he sat upright in his chair and fixed Denzil with a long hard look over his rimless glasses before speaking,

"So you have been working for some four weeks" he mused almost to himself,

"I am going to ask you a personal question if you don't mind. How much are you paid?" Denzil replied -" I get nine shillings a week living in, Sir"

Finkelstein reflected on that for a moment or two before firing another question at him. "Nine shillings a week, that's good going for a young man like you. Now tell me how much have you saved in that time?" Denzil was puzzled "Saved, Sir - I'm not sure?" his voice tailed away.

Finkelstein smiled understandingly, "How much do you save a week from your nine shillings?"

"Not much, Sir " Denzil confessed " I seem to spend it all."

"Don't worry that is what most people do" Finkelstein assured him. "I want to give you a bit of advice that may well help you as you set out on your working life. Will you allow me to do just that?" Denzil was happy to agree not wishing to be disrespectful to the elderly man. "Right then" pursued Finkelstein leaning forward in his chair, his voice taking on a more resolute tone, "Here is what I would like you to do. I will have to explain a certain plan of action. This will take some time. I do not want to interrupt your working day so tomorrow is Wednesday when my shop is closed for the town's half day. I find it a good time to catch up with any backlog of work. You say you are free in the afternoon so call in at my shop after 2pm and I can talk things over with you. Will you do that?" Denzil agreed that he would present himself at the stated time.

As he left the lounge he did wonder just what he was letting himself in for. Perhaps he would discuss the matter with Monty but on second thoughts decided not to. He would simply attend the meeting tomorrow and take it from there. He reflected on how Finkelstein had asked him about saving money and realised that he had actually spent his pay knowing that Friday would bring another pay packet. His final thought that night before he fell asleep was that how much Monty was more in need of financial advice. Tomorrow was another day when he would take on board whatever advice this eccentric old man would dish out to him. He didn't have to take it after all.

CHAPTER 8   The Finkelstein Plan

On Wednesday afternoon he set off for North Bridge street to be there for exactly 2pm. The Town Hall clock was chiming the hour as he knocked on the closed door of Finkelstein's shop. Finkelstein himself opened the door for him and invited him inside

"Come away in my boy and I see you are dead on time. That's a good sign."

The shop was brightly lit with glass cabinets all round filled with silverware, watches and crystal items. In one corner a large grandfather clock stood with its brass pendulum moving to and fro. Finkelstein was jacketless with a black apron tied round his waist clearly having just risen from his work bench. A display counter dominated the room with a till on top and beyond Denzil saw another room, the doorway obscured by a curtain. The jeweller led the way brushing aside the curtain so that they were now in a back room with a work bench on one side covered in various tools and watches. On the wall was a huge chart with various numbers and letters in bold black type. Clearly an eyesight testing chart as the figures diminished in size in a downward direction. A chair was pushed forward for Denzil to sit on beside the old man as he started his talk.

"Thank you for coming," he commenced, "now the advice I am going to give you is free but you are equally free not to take it. However, I was given such advice when I was roughly your age and it has stood me in good stead. You are just starting work and there is no better time to learn good habits. Most people earn a wage and promptly spend it, just like you are doing with your weekly pay. If they get promoted or given a rise in pay then they adjust their spending accordingly. So people become wage slaves. If they do not save then when they lose a job or fall ill they have nothing to fall back on.

Denzil listening attentively thought to himself how Monty would benefit from this talk.

"Now as a living in hotel worker you are in an unique position. You have no rent to pay and your food is supplied so your money is really spending money. Now I have to ask you a question, you earn nine shillings a week, so could you say learn to live on say five shillings a week and save four shillings each week?" He paused and looked directly at Denzil as he posed the question. Denzil nodded without giving the matter too much thought. "Very well then" Finkelstein continued "Consider this. If you did that you would have saved one pound per month and after a year have a small nest-egg of twelve pounds. Hopefully after a year the good habit of money management would have set in and you would go on from there. Do you think you could do that?

The idea appealed to Denzil so he spoke, "Yes, sir, I don't see why not." Finkelstein adjusted his glasses. "Excellent! I take it you do not have a savings account so what I propose is that I will help you open just such an account and you will invest your four shillings a week. Now I know only too well it is very easy to embark on such a scheme and after a few weeks or months, for whatever reason, it falls by the wayside. I will therefore give you some moral support. You bank your money every Friday and bring the book here to me in this shop to initial. This is a form of discipline that is very essential and I am always there if some problem arises. After one year you will no longer report to me and be master of your own affairs. I would also stress that this arrangement is kept strictly private between us." Once again he paused to let this sink in. Denzil thought quickly. The idea appealed to him. He would have some money put by plus, after a year, he would be a free agent and anyway it would do no harm to humour this well meaning old man.

The agreement secured Finkelstein leaned over and gravely shook Denzil's hand. "That seals our deal my boy. Now, I could put some money into your account to formally open it but I want it to be your own money so that you stand at all times on your own two feet. That is important. So you get paid on Friday coming, what say that afternoon we meet up and I will escort you to my bank to open an Account in your name?"

Denzil had a sudden idea. He told about the two ten shilling notes in his wallet back in his locker that he would be willing to use to open his account. Finkelstein's eyebrows were raised at this revelation and the meeting soon concluded with an agreement for Denzil to report back to the shop the next day. He returned to his room to find Monty lying on his bed. He was moaning that he was broke with no money for fags and unable to borrow any further funds until he had repaid what he owed already.

His financial plight combined with what had passed that afternoon gave Denzil much food for thought. Next day he extricated the money from his wallet without Monty seeing what he has doing and, after his shift was over, made his way back to the jeweller's shop. Today it was open with Mr Finkelstein's wife dealing with a customer. Finkelstein appeared from the back shop slipping his jacket on, hat and stick in hand. Telling his wife he would not be long, they left the shop and walked along the busy street until they reached the imposing frontage of the Bank of Scotland. Once inside Finkelstein approached a reception desk and, raising his hat, spoke to the clerkess seated there for a brief moment. He returned to Denzil and they took seats in a waiting area. Never having been in a bank before, Denzil watched with interest as bank customers came and went to the tellers behind glass screens. A few minutes elapsed before a door opened and a man in a dark business suit waved them in.

"Well Isaac" he greeted the jeweller "Good to see you and trust business is well."

Once seated, the two men conversed for a few minutes about local business gossip. They touched on the recent activities of the Stern gang in Palestine so Denzil switched off and looked out the window at pigeons sunning themselves on the roof opposite. He suddenly came back to life as he realised

Finkelstein was introducing him to Mr Holland the bank manager. "So this is my latest customer is it? Well you can never start too young I always say." The bank manager stated pressing a bell on his desk. The door opened and a lady appeared almost immediately. Denzil produced his two ten shilling notes handed them to the lady as directed. Mr Finkelstein handed her a note with Denzils details and she withdrew only to return some minutes later with a brand new red bank book in her hand. Mr Holland gave it a cursory look over before handing it over to Denzil. He saw them both to the office door, shook hands with Mr Finkelstein and, much to his surprise, with Denzil. It made him feel very grown up. They walked up the street together, Denzil clutching his new bank book. They parted company at the top of North Bridge Street but not before Finkelstein had a parting shot. "Well Denzil - that is the first step on hopefully a long and worthwhile journey. Now remember your pay day this Friday is the next step. See you then." He walked off up the road back to his business in North Bridge Street.

Back in his room Denzil was relieved to find that Monty was clearly out on the town. He sat on the edge of his bed to study the new bank book. He opened it and saw his name inscribed in the inner page. There were many blank pages all ruled off with room for dates and monies lodged but his eye was fixed on the first solitary entry that read "11/06/47 - One Pound Sterling - £1 - 0s – 0d." He looked at it for a long time before placing the book securely and safely in his locker. Thursday was his day off that week and as Denzil relaxed back at the croft with Jean again telling her all about the past weeks happenings he realised with a certain pang that he was unable to tell her about his meeting with Finkelstein and just what had evolved from it. Back at work on the Friday he had an encounter with Mr Scott. Quite clearly in a foul temper he took it out on the two boots porters over some imagined mishap that was none of their doing. They were happy to escape with a major dressing-down from the head of their department. Still smarting from this injustice they reported for their wages to the office. In front of them was a woman in a shabby raincoat and head scarf signing for a pay packet. Denzil had never seen her before. Monty as always had the answer. "See her" he pointed to the woman in question - " Know who she is?" Denzil shook his head." She is the wife of our esteemed and deeply loved head porter."

Puzzled Denzil whispered to him "Mrs Scott. 1 didn't know she worked in the hotel as well."

"Work here no way, you daft bugger!" Monty punched him playfully on the arm "She is just here signing for her old man's pay as usual before he gets his grubby hands on it."

He went on to explain that in the past Scott had arrived home on many occasions with a prolonged stop at the 45 Bar having laid waste to his money. In desperation his wife with a family to feed sought an interview with the manager to see what could be done. Miss MacLean intercepted the matter and in her usual common sense way found a solution in as much as that Mrs Scott would collect and sign for his wages weekly. Matter resolved to everybody's satisfaction save that of the head porter who just had to wear it.

Monty prepared to repay Archie the money he had loaned him adding that his old lady would have to wait until next week when he would be in a position to repay at least one of her advances. He grumbled that he faced a few hard weeks. Just like the hard pressed nation he would be facing his own austerity programme.

Denzil fished out his bank book after Monty had departed. Once at the bank he queued up and finally faced a teller handing over his book and four shillings. The teller took the money, stamped the book and returned it. Denzil was surprised how quickly the transaction had taken. Outside the bank he opened the book to see that the new entry read ' 13/06/47 - four shillings - £1 - 4s -0d.' Well satisfied his next step was to call at the jewellery shop as arranged.

Finkelstein emerged from his work shop area and invited him to come in. The bank book was duly initialled by him and returned. Finkelstein leaned back in his chair with a quiet smile, "Well Denzil - we have got off to a smooth start - wouldn't you agree? Keep it up and see you here next week!"

So a weekly pattern emerged and by the end of June the bank book total read £1 - 12s - Od. July got off to a flying start. Two surveyors were booked into the Royal for two weeks engaged in surveying work high up in the hills for a new hydro dam project. Nightly outside their bedroom doors they placed their mud encrusted boots for attention. Monty in a bad mood with his financial problems pulled rank on Denzil, "Right Dez - as you're the junior boots these are your problem."

Denzil decided that he would give this task his best attention. He carefully washed the mud off the boots in the pantry, rubbed them dry before applying the boot polish and finally bringing them up to a shine with a soft cloth. Once or twice as he replaced the boots at the door one of the occupants in a dressing gown heading for the toilet acknowledged him. On the final day of their stay, as he replaced the boots for the final time the bedroom door opened. The guest emerged to thank him for the care he had taken of their footwear during their stay and handed him two shillings! It was Denzil's first tip. He decided not to tell Monty. So on the 4th July it was with some satisfaction that he lodged six shillings into his account. In the jewellery shop Finkelstein as he initialled the book nodded quiet approval as Denzil explained his windfall. He found living on five shillings a week manageable. With having every afternoon free it was quite tempting to enjoy an ice cream slider from the Bonnacorsi cafe or a bag of chips. He had been going to the pictures twice a week but this he curtailed to once a week. He stopped buying magazines as he discovered that guests discarded them in their rooms and while clearing pantry rubbish he could salvage plenty of reading material. There was a final twist to the surveyors boots saga. The surveyors had written to the Royal manager saying how much they had enjoyed their stay with excellent food and in particular the care extended even to their footwear! Apparently in another hotel they stayed in the staff had refused to clean them. Miss MacLean sought Denzil out at the lodge and congratulated him while Mr Scott and Monty ground their teeth in the background for different reasons.

The July flying start continued. On Friday 18 Denzil was in the back room of the jeweller's shop as Finkelstein handed him back his bank book. "Two Pounds, six shillings. It's going very well Denzil" he commented "Now I have got something that might interest you. You say you are free most afternoons so this might appeal to you. Here in North Bridge Street some of us have had our windows cleaned for many years by old Bob Wright. He's a bit of a character - a First World War veteran. Now he is due to go into hospital for a few weeks for some operation or other. He has a fairly sizeable round and one of his colleagues had agreed to take on most of his round until he returns. This gives his friend a very heavy workload on top of his own round. I had an idea and see what you think about it. If the four shops in our street were taken off his hands it would ease his burden? How about if you take on these fours shops until Bob returns? He will show you the ropes and it will not only fill your afternoon but earn you some more money into the bargain." Denzil was only too happy to go along with the proposal.

Next afternoon Bob limping badly showed him what it entailed. The four shops were Finkelsteins, a high class ladies fashion shop called Morgan Charles, the Inverdeen Building Society office and Hetty's, a small corner shop trading as a general store selling newspapers, cigarettes, sweets and sundry items. Bob explained that the three major shops were cleaned once weekly on a Wednesday or Thursday so they looked their best for the busy week-end trading. Hetty's was done once a week on no fixed day.

He had organised payment along the following lines. The Fashion shop and Building society paid 1/6d as they both had two large show windows whereas Finkelsteins and Hettys with only one display window would be 1/0d. This would be a total of 5 shillings per week collected in cash. Bob prevailed on Denzil to do a good job always ensuring after doing the windows that the sills were cleaned thoroughly with a soft chamois leather. He had no wish to come out of hospital to face the fact that he had lost some very valuable clients. Denzil assured him of his best efforts to keep the flag flying. His last task was to show where the tools of his trade were stored in a yard at the back of Hetty's shop. This involved going through Hetty's packed shop. Bob introduced Denzil to the shop owner. Hetty turned out to be a very obese lady who moved about her cramped shop with considerable difficulty but made light of things with a hearty smokers laugh. In the yard Bob, among all the buckets, ladders and bric-a-brac of his trade, showed him how to work the long poles with soft mop heads and one with a broad rubber blade to remove the water from the window. The poles had extensions that could be fitted so that they could reach the higher parts of the show windows. Satisfied that things would be done his way Bob made his departure saying that he was looking forward to seeing them again once the doctors had finished with him. Denzil made a note that he would do the windows on the next Wednesday and Thursday as his start date. On his way back to the hotel Denzil did some mental arithmetic, working out that for the next few weeks until Bob returned he would enjoy an income of some fourteen shillings a week. He would for that period bank eight shillings per week and retain six shillings for personal use giving himself a rise of one shilling.

July had proved to be a rewarding month! The two boys did not take much note of world news as it all seemed so far away, never appearing to have much impact on their lives. In early July they broke off for lunch to find the staff hall table in a fervour of some considerable excitement. The news had just broken that the King's eldest daughter the Princess Elizabeth had become engaged to Lt Philip Mountbatten. The housemaids all thought that it was so romantic and could hardly contain themselves. Male staff members were a bit more phlegmatic about the event. Old Willie the hotel handyman, pipe in mouth, voiced a concern,"See here. She is going to be the next Queen but does that mean this Philip fellow will be King?"

The conversation raged long after the two boots had left to finish their shift. July saw Denzil complete two window cleaning sessions. He found the outdoor work enjoyable and soon got the hang of carting the water buckets about and using the brushes not forgetting the chamois leather finishing touch. What was even more enjoyable was the extra money that came his way. He would certainly have to come down to earth with a bump when old Bob returned to claim his round. He had to tell Monty about his extra activity but stressed it was just for a few weeks while Jean when he told her was concerned that he was doing too much. Friday 1st August he presented himself and his bank book to North Bridge street as usual. Finkelstein almost purred with satisfaction as he noted the new total that now read £3 - 2s - Od. Things may have been looking rosy on Denzil's financial front but the same could not be said for the nation. The placard outside Hettys read " CABINET IN URGENT TALKS ON ECONOMIC CRISIS" Prime Minister Atlee warned Parliament of " peril and anxiety" in the country's inability to pay for imports. Among food cuts the total meat ration is reduced by two pence to one shilling per week, ration books would be needed in hotels after two nights, foreign holidays banned from next month. Businessmen going to Europe not allowed any more than £8 in foreign currency.

The Prime Minister ended by calling for sacrifices akin to wartime stating, "I have no easy words for the nation. I cannot say when we shall emerge into easier times." Little wonder that the royal engagement discussion around the staff hall table was summed up by Grace Salmon one of the cleaners, "Thank God for something to bring a bit of cheer into our lives!" All this was totally lost on Denzil as whistling happily he locked away his bank book securely in the locker. His only concern was to ensure that Monty did not come to know of its existence!

CHAPTER 9   Paddy the Barman

August was the peak month for the struggling tourist trade and increasing business activity meant that the Royal, despite the prevailing national hardship, was trading well. Denzil had by now checked out most of the working areas of the hotel. The hotel still-room where tea and coffee was brewed along with sandwich preparation and cakes for afternoon teas supplied by the kitchen pastry chef was a well recognised ' no-go area' Five formidable housewife friends from a fairly rough estate in the town ran the still-room on a rota basis. Monty referred to them as the Five Wise Virgins but never in their hearing! A combination of Monty's banter and an occasional couple of rabbits, victims of the Cabrach snares, gained them access to the odd off duty cup of tea and sometimes even a cake.

Word about the still-room rabbit soon got about as very few things in an hotel environment stayed private for long. Sous chef Jock McIntosh buttonholed Denzil one morning. "Here boy. I hear you're a rabbit trapper in your spare time, is that right?"

Denzil's first thought was that he might have broken some hotel rule and he slowly nodded his head waiting for some rebuke. Jock then explained to him that, as sous chef, he was responsible for the staff hall catering and it was always a struggle, what with rationing and everything to provide a varied diet. Most of the professional rabbit trappers seemed to get a better price for their catch down south. Could Denzil provide six to eight rabbits weekly that he could use for staff meals? If so the hotel could pay 9d a rabbit paid through petty cash. A relieved Denzil quickly agreed to this deal and so another money making venture fell into his lap.

He purchased more snares as an investment in his new venture. On his next day off he told Jean all about it. She agreed to help him out by setting snares the day before he came home so that some rabbits lay on the bottom shelf of the outside milk larder awaiting his attention. Next morning his own catch was added. Jean insisted on skinning and gutting the rabbits although he tried to assure her that there was plenty of Royal kitchen staff to attend to that side of things. The net result was that Denzil returned to the Royal after his day off with a carrier bag filled with rabbit carcases individually wrapped in newspaper. He soon found himself collecting the petty cash payment for this supply weekly from the same office as hotel staff was issued. The payments could vary between four shillings and sixpence and six shillings. The clerkess suggested to him that he should collect this payment at the same time as he collected his pay. Denzil politely declined this helpful suggestion. No way did he want to have Monty come to know about his additional income stream! His first supply was eight rabbits so he collected a very welcome six shillings on the Friday morning. He made some excuse to Monty before slipping away to complete the office transaction. In the bank that afternoon he passed over fourteen shillings along with his bank book. He got quiet satisfaction at Finkelstein's surprise at the latest entry. On learning about Denzil's latest enterprise the jeweller removed his glasses, slapped his thigh and laughed out loud. He handed back the bank book remarking that this would help to cushion matters when Bob Wright came out of hospital to reclaim his round. Just about this time Denzil met up with the final character in the Royal when Monty and himself were roped in one morning for a new task. The porters were busy and under strength as Andy Bremner was down with flu. A porter was detailed on a daily basis to transport beer and spirits from the Liquor Store to re-supply the Cocktail Bar.

The two boys used an old fashioned staff lift to transport the items from the secure store in the basement. The Cocktail bar was impressive. The bar like a high altar with subtle lighting and inverted bottles glistening on the optics in neat array as well as on the glass shelves. A cleaner was hoovering the carpeted area while, behind the bar, the cocktail barman prepared his bar for service. The barman looked up at their arrival. Denzil guessed that he was in his late thirties with a ready smile. He was in shirt sleeve order as he sliced oranges and lemons into a silver dish. Philip Aloysius Tomkins was a man of mystery. In point of fact he had been one of the first members of staff that Miss MacLean had ever interviewed when she had been appointed personal assistant.

The hotel had experienced some problems during the war years finding a suitable cocktail barman. Miss MacLean was just finding her feet in her new role when a regular customer, a retired lawyer Iain Smith who called in almost daily at the same time for a large malt, stopped her one day. He complained that his malt whisky was not as it should be in his opinion so would she look into the matter forthwith. She assured him that she would. After thinking things over she decided to call in the hotel stocktaker a Mr Val Boyling whose office was in Carlton street. Major Drysdale approved this action. Boyling called in one morning without warning and it did not take long for him to uncover the problem. The barman turned out to be a secret alcoholic. His party piece was to take a bottle of whisky and pour about a third of its contents into an empty lemonade bottle to take away and consume at his leisure. He then filled the whisky bottle with water so it looked full before returning it to the optic. Boyling's hydrometer that showed the density of spirits soon revealed that the bar was awash with watered down liquors of all kinds. The barman was dismissed on the spot and his position advertised. Meanwhile a barman drafted in from the Ballroom bar staff held the fort. Miss Maclean conducted the interviews. Tomkins stood out from the other applicants. His friendly, confident manner backed up by an impeccable reference from the Gresham Hotel in Dublin and his membership of the United Kingdom Bartenders Guild landed him the job. On his first day in his new appointment he looked with distaste at the white patrol jacket that the previous incumbents had worn. He showed Miss MacLean a dark green lightweight blazer with an ornate crest

75

on its breast pocket that would be his preference. She had to agree that it added more class and asked what the crest stood for. Philip declared airily that it was his old alma mater and that was very much that. Within a day or so he had completely turned the bar into a new league. The bar had lapsed for many years in inefficient hands and the turnover was to say the least disappointing. The new barman informed Miss MacLean that he would like to be known as Paddy and so it came to pass. She kept a close eye on developments as Paddy settled into his new post. Drysdale returned from a weeks golfing holiday asked her anxiously how their new charge was settling in. She had sufficient confidence by this time to inform him that a star was born'!

It was no exaggeration to say that the bar exploded into action. Paddy ran it like a stage actor and the bar for its part reacted favourably to his stage management. It started like most major events in a minor fashion. An harassed businessman who dropped in for a reviving drink would find himself being introduced by Paddy to somebody else who had dropped in for the same reason. Several drinks later they would part agreeing to meet up in the same venue. Paddy greeted anybody who entered the bar like an old friend in a slightly raised theatrical voice that dominated the bar. "Good morning Sir, nice to see you again. Please have a seat and I will attend to you shortly" to a regular "Afternoon sir - Your usual diet I presume?" to a lady entering on her own, " Good day Madam it was a dull day until you came in like a ray of sunshine, please have a seat and I will attend to you shortly"

His art was to make people not only feel welcome but perhaps, more importantly, to feel important. Local businessmen entertaining important clients loved the feeling that on entering the bar they were greeted in a welcoming and respectful manner. It was as if it underlined their standing in the community. Individuals who came in to sit at the bar stools that fronted the bar would find themselves unloading their problems on to Paddy who always seemed to have a sympathetic ear. This would involve downing several drinks and in the end they invariably stood Paddy a drink. Indeed Paddy once complained to Miss MacLean with some humour." You know Miss MacLean - I'm thinking of seriously taking holy orders - they seem to think at times that this is a confessional with their marital and business problems." Miss MacLean looked at him shrewdly before replying, "I see most times they pay for their confessions!" Paddy just smiled at this observation.

Nobody ever saw him take a drink. Whenever a client offered him a drink he would invariably reply with his standard reply "Sir you are too kind!" This could vary when a group placed a large drinks order and ended by saying, "Oh and have one for yourself!" Paddy would come back with "Thank you sir, as you know I do not drink on duty but I have to confess a large brandy at the end of the night is a great comfort!" The money for drinks offered to him ended up in a special compartment in his till known as Paddy's Poke.

Lunch time clients who dropped in for a drink as they looked at the racing news found Paddy to be something of an expert on the racing scene. He had a unique sense of humour and stories soon abounded about him. An example was a young vet in a local practice called Robertson who became a regular and once called on his services. He had been attracted to a very superior young lady who was a secretary in a local legal firm. After much soul searching he had invited her out to dinner and much to his surprise she had accepted. The young vet asked Paddy to look after them when they came in for a pre-dinner drink and build him up. Paddy assured him of his best attention. On the night the young vet sat down with his new date making small talk. Paddy let them settle down before bearing down on them with his silver tray in hand. He greeted the young couple in his best theatrical fashion, "Good evening Mr Robertson sir. How nice to see you again now what would you and the future Mrs Robertson care to partake of ?" Amidst much laughter, joined in by a blushing secretary, the ice was truly broken. The popularity of the bar spread like wild fire. Miss MacLean had to engage a part time waitress to assist in the busy bar at weekends. Soon she had to engage another such waitress. One waitress covered a weekday night while both were employed at the weekends. She was fortunate to secure the services of two identical twin sisters, Angela and Paula MacLaren, one dark haired and one blonde. The bar activity on busy nights over-spilled into the lounge area in the main foyer. Within a month or so the bar became known as Paddy's Bar and Philip referred to as Mr Paddy. Paddy did not confine his activities to promoting his bar. Couples dropping in for a drink were soon informed of what the kitchen had to offer that night and soon the Maitre d' would appear at their shoulder with menus for their perusal. Jack Mitchell with his own professional approach to his calling appreciated the way Paddy operated.

There was however a downside to this relationship. On many occasions a party booked in for dinner would gather in Paddy's bar for an aperitif before proceeding to the restaurant. Paddy's attention and performance would usually result in this process being somewhat delayed. Jack Mitchell would find himself having to enter the bar to rescue his overdue diners and addressing Paddy with mock severity, "Mr Paddy, have you kidnapped my guests?" The party would then rise amidst much laughter having consumed more drinks than they had anticipated. The cost of several large brandies would also be nestling in Paddy's poke. Miss MacLean could only estimate just how much Paddy derived tax free but in a week he could easily quadruple his weekly pay and that was only an estimate!

The increased turnover and profit percentage returned by the bar broke new records. The strange thing was nobody knew very much about Paddy. When asked where he hailed from he said vaguely that it was somewhere just outside Dublin. As the war had just ended most people had seen service one way or another so, if Paddy was asked if he had served, he would simply reply, "Army service, what me? With my flat feet, 1 don't think so!"

He never spoke about himself in any respect. A couple of months after he had transformed the bar Miss MacLean was struck by a sudden thought about their mystery barman. She dug out from her files the letter from the Gresham Hotel and the United Bar Tenders Guild certificate. At the interview she had taken them at face value but now she took the trouble to contact both parties for confirmation. They both replied within a week and neither had ever employed or had a member of that name. She gave the matter considerable private contemplation before replacing the correspondence back in her file and decided on no further action.

One particular action took place that cemented Paddy's place in Royal folklore. It took place one busy November night and, as it so happened, Major Drysdale and his wife were entertaining the Royal's managing director and his wife. They were working their way through a bottle of vintage champagne in Paddy's bar prior to dinner. Paddy was behind the bar dealing with a bar lined with clients while Angela MacLaren tended to the crowded table area. A man entered the hotel front door. He was about six foot tall, casually dressed, unshaven with a surly, unpleasant expression. Roddy at the porters desk was first to spot him. He went forward to challenge the unwelcome guest but the man simply brushed him aside as he made for the welcoming haven of Paddy's bar. Roddy decided that discretion was the best part of valour and retreated back to the lodge. The man stood now at the entrance to the bar and conversation dried at several tables nearby at his presence. Drysdale spotted him and knew with a sinking sensation that here was going to be trouble big time.

Paddy spotted the intruder at the same time and moved smoothly into action. Leaving the bar he approached the man who was standing swaying slightly, surveying the room. Paddy realised that here was a drunk who would be difficult to deal with. "Good evening, sir" Paddy addressed him - " Sorry we are a bit busy tonight, perhaps if you have a seat in the lounge then I can attend to you." The drunk stared at him for a moment before saying in a loud voice "Fuck off!"

Conversation died away as everybody took in this confrontation. The drunk looked around. Two ladies sitting with their gin and tonics had a spare chair at their table so he plonked himself down there effectively blocking the two ladies from vacating the table. He fished in his pocket, drew out a crumpled five pound note, threw it down on the table before speaking to Paddy, "Hey you gie us a fucking large whisky and make it snappy!" He accompanied this demand by slamming his open hand on the table so forcibly that one of the ladies glasses spilled over as they recoiled in some alarm.

Drysdale closed his eyes at what he was witnessing. It was clear that if the police were called trouble would probably kick off long before they arrived. Paddy appeared to heave a slight sigh as he bent down to pick up the crumpled five pound note saying "Certainly sir, I shall look after you right away!"

Drysdale could not believe his ears. Had Paddy taken leave of his senses? Paddy turned the bank note up to the light and squinted at it, "I'm sorry sir but this note is a fake!"

The drunk sat up in his seat. "A fake. What the fuck are you on about?"

Holding the note up Paddy continued "Here see for yourself." The drunk lurched to his feet, took the note in his hand with a puzzled look on his face, clearly no longer in charge of the situation. What happened next has often been discussed by those present. It was evident that Paddy had got the distracted drunk up and out of his seat. There was a sudden blur of movement as Paddy moved into action. His right hand crossed the drunk's chest to secure a firm grip on his jacket's lapel. His left hand took hold of the drunk's arm gripping it by the wrist so that it was braced hard against Paddy's rigid forearm. The bank note fluttered down onto the table as the surprised drunk took stock of this new situation.

"What the fu..." was as far as he got before Paddy twisted and pulled firmly on his wrist. An excruciating pain clearly took over the drunk's world as speech and physical reaction were beyond him. His body was arched, his mouth fell open and he tried to stand on tip toe to escape from this agony. Paddy relaxed his grip for a moment saying "Now sir, I think it is time for you to leave." The drunk now his pain subsiding clearly had other ideas, clenched his free fist and attempted to strike his captor. Paddy simply applied his wrist twist and the drunk sharply re-entered his world of pain. Standing locked together Paddy decided that matters had gone far enough. "Shall we dance sir?" he enquired in his stage voice before setting out of the bar propelling the transfixed drunk who was walking backwards clearly wracked in some distress. They passed the porter's desk where Roddy stood wide-eyed observing their passing. The two figures eventually disappeared out of the swing door leaving a stunned and silent bar in their wake. What happened outside would forever remain a mystery. Did the drunk offer resistance once released or, as Paddy maintained, suffer a bad fall on the pavement after he left him? Certainly Paddy was outside for less than a minute before returning commanding Roddy to summon an ambulance. A relieved Roddy scurried off to do as he was asked.

Paddy's return to his bar was greeted by a spontaneous round of applause which he acknowledged with a slight bow. He went immediately to the table occupied by the two ladies who had been trapped when the drunk had claimed the spare seat. Angela the waitress had already mopped up the spilt drink although the banknote still lay on the table. His voice carried over the still hushed bar." Ladies - the gentleman in question sends you his profound apologies. He was not quite himself tonight. He would like to stand you a refreshment to make some amends." The banknote was plucked up as he strode back to the bar as normal conversation broke out. Drysdale discovered that he had downed his champagne in one relieved gulp. The two gin and tonics were delivered by Angela to the grateful recipients. Paddy rang up the drinks on the till and the balance of the fiver ended up in Paddy's poke.

As Angela deposited the drinks on the lounge table the sound of a siren could be heard in the background as an ambulance arrived at the hotel entrance. The medics discovered a body slumped against the hotel wall, moaning gently clutching a broken elbow and badly dislocated wrist. There had to be a post script. Once in A & E the drunk had complained that he had been assaulted. The police were informed and, duty bound, had to make an investigation. They called at closing time when Paddy confirmed that he had escorted the man out of the hotel quite peacefully. Once outside the drunk had suffered a bad fall so he had summoned an ambulance in case he required medical attention. Major Drysdale confirmed events so the police closed their notebooks, wished the two gentlemen well and took off into the night. Naturally the night's event was much discussed in homes and offices by those present. It only served to add to the aura that surrounded the Royal cocktail barman. Drysdale recounted what had happened to Miss MacLean over morning coffee in the office next day. His military training told him that the hold that Paddy had immobilised the drunk with showed a certain proficiency in unarmed combat in his opinion. Miss MacLean decided to share this observation with Paddy to see his reaction. Paddy professed to be deeply shocked, "Unarmed combat. Whatever next? I don't understand why everyone is making such a fuss. The poor fellow was so drunk I practically had to hold him up."

Miss MacLean smiled to herself and thought there would be little point in ever raising the question of the highly questionable references in her file. Somehow Paddy she imagined would have some glib answer to even that.

Chapter 10   The Window Cleaner

Denzil settled into a fairly busy pattern of activity that August. His hotel job kept him active until he was free in the afternoon to tackle his window cleaning routine. He had to work that activity around his day off but as he was not tied to any specific days that was easily managed.

His day off came as a pleasant break as the crofting chores were tackled. His snaring enterprise established, he asked permission of neighbouring crofter Jack Munro to operate on the steep hillside running up from his croft house. This hillside on a summer's evening was alive with rabbits cavorting about so Jack was only too happy to let Denzil exact a toll on its population. He always ensured that a rabbit was handed into Mrs Munro as he cleared his snares.

Jean loved to hear him talk about life in the Royal as it opened a window into a life beyond her crofting world. The Cabrach rabbits featured as a weekly treat on the staff hall table in the form of a savoury stew with dumplings. Denzil managed to collect his rabbit money usually on Monty's day off, a wise move as Monty seemed to be eternally involved in struggling to live within his means.

In mid-August one Tuesday morning the boys were at the Porters' lodge collecting the papers to distribute to the guest bedrooms. Finkelstein made his usual descent of the main staircase heading off to start his working day. Scott who was strutting importantly in front of the desk greeted him effusively

"Good morning Mr Finkelstein!" Finkelstein barely acknowledged him as he appeared to be deep in thought with his head lowered. He passed Scott then looked up and beckoned to Denzil. He went forward to meet the old jeweller meeting with him in the main foyer. Finkelstein lowered his voice "Denzil, sad news I'm afraid to tell you. I have just had a call from Bob Wright's daughter to tell me that her father passed away in hospital earlier this morning. I thought you should know. See you on Friday, my boy." He walked slowly off towards the front door.

Denzil was taken aback at this news but before he had time to properly take it on board Scott was in his face snarling-" What's the likes of you chatting to Finkie for? My God, you're getting a bit to big for your boots around here?"

Denzil was glad to escape with his bundle of papers. On Friday Finkelstein informed him that he would be attending the funeral the next day. The following Friday, as Denzil attended with his bank book once again, the jeweller had some news to impart. "Denzil, I was speaking to Chalmers at the funeral, he is the one who took over Bob's main round when he went into hospital. He has taken on somebody part time to handle his now enlarged round. However he is more than happy for you to retain the Bridge street shops on a permanent basis. Looks as if you have fallen heir to Bob's equipment as well. I told Chalmers that you would be happy with that arrangement. Are you happy with the outcome?" Denzil nodded his agreement. This was the last Friday in August and the total of £5 - 14s - 0d in the bankbook was duly ticked as they moved into September. Denzil had a certain routine after he had cleaned Hetty's window and stored his equipment away in her back yard shed. He bought his sweet ration with his ration book in her shop. Hetty, with her big bulk perched as always on a reinforced stool behind her till, grumbled at her lack of mobility. Many customers served themselves while Hetty sat at the till waiting to take their cash, One afternoon she asked Denzil if he would do one afternoon per week to assist her. It would involve stacking shelves, general cleaning, sorting out cardboard boxes and other rubbish for the twice weekly bin collection. His pay would be one shilling and his sweet ration would be free. They shook hands on the deal and yet another of Denzil's free afternoons was taken care of. The newspaper placards outside her shop kept Denzil in touch with world news as he prepared them for the weekly rubbish collection. One placard read in bold lettering "SUN SETS ON BRITISH RAJ!

" Apparently British rule had ended after some 163 years and two new dominions, India and Pakistan, were born out of Britain's Indian Empire.

He found that he was now banking a total of fifteen shillings a week. Once or twice he had to buy new shoes and underwear so that the total could fluctuate but Finkelstein ticked his book weekly expressing satisfaction. His September 26th running total now read £8 - 5s - 0d. Alongside the Joe Louis picture on his wall Monty had a new hero. A black and white action photograph of a debonair cricketer Denis Compton performing his trade mark sweep stroke. That glorious summer he had scored record figures of 18 centuries and 3,816 runs that did much to lift the nation's morale.

In early October, as austerity tightened its grip, it was announced that the bacon ration was to be cut to one ounce per week. There were harsh words around the staff hall table by the housewife element at this latest cut. Monty tried to lighten the general gloom by announcing that his assistant Dezzy in addition to supplying rabbits was starting up a herd of pigs. He advised those present to place their orders early!

The tourist season had all but wrapped up by early October. Business activity took its place and stock room action boomed as agents displayed their wares to catch the hoped for Christmas bonanza. The boys were for some weeks steady callers with their hand barrow at the railway station. It was a case of either collecting agents cases from the trains or transporting a laden hand barrow with cases for departure back from whence they came. Mr Scott made a point of meeting an agent on arrival at the hotel and seeing them off when their time was up. As a result he collected the agent's tip although he had very little to do with the work involved. This was a bone of contention amongst the other porters. A few agents like Frank Malone were aware of this and got round it by giving Scott half of the tip and then giving the other half to the porters at the station prior to departure. The boots never received any share of this tip and were told that they would only qualify once they in turn had graduated to becoming a porter and it was something to look forward to!

In late October the town mart was busy for three days as a major sale took place every year. Many farmers selling livestock that they had fattened up over the summer before the winter months set in. One morning Denzil observed a strange happening. An elderly unkempt man in a shabby, stained raincoat carrying a shepherd's crook marched into the foyer making straight for the reception desk. He saw Mr Scott make a bee line for him and waited for the altercation that was surely going to come about. Instead to his amazement Scott greeted the man warmly even shaking his hand and conversing in an animated fashion. Archie marched into the lodge where the other porters were having a tea break. Denzil followed him, his curiosity aroused.

"Look out - look out! Old Abrach is in town! Lock up your daughters!" There was general laughter.

"Well - that will make Mrs Mac's day with her favourite guest back in town and I don't think!" added Andy Bremner to further gales of laughter. Denzil learned that Abrach Mackay had a farm over in the west coast and hit town every October to sell his livestock. An eccentric character well into his seventies he lived alone. He booked into the Royal every year and the tale was told that when he first booked in he had to be persuaded that his collie dog was not exactly welcome. In the end a cattleman employed at the mart looked after the dog for a handsome retainer every year. Abrach booked a top quality room for himself but that was it. He never used the bar or restaurant preferring to drink with his cronies in a spit and sawdust pub close to the mart. All his meals were snatched at some dingy workman's diner.

Archie said that always on his departure Scott would receive a substantial tip so that explained his warm welcome to this particular guest. There was a downside to this guest. His personal hygiene left much to be desired. The bath in his special room was totally unused during his stay and, after his three day stay was over, Mrs MacBeth claimed that she had to have the room fumigated and his bed linen laundered twice! Archie told the story of one year he was coming down in the lift with an expensively dressed American couple from the second floor. The lift doors were about to close when old Abrach came shambling along in their direction. The American guest paused the lift so that old Abrach could travel down with them. Once inside the lift door closed on the quartet. The hotel central heating was on and soon this reacted with Abrach and a certain miasma seemed to surround him. Archie knowing the form, held his breath. The American couple were not so fortunate and a minute or so later on the ground floor they reeled out of the lift green at the gills. A can of air freshener was always at hand in the porters' lodge during Abrach's stay.

By this time Denzil was a recognised figure in the bank as he did his weekly banking. One occasion when he was waiting in the queue Mr Holland passed by ruffling his hair and commenting "Well young fellow - how is the first million coming along then?" His entry for Friday 31st October 1947 read £11 - 6s - 0d . So he had breached the £10 barrier! Finkelstein smiled in quiet satisfaction as he ticked it off saying almost to himself "Remarkable, quite remarkable!" He almost felt guilty when he heard Monty moaning about his financial plight and thought of the bank book secure in his locker.

Monday 10th November Denzil celebrated his fifteenth birthday. As a celebration it was a muted affair as he told nobody not even Monty. That morning to his total surprise as he passed Miss MacLean, who was on her rounds, she stopped and said, "Happy Birthday Denzil. Many happy returns!" She made a habit of entering in her diary the birthday dates of staff members. It made them feel part of the hotel family and especially important to the younger members especially young housemaids from the islands who were away from home for the first time in their first employment. On November 20 Princess Elizabeth was married to Prince Philip now styled as the Duke of Edinburgh, in a glittering service at Westminster Abbey before a congregation of some 2,500. In London crowds, some who had slept out overnight, were 50 deep along the Mall and Whitehall to cheer the young couple in the impressive state coach. It was a colourful and welcome break as the nation struggled in the aftermath of the War. Miss MacLean arranged for a wireless to be installed in the staff hall so that staff could listen in and feel part of the national celebration.

However Denzil was to remember that royal wedding for a very different reason. On Friday 28th November he had banked ten shillings now making a total in his bankbook of £13-lls-0d. Back in the hotel Calum asked him if he would deliver some mail and newspaper to the Manager' suite. He took off his jacket in the lodge and quickly donned his uniform to do the task. Later back in his room he went into the usual routine of locking away his bankbook in his locker. He felt in the usual pocket. No sign of the book! He checked every pocket with growing alarm but no sign. Perhaps he had dropped it in the street or maybe even the lodge when he changed jackets. He made the lodge his first port of call. Just his luck the only person in the lodge was Mr Scott checking the staff rota. Denzil looked around and checked his uniform pocket but no sign.

Scott turned at this point as if he had just become aware of his presence. "Looking for something, boy?" he queried. Denzil was stammering out some excuse when Scott suddenly reached in his pocket and produced the bankbook, "Could this be what you are after?" Denzil felt an enormous wave of relief, taking the book and expressing his thanks he was glad to escape to the sanctuary of his room where the bankbook was secured. Lying in bed that night he was glad that the incident had passed off well and that Scott did not seem to have looked at the book as he had made no comment.

Next afternoon he realised just how wrong he had been in this assumption. Scott asked if he could have a private word with him in the lodge. Once in the lodge with the door closed he opened up to Denzil "Look Denzil lad" It was the first time he had ever addressed Denzil by his first name. "I couldn't help noticing that you have managed to save a wee bit of money in your book. I have a favour to ask of you could you lend me say £9 as I have Christmas presents to buy for my family this week? The loan will be only for a few weeks as I get a good Christmas bonus in mid December and I will repay you in full. I wouldn't normally do this but it would help me out and I would be very grateful."

Denzil had an initial feeling of unease but he reasoned with himself that to lend Mr Scott some money for a few weeks until he was repaid would work out. Perhaps it would mean that the Head porter would view him with a more kindly attitude in future as he had helped him out.

He agreed to Scott's proposal. Scott suggested that if he withdrew the money that afternoon it would be really helpful and he asked if Denzil would not discuss their arrangement with anybody. So Denzil found himself back in the bank withdrawing nine pounds and handing it over to Scott who expressed his gratitude. He looked at the bank book entry before he locked it away. It now read £2 -1s -0d - and Denzil thought it was good to have money saved up so that one was able to help somebody out even for a few weeks. Friday 5th December he paid in fifteen shillings before heading for the jeweller's shop. It was on his way there that it dawned on him that he would have to explain why the entry now read a meagre £3 - 6s -Od. Mrs Finkelstein smiled he he entered the shop while Finkelstein called out from his workshop, "Come away in my boy." Denzil passed the book over without comment. Finkelstein opened the book to apply his usual tick, he paused and Denzil saw his face darken with a look of disappointment. He looked at Denzil over his gold rimless glasses, "What's this Denzil. Are you throwing a Christmas party for the staff?"

Denzil explained how the withdrawal had come about. It did not do much to dispel the dark look that had crossed the old man's face but he ticked the book entry as usual before Denzil went on his way. Over the next couple of weeks Denzil observed that Mr Scott seemed to be in a good mood even to the extent of calling him Denzil. However that Friday as Monty and himself were signing for their wages he found Mrs Scott ahead of them signing for her husband's pay and that initial feeling of unease returned never quite to go away. Two weeks passed and Mr Scott made no mention of repaying his loan. On Friday 19th December Finkelstein asked him if the loan had been repaid and did not seem unduly surprised when Denzil gave him a negative reply. "Right,my boy. Time for action. Go back this afternoon and ask Scott point blank when you can depend on the loan being returned. Then return here and advise of me the situation. 1 know you don't like doing it but remember it's your money."

Denzil returned to the hotel with a heavy heart. He asked Scott if he could speak to him in private and had to wait some time in the lodge before the head porter came in shutting the door behind him. Denzil summoned up his courage and enquired when the loan would be repaid in a faltering voice. Scott gave him hard look before replying, "Well I have been giving the matter some thought. Where did a boy like you get that kind of money eh? It must be stolen I think. A lot of tips have gone missing recently. I should by rights have you reported to the manager and have you fired. However I am going to give you another chance. Keep this matter quiet between the two of us but if any more money goes missing, then that will be that. Let this be a lesson to you. Now off you go and let's hear no more about it!"

Denzil knew that there was no use in protesting further and left the lodge with a sinking feeling in the pit of his stomach. He trailed back to North Bridge street to report back as instructed. Finkelstein listened to him impassively as he reported what had happened. He seemed to come to a decision. Reaching into a drawer on his workbench he handed Denzil nine pounds in one pound notes. Denzil looked at it in surprise. Finkelstein spoke "Right Denzil there is your loan repaid. Let me explain to you what course of action I have decided to take.

Every Christmas as a permanent resident I have got into, the custom of giving the various heads of department a Christmas bonus. Usually it is £10 and a reward for the various extra services they do for me over the year. Now I intend to speak to Scott and tell him that I understand he has a debt due to you that he has been unable to settle so I have paid it out of his bonus to save him any embarrassment. He will receive therefore a bonus of £1 instead of the £10 he will expect." Denzil picked up the money and started to thank Finkelstein but he was cut short. "Denzil, you will find to every action there is a reaction. You might be lucky and Scott will accept the outcome and that will be it. On the other hand he may well react so be prepared for that. Whatever happens we will have to handle it as it comes. That should teach you a lesson for life. Never let anybody know your financial position. If you do people like Scott will forever be tapping you up for loans or inventing schemes to relieve you of your money. Now off you go and bank that money forthwith."

Denzil went to the bank but back in his room Monty was lying on his bed ready for a chat so he could not return the bankbook to his locker. Later when Monty had left to hit the town Denzil got ready to go to Hetty's to do his stint and had an opportunity to look at his bankbook entry. It read £14 -12s - 0d - so things were back to normal. He felt a surge of relief that the matter was finally settled as he secured the bankbook in his locker.

A day or two passed and the hotel was busy as Christmas loomed up. Office parties were a growing business that kept Paddy's bar and the restaurant humming. Denzil had avoided Scott after his meeting with Finkelstein and in the end relaxed confident that the matter was over. On Wednesday, back in the hotel after his day off he was replacing his boots box back in the porters lodge when he became aware of somebody entering the lodge and closing the door. He had half turned thinking he was about to greet one of the porters when his head seemed to explode as a heavy blow to the back of his head sent him sprawling on the floor. Literally seeing stars he looked up to make out standing above him, the head porter with his red face contorted with rage. Two hefty kicks in his ribs left him retching for air as finally, the assault over, Scott shouted at him."

"Right you black bastard. I'll teach you to go running to Finkie with your sob story. Rob me of my bloody bonus would you! I'm going to have you fucking sacked out of here and see how that suits you." Denzil scrambled to his feet, holding his bruised ribs he left the lodge as fast as he could. Scott true to his word sought a word with Major Drysdale that very afternoon. Drysdale for his part talked it over with Miss MacLean next day in the office. She was immediately interested and persuaded the manager to have a cooling off period so she could look into the matter in some depth. Scott tackled Drysdale again and was told that as it was Christmas to give the boy a second chance but if the boy did not sort his ways then he would have to go.

Scott made a point of cornering Denzil in a quiet spot and telling him that just after Christmas he would report him again on some imagined wrongdoing and that that would be that as far as Denzil was concerned. Miss MacLean made a point of talking to Denzil but he closed up and she learned very little about the break down between Scott and himself. Denzil did however open up to Finkelstein on his next bankbook trip and told him in detail of what had taken place. The jeweller was quiet for a while as he took in what he had been told. He removed his glasses and rubbed his eyes in a tired fashion. "Denzil my boy, I feared that this might happen. It was a calculated gamble on my part but I felt that we could not let Scott get away with his theft, for that is what it amounted to in my opinion. It would be nothing short of tragic if he used his position to get you dismissed. I have found in life that if you do not stand up for yourself then nobody will. Often when you are up against an opponent you have to look for his weakness and exploit that. In many cases that is the only vulnerable way of striking back at them. Do you understand what I mean?" Denzil nodded but really was not at all sure what this high minded advice had to do with his situation. They agreed to keep each other posted of developments and parted with Finkelstein telling him to keep his spirits up.

A busy festive period helped to keep his mind off things but, as they moved in to the New Year, Scott again cornered him and said to enjoy his last week in the hotel as he would ensure that in a few days time he would be contacting Drysdale.

That night Denzil found it hard to sleep. He tossed and turned trying to imagine being dismissed and having to trail back to Jean and the croft, trying to explain things. He thought of the words uttered by Finkelstein about looking for a man's weakness if you came up against somebody. Tired and dispirited he fell asleep at last. He woke with a start sometime in the middle of the night with Monty snoring peacefully in the background. All he could see in his mind's eye was Mrs Scott signing for her husband's wages!

That was it! An idea was born but he dismissed it at first as too fanciful, until he realised that he had little or no alternative. His mind made up, he fell asleep. The die was cast.

Next day he cornered his friend commis chef Brian. He explained that he had to take a half bottle of whisky back to his mother. His problem was neither Brian or himself could buy liquor as they were under age so could Brian get one of the kitchen porters to nip out and do the necessary. Brian said no problem as old Walter was quite used to running errands for the chefs. Denzil handed over the money that he had withdrawn from the bank that morning for this purpose and, in due course, Brian handed him a half bottle of White Horse whisky wrapped in tissue paper. That afternoon Denzil volunteered to assist in clearing away coffee cups from the Residents lounge. The half bottle nestled in the inner pocket of his uniform. He had an unreal moment when Finkelstein rose from his afternoon siesta and spoke to him briefly as he left to go back to his business. Denzil thought to himself if he only knew what was lurking in his jacket!

The last three businessmen left the lounge and Denzil moved into action. He placed the half bottle on his tray along with some used coffee cups and headed direct for the lodge. The head porter glanced up as he passed by saying "What's that on your tray Sambo?"

Denzil replied "Somebody left this tucked down a seat in the lounge, I'm just going to enter it in the Lost Property book."

"I'll take care of that. You get yourself back to work 'cos you won't have a job for much longer!" Denzil handed over the whisky as instructed and made himself scarce.

Next day was his day off so once he had finished his shift he prepared to head home to the croft. His lorry lift dropped him off at the bus stop so as he trudged along the road he had plenty of time to reflect on just what he had done. The outcome was anybody's guess but he consoled himself that even if it backfired well he had gone down fighting. Soon he climbed the path and Moss bounded down with his usual rowdy welcome.

CHAPTER 11   Exit Mr Scott

Next day on the late afternoon bus he tried to relax as he headed back to the hotel wondering just what lay ahead of him. Monty was missing so he lay on his bed for an hour or so trying to read a book but finding it almost impossible to concentrate. At last Monty burst through the bedroom door in his usual fashion, bursting with excitement. He plumped himself down on the edge of his bed exclaiming, "Dezzy, boy, trust you to have a day off when it was all kicking off here! It was great! You really missed yourself!"

Denzil sitting upright in his bed had dropped his book. Trying to keep his voice normal he tried to calm his excited workmate, "Hey Monty, hold on. What exactly did I miss?"

Monty was on a high, "Dezzy, Scottie got pissed while on duty. Apparently there was a bottle of whisky in the lodge and he had been tippling away at it. Some elderly couple came to book in and Scottie got up their nose in some way and they took exception to him being under the influence. The guest went to reception to report the matter and who appears but Cleano herself. She told Scott to go off duty but he objected asking her who did she think she was. She took a firm line with him as other guests were standing about watching the set-to. Scottie then started swearing at her until Paddy was alerted from his bar. He calmed Scott down and persuaded him to go home. Cleano had the last word telling Scott to report to her office next day at 9am sharp.

He called in this morning a bit hungover and went to put his uniform on before reporting to Cleano and Drysdale. Cleano however had been in earlier and removed his uniform. She doesn't miss a trick that woman! So the poor bugger had to appear without the comfort of his status symbol wrapped round him. I've no idea what took place there but it appears Scott was fired on the spot. Scottie - fired! Now there's a real late Christmas present and no mistake! Oh, Dezzy boy, you really missed yourself!"

Denzil sat back on his bed agreeing with Monty that he had indeed missed out. Monty was heading out on the town on yet another hot date but had wanted to be the first to tell Denzil the breaking news. Next day Denzil found that Scott's departure was the main subject of conversation in all departments. Calum was summoned to a meeting with Miss MacLean mid-morning. He returned and called all the portering staff for a short meeting in the lodge. His appointment as new head porter would be confirmed shortly, at which they all cheered. The vacancy for porter would be filled by Monty after a week until a new boots had been appointed. End of meeting and back to work.

Monty was exultant at his promotion and the extra money it would entail. "Hey Dezzy," he remarked "You've only been six months here and you are now senior boots! That must be some kind of record." Denzil was only too delighted that the dark cloud of Scott had been removed from his horizon and everything seemed to have worked out so well. Miss MacLean had taken quiet satisfaction from Scott's departure as he had been a malignant influence on the whole portering staff in her opinion. One thing bothered her was why Scott had taken a half bottle of whisky into the lodge for his consumption whilst on duty. It was not to remain a problem for long. One afternoon shortly after the event she had occasion to go into the kitchen. The chefs had knocked off for the afternoon leaving the three kitchen porters to clear up ready for dinner service. One was busy washing cooking pots at the double sink, the other was peeling potatoes leaving old Walter mopping the floor in his bare feet, swearing and speaking to himself.

Miss MacLean always spoke to the KPs again simply to make them feel that they mattered and that the job they did was important to the smooth running of the Royal. Walter grunted in reply and then leaning on his mop declared, "Aye I'm fine, but I want to bring something to your notice! Young Brian and yon black boots boy are drinking whisky! They made me fetch it for them, half bottle of White Horse! They're far too young for that carry on. I hope you'll have a word with the pair of them?"

Miss MacLean assured the agitated kitchen porter that she would do just that. She left smiling as part of the jigsaw had just fallen into place. Friday 26th was Boxing Day. It was a Bank Holiday also so Denzil was not able to do his normal banking until Monday 29th. The Finkelsteins had gone off to London for the festive period and closed their shop for that period. His banking on the 29th would have been fifteen shillings but to his surprise his window cleaning Clients, and even Hetty, gave him small Christmas bonuses so that he banked his best ever total amounting to £2 - 17s - 0d. His running total as he prepared to enter 1948 was £16 - 19s - 0d. Friday 2nd January fell on a Friday so banks were once again closed as part of the Scottish New Year celebrations. It was 9th January before things returned to normal on his banking front and he lodged £1 -1 - 0d for the two weeks.

He entered the shop in North Bridge Street to be welcomed by Mrs Finkelstein wishing him a happy New Year. On the way to the shop Denzil knew that his bank total was more than satisfactory but what comment would Finkelstein pass when he saw the withdrawal he had made to purchase the whisky. Finkelstein was seated at his workbench looking at some watch part with a magnifying glass. At Denzil's entry he put the glass down on the bench and turned to give him his attention.

"Well Denzil, my boy, Happy New Year to you and may good luck continue to shine on you. It was certainly a piece of good luck that removed Mr Scott from the scene and no mistake." He ticked the book as usual. "I think Denzil, at the outset I believe I said, if you saved diligently, you could have a nest egg of £12 or thereabouts. Now here you have a total of £18 - 5s- 0d and still have six months of the year to run. Very well done and keep it up. I note here you have a small withdrawal a few weeks ago. I trust you were not buying a going away present for our departed head porter?" Denzil laughed. The old jeweller sat in silence for some time after

Denzil had departed then he burst out into a peal of laughter, so loud that his wife came into the workshop in some concern.

Monty moved his gear out of their room to make way for the new boots. He turned out to be a small boy with spiky fair hair and a cheeky face. His name was Jimmy Grant but due to his Germanic appearance everybody called him Fritzi. His father was a game-keeper in a remote glen some thirty miles to the west and head of a staunch Catholic household numbering eleven children. Monty remarked to Fritzi when he learned this that his family must have been only too happy to kick him out to work.

A better working atmosphere now operated under Calum. His first move was to inform everybody that from now on tips would be shared instead of everybody looking out for themselves as happened under Scott's regime. A padlocked box or "tronc" was placed in the lodge and everybody lodged their tips in it and once a week Calum would pay out to the porters based on a points system. Points were determined by position and length of service. He even went so far as to include the boots in the system as in his opinion they often had to assist the porters in their duties. Life in the Royal soon settled back into the usual routine now that the festive period was behind them. Fritzi turned out to be an eager learner and thankfully did not talk as much as Monty. Monty for his part settled into his new role and increase in weekly pay but Denzil soon discovered that his spending pattern increased accordingly and he was soon back to living on advances as before. Hetty came to rely on Denzil more and more and he soon found himself doing extra work in her shop. He never asked her for money for this additional work and managed to fit it in round his fairly full working cycle. Another client emerged for his window cleaning round when a vacant shop beside Morgan Charles fashion shop was taken over by a national shoe company called Troughtons. His weekly take from window cleaning was now 6/6d which was very heartening. His share from the porters tronc was usually about 2/-. Monty never stopped telling Fritzi how lucky he was to have started working under Calum and the hardship he and Denzil` had endured under Scott's reign. Denzil was now banking in the region of one pound per week subject to the amount of rabbits he delivered or his share of the porters' tronc.

At the end of January as Denzil took in a newspaper placard from outside Hetty's shop, he noticed that it read "GHANDI ASSASSINATED!" He found that that this often led him to read the unsold paper in the shop and slowly he developed an interest in world affairs. He was able to add to the discussions that often ranged about the staff hall table. January's end saw his bankbook total stand at £21 - 2s - 0d.

One afternoon in early February, a group of the staff were relaxing, some smoking, round the staff hall table after lunch. Donnie Smith, the hotel boilerman and electrician was reading a newspaper with a mug of tea in hand. He flung the paper down on the table saying angrily, "What a bloody world we live in. I thought when I was demobbed in 1945 that we would all live in peace. See this paper! Problems among the Allies over Berlin, Russia backing the new Republic in North Korea, trouble in Palestine, trouble in India in a big way and now the Royal Navy is sending a frigate off to the Falkland Islands to sort out some problems there!"

One of the cleaners enquired, "The Falkland Islands, where's that?"

Nobody seemed to know but Donnie said that Argentine seemed to be involved in the problem. Denzil was able to supply the information. Duncan MacGillivray's older brother Angus had gone out as a shepherd away back in the early 1930's and married and settled down there. His occasional letters home gave them all the news and Denzil had collected the stamps. The letters however had ceased after Duncan's death in 1944.

Denzil's week had settled into a comfortable if busy pattern. He saw Mr Forrest from time to time on his bus journeys to work and who always asked him how he was getting on in the Royal. In March old Jessie MacLeod suffered a stroke and ended up in a nursing home with Jean taking on the task of informing her son and family in New Zealand. As Denzil trudged up the path on his way home each week the cottage looked very forlorn without the usual plume of smoke coming from its chimney. The months slipped by and soon another spring heralded the slow start to yet another tourist season, Rationing was slowly slackening but in early April Hugh Gaitskell, the Fuel Minister announced that motorists would be rationed to 90 miles a month from June 1st.

Denzil kept up his banking routine and visits to North Bridge Street on a weekly basis with his pay-ins being usually £1 or slightly under each week. On Friday 11th of June he presented himself to Finkelstein as usual to have his book ticked. The jeweller was waiting for him as always in his workshop.

He smiled as Denzil came in exclaiming, "Well, Denzil, this is a red letter day!"

Denzil was not too sure what he implied by that. That week it had been announced that Princess Elizabeth was expecting a baby in the autumn and his first thought was that this was what Finkelstein was meaning.

Finkelstein opened up his bank book and said, "Read the date of the first entry, my boy."

Denzil looked and realised that it had been 11/06/47, exactly a year ago. At that moment Mrs Finkelstein entered the workshop with a cake on a silver salver with a single candle light. Denzil had to laugh. Later he blew out the candle, cut the cake and they each had a slice, the Finkelsteins with their tea a generous glass of lemonade was poured for Denzil. They talked about how much had happened over the past year and Finkelstein complimented Denzil on the way he had stuck to his routine.

Now he said, "You are on your own and do not have to come each week to me to countersign your bankbook."

He solemnly ticked off the last entry that now read £37 -8s - 0d. Before Denzil left Finkelstein stood up and shook his hand saying that if he ever needed financial advice then his door was always open. It was not a complete farewell as he said, "You still clean my windows and I will no doubt see you from time to time in the Royal."

Denzil walked away from North Bridge Street with his bankbook for the last time, determined to maintain his saving routine. He had never told anybody about his arrangement with Finkelstein not even Jean.

He had offered Jean some money for herself but Jean would have none of it,"Och away with you! I have more than enough money what with my pension and the odd calf sale, more than sufficient. You look after yourself, son."

In June Andy Bremner the porter with the bad leg took a thrombosis and was signed off work on a permanent basis. Denzil found himself promoted to fill the porter's position while a new boots applicant was sought. The downside was he had to move his room as the two boots lodged together so he found himself sharing a room once again with his fellow porter, Monty. His promotion meant a wage increase to twelve shillings per week and some more points towards his porter tips share out. He had been finding living on what he retained quite tight so the extra money was very welcome. It also meant that he was now banking never less than £1 per week. Monty still tapped him up for money on a weekly basis but he pled poverty and having to support his widowed mother. Monty, in friendly fashion, called him a tight bastard but knew that Denzil and money was a no-go area.

In June an event happened that was to have a profound effect on his life. Again it started in a very understated way. One hot summer's day some of the chefs were sitting outside on the stone steps that led to the kitchen having a breather before lunch service. Down the street marched a boy about Denzil's age with a thatch of red hair and freckled face carrying a large heavy wicker basket. The chefs watched him with interest as he stopped in front of them. "Can I see the head chef," the boy enquired of the group.

Denzil and Monty who were relaxing with the group looked on with interest. Manfred, one of the chefs stubbed out his cigarette before asking, "What are you after him for?"

The boy replied, "I have got some salmon for sale."

"Oh, Chef doesn't see poachers, son " Manfred responded.

The boy flushed red and replied fiercely, "Ah'm no poacher!"

The chefs all laughed at him. Denzil rose to his feet.

"Come on, I'll show you to the kitchen" he said and led the boy into the building.

On the way Denzil told him to ignore the chefs as they were a bunch of jokers. Chef Bonnacorsi was interested in the bag of fresh salmon but said that he would be more interested in a steady weekly supply and that each supply would need a headed invoice.

The boy introduced himself as Rory McCulloch from a fishing village called Ullamore on the west coast. He worked with his father who had his own boat and supplied fish in his local area. His visit to Inverdeen was to see if a new market could be opened up. A weekly supply would be no problem along with an appropriate business invoice. A price was negotiated and Denzil was quite impressed with the way young Rory conducted his business. Chef, at the conclusion, said he wished he could get some smoked salmon and Rory assured him that his father specialised in that product with his own smoke-room. So the deal was done and Rory handed over his first invoice. The two boys walked out together with Rory thanking Denzil for his assistance.

Over the next few weeks Rory made his weekly delivery and became a recognised supplier. Once or twice the boys met by chance in the kitchen. Rory travelled by the west coast mail bus to deliver his goods and then caught the afternoon bus back so that most of his day was spent on the road. He usually had a good few hours to kick his heels waiting for his return bus. One afternoon on his fifth delivery Denzil invited him to The Merry Thought cafe for an ice cream. They stood outside the cafe sitting on a wall enjoying their sliders with Rory remarking that although he was glad to have the Royal as a customer, the travelling made it a long day.

Denzil had an idea. "Why don't you put the fish on the mail bus and I collect it at this end from the depot and deliver it to the kitchen for you? Seems to me it will not only save you money but also your time." Rory jumped at the idea immediately. So it became a weekly task for Denzil to meet the bus and collect the fish supply. Rory came down once a month mainly to collect his payment from the hotel office.

On his first monthly meeting he handed Denzil an envelope with £3 in it as payment for collecting the fish. At first Denzil refused until Rory insisted saying that he had cleared it with his father as Denzil's role meant that not only did he save on bus fares but it left him free to work on their boat.

In mid June the main talking point in the hotel was a change of manager. Major Drysdale and his wife had purchased a small fishing hotel up north and would be leaving on 1st July to take up their new business. There was much speculation that Miss MacLean might step into his shoes but in the event a new manager, Mr Nigel Jennings was appointed. He and his wife had two young children so an additional guest bedroom was added to the management suite. Miss MacLean organised a collection for a going away gift for Drysdale at a small party attended by the heads of department. She welcomed the new manager who wanted to be more hands on than Drysdale had been which was easily achieved. He too quickly realised that he depended on her to a great extent and so she found that her role was pretty much as before and the staff also quickly knew that not much had changed.

Chef Bonnacorsi challenged Denzil one day. "Denzil, what are you all about? I go into Hetty's for my paper and you are working there. Next day you are cleaning windows on North

Bridge Street. You are still working here as a porter full time. You supply rabbits to this kitchen and now you seem to be a partner in crime with that young fishboy from the west coast. Do you ever get a chance to sleep?"

Denzil laughed it off. Calum also noticed his work load as Denzil had to organise his working shifts round his other jobs and told him not to overdo things. His working week was full with very little time to hang about getting bored and that was just how he wanted it.

CHAPTER 12   Ullamore

One day in early August Denzil met up with Rory on his monthly trip and the usual £3 envelope changed hands. To his surprise Rory opened up "Denzil - have you ever been over to the west coast? My mother suggested that I invite you over for a few days to see how we operate. How about it? Think it over."

He was due two weeks holiday and Calum had asked him to take it before the end of September. He had not given it much thought except for arranging cover for his various jobs and expected just to spend the period back at the croft. The idea of using part of the holiday to explore somewhere different appealed to him and he was sure Jean would understand. He accepted Rory's offer. It was arranged that at the end of August on Rory's monthly trip he would return with him to spend a long weekend in Ullamore.

Denzil had a word with Fritzi about covering his window cleaning round on his holiday period. No problem said Fritzi who was only too keen to earn some additional cash. Hetty could cope without him for the fortnight and the rabbit supply would also go into cold storage until he returned. Jean was only too delighted that he seemed to have made a good friend and also that instead of spending his whole holiday at the croft he would have a real break from routine. He would also show Fritzi the window cleaning ropes for a couple of weeks before the holiday. So it was all arranged. The month of August proved to be very busy with more tourists on the go.

The porter's department was a changed place with Calum in charge. He was strict but fair in allocating duties and Miss MacLean was very satisfied that this department was operating to a very high standard. After all in many instances this was the first department that guests made contact with in the hotel. First impressions in her opinion could be important.

Denzil hit a personal milestone on 20th August with his banking. His weekly £1 - 0s - 0d entry brought the total to exactly £50! Later that day he met Finkelstein on his way back to business after his usual post lunch siesta. They spoke to each other in passing and for one moment Denzil felt like telling him about his new banking total but thought better of it. Strangely, he never thought of the total as money. He could not relate it to the actual minor amount of cash he lived on weekly. It was just something that existed in a different league.

Monty was still labouring with his financial situation as usual. It made Denzil realise just how fortunate he had been to have that early contact and advice from Mr Finkelstein. The day of the holiday came about. He banked his £3 from Rory along with £1 - 2s - 0d and ensured that his bank book was securely locked away in the locker. His locker key he kept tied to a cord round his neck at all times. Late afternoon saw the two boys catch the bus for the west. As it headed north out of Inverdeen Denzil found it difficult to contain his excitement as this would be his first real trip away to a different part of the country. He pointed out Jean's croft to Rory as they passed by on the main road. It seemed so small tucked away on the hillside among the scattering of other houses and the patchwork of fields. He was fascinated at the different countryside they passed through until the bus started to climb out of the cultivated fields and villages into the barren, heather covered hills that led to the west. The bus climbed slowly until at last they seemed to be on a level part of the hillside. The road meandered alongside a loch fringed with birch trees. Rory pointed out a large hillside on the other side of the loch saying that in winter it was literally moving with red deer who had descended from the tops in search of winter feeding. The road was single track dotted with many passing places. Alongside the road at regular intervals Denzil spotted wooden poles some five foot high. Rory explained that in winter they were essential when drifting snow covered the road to mark out just where the road was.

The high mountains to the west in the distance fascinated Denzil and Rory seemed to know all their Gaelic names. At last the road started to descend from the high plateau they had traversed. The road wound down in tight bends for some miles until at last they were back in cultivated fields and houses once more. They rounded a bend in the road and Rory suddenly clutched Denzil's arm, "Look there's the Atlantic!" he exclaimed. Sure enough in the distance Denzil could make out in the early evening sunshine the glint of blue water with steep hills rising on either side.

The road continued to wind along the sea loch for some miles then another steep climb and round another bend. Suddenly there before them Denzil saw Ullamore for the first time. The hillside made a sudden sweep so that the sea loch narrowed. In this sweep of hillside the village sheltered with white washed houses fronting the sea shore and a harbour nestled to its front with a variety of boats tied up. Other houses backed up the ones on the sea front and one or two larger buildings dominated the skyline. The village seemed to sparkle in the early evening sunshine and as if to complete the picture a lone yacht with white sails was tacking round the headland clearly heading for a night's mooring. The bus came to a halt close to the harbour and the passengers alighted. Denzil wanted to have a close look at the harbour so they strolled around and Rory identified some of the different types of boats. Cold eyed seagulls strutted on the harbour pecking away at fish debris or roosted on the iron bollards. It reminded Denzil of the gulls that haunted the Royal bin area. They set off along the sea front road and at one point Denzil stopped short when he saw in a small front garden what appeared to him to be a palm tree. Rory explained that it was indeed a sub tropical tree that grew there thanks to the warming influence that the Atlantic Gulf Stream had on the west coast of Scotland. At the end of the road a well worn path led round the headland to a scattering of croft houses on the steep hillside overlooking the sea loch and the mountains on the other side. Denzil almost laughed out loud as it was as if Cabrach had been transplanted to the other side of the country.

The McCulloch croft was on the lower level so they were soon in the house being welcomed by Rory's mother while his young sister Fiona was shy at meeting this newcomer. Once the initial welcome was over Rory enquired "Where's Dad?" His mother busy laying the supper table gave a short laugh, "Och he had some overseas visitors out on a boat trip this afternoon so no doubt they will be entertaining him to cocktails in the Victoria Bar - as usual!" Denzil had to field a lot of questions from Rory's mother about his own background and his job in the hotel. She said how grateful they were for his services at collecting fish from the bus on a regular basis as it not only provided them with another outlet for their salmon but enabled Rory to have another day on the boat. Denzil observed that Rory handed over the salmon money to his mother and guessed that she must be the one in the family that handled the finance. They were relaxing round the supper table with supper well over when Rory's-father entered the house. Duncan McCulloch was a tall man dressed like a game-keeper with a deer stalkers fore and aft hat on his head with a reddish face set off by a bushy moustache. He greeted Denzil warmly as his wife rescued his supper from the oven where it was being kept warm. The conversation started up again and Denzil soon learned that the McCulloch family had lived in Ullamore for generations and was a well respected family in the community. Duncan or Duncy as he was usually called ran a boat that not only earned a living by fishing but was also used increasingly in taking tourists out on trips down the sea loch to where it opened out into the ocean proper. Only last year they had invested in another boat so that Rory could operate independently from his father and increase their income. The croft boasted a cow for milking, two goats for cheese making and the usual flock of hens. Rory's mother looked after this aspect of the family set up and her goat's cheese was selling well in Macleod's general store in the village. Her maiden name by coincidence was Morrison and she belonged to a large Lewis family. She had trained as a primary school teacher and had come to Ullamore to join the staff of the school there before meeting her husband and settling down with him. She soon realised that her husband was what is known in the west coast as a character. He knew everybody in the village and surrounding area but had no business drive or real ambition in life. His love of the easy life coupled with a fondness for a dram or two in convivial company was quite sufficient for him. She decided early on that she would need to direct Rory's path in a different direction.

Denzil was seated close to Duncy as he ate his belated supper and sensed a mixed aroma of fish, tobacco smoke and whisky that seemed to emanate from him. Rory's mother talked about them having a full house this weekend as her nephew Dominc who lived in Edinburgh was due to arrive tomorrow and she had squeezed another single bed into Rory's room so the three boys could sleep together. Dominc was the son of her younger sister Ethel who trained as a nurse in Edinburgh as a young girl. Later she attracted the attention of a young doctor Howard Greening who had turned up at the hospital where she was based to do his Houseman's year. The mutual attraction led to marriage and four children, three boys and a girl of whom Dominic was the youngest. They all came to see their aunt in the west coast when they were children until their various careers dominated their lives. Dominic was the exception and he took every opportunity to head to Ulllamore and enjoy the way of life it presented. His father had become a distinguished surgeon and the family lived in some style in Morningside. Dominic for his part had graduated as a lawyer with distinction from Edinburgh University and was currently serving his apprenticeship with a prominent legal firm in Charlotte Square.

The table conversation drifted on until darkness slowly came down and Mrs McCulloch lit the Tilley lamp. Denzil talked about the hydro electric engineers who used the Royal as a base while work continued on two new dams that would eventually provide electricity for a wide area of the Highlands. The talk then ranged on now that the war was over what other changes would be brought about to affect their lives - until it was time for bed. Denzil woke early the next morning and the silence reminded him of the croft at Cabrach. If he listened carefully he could make out the faint calls of sea birds down on the sea shore and the distant lowing of a cow. After breakfast they set off for the harbour with Rory carrying their sandwich lunch prepared by his mother. Duncy was already at work in a dilapidated shed close to the harbour that he owned. At one corner of this shed was a smoke room roughly screened off with a pipe set into the roof to release the smoke. The floor of the smoke room was littered with wood chips that smouldered away. Above on several wooden spars several salmon were secured so that the smoke could do its work. Rory explained that his father had a special process before he smoked the salmon that gave it its unique flavour. The fish were placed in a special marinade for 24 hours before being subjected to the smoke house treatment. The rest of the shed was an untidy mess of creels, baskets, fish boxes and other tackle. In one corner was a huge barrel of salted mackerel that Rory explained was used as bait for the lobster creels. Once Duncy had satisfied himself that the smoke house process was well under way the three of them set off for the harbour where their boat was tied up. They made slow progress as Duncy stopped to chat to other fishermen and people he knew. It was a beautiful summers day with a calm sea reflecting the sunshine. The boat was some 20 feet in length with a 5 horsepower Seagull engine and bore the name "Morning Mist". Once aboard, the engine fired and they moved away from the harbour out into the sea loch making for the headland. It was Denzils first time on a boat of any kind and he was thrilled at this new experience. He looked back as the village receded in their wake and the high bare bills crowding the water seemed so close he felt he could touch them. Duncy and Rory were busy sorting out things around the boat so conversation was limited.

They rounded the headland and after half an hour entered a sheltered bay where a series of buoys floated on the water. The boat throttled back as they approached the buoys and Duncy and Rory prepared for action. When they reached the first buoy Rory leaned over and hauled away at a rope attached to the buoy so Denzil came forward to give him a hand. They worked away with the rope coiling round their feet on the deck until eventually out of the translucent waters a creel came into view and was hauled aboard amid a shedding of sea water. Inside was a huge dark blue lobster moving slowly in its creel prison. Rory expertly removed the lobster into a fish box on the deck. Duncy had prepared a fresh mackerel bait and secured it back in the creel. The creel was then placed over the side of the boat and the rope paid out as it slowly sank back into the depths.

The boat moved over to the next marker buoy and the process repeated but this time the creel was empty so once the bait was checked it was returned back into the water. They had fifteen such creels to check and in the end their haul was ten lobsters, by which time Denzil had become more than proficient in not only hauling the creels but also fixing the mackerel bait. The lobster session over the boat engine was switched off. Sandwiches were issued and Duncy produced three bottles of McEwans export from a supply he kept stashed away in a corner of the boat. Bathed in sunshine, lunch was enjoyed as the boat rocked slightly in the gentle swell.

Denzil could not resist teasing Roy about this ideal way of life that he enjoyed but Duncy brought him back to earth by saying that he should enjoy it while he can as the weather was not always as kind as this. He also made the observation that this settled weather could mean that the salmon were running so they would give that a try in the afternoon.

Lunch over and with the newly caught crustaceans slithering around in the fish box on the deck they set off for a point down on the other side of the seal loch. Once there they tied up at a small cemented landing area. A small rowing boat was beached on the shingle and was quickly dragged into the water. Coiled up in the boat was a bulky fish net that Rory referred to as a splash net. This was brought into play and one end secured to an iron stanchion set into the cemented landing platform. They got into the boat and with Rory and his father plying the oars rowed away from the shore playing out the net as they went. The boat went in a slow circle until they rowed back to their starting point with the net fully paid out. The boat was beached and the three men started to haul in the net that had been paid. It was reasonably hard work as the net was resisted by the water but gradually it came nearer the shore. A salmon suddenly broke the surface of the water inside the net and Duncy grunted in approval. As the net eventually closed in Denzil experienced a thrill of excitement as several silvery salmon threshed about in the splash net. The net was landed to reveal seven large salmon with sea lice clinging to them. Another fish box was taken from the boat and the salmon safely deposited in it and placed alongside the lobster box. The splash net was neatly rolled up and secured in the beached rowing boat before the Morning Mist headed back to Ullamore harbour with Duncy professing himself happy with the days haul.

Back at the harbour they unloaded their catch. The lobsters were carried back to the store and in a back room was an old iron bath filled with seawater that provided a temporary home for the crustaceans. Duncy had other plans for the salmon and six were put into a wicker carrier bag to be taken to supply an order for the Braes Hotel one of the large buildings that sat on a higher street back of the sea shore. The two boys took the other salmon back home with them. Rory said that they would not wait for his father as after he delivered the fish he would no doubt spend an hour or two with his cronies in the public bar.

Back home they washed and changed prior to supper. It was somewhat delayed as Duncy took his time before he rolled home in a mellow state. Dominc had arrived from Edinburgh during their absence. He was a tall fresh faced twenty two year old and was soon telling them about his first impressions of his new law firm employers. Dinner was served with a first course of homemade cock-a-leekie soup followed by grilled salmon steak, vegetables and new potatoes. Denzil was taken by the fact that the salmon they tucked into was one of the batch they had hauled in on the splash net that very day. Homemade apple pie and custard completed the repast and Duncy solemnly raised his whisky glass at the end and ironically proposed a toast to all those whose life was ruled by rationing. Later they sat outside the croft house as it was still bright looking down on the sea loch where a large yacht was slowly heading out with sails billowing for the open sea.

Eventually Duncy with glass in hand turned to Rory, "Hey boy. How about getting the pipes out and send them a message!" Rory did as requested and emerged from the house with a set of pipes that he proceeded to warm up with much blowing and patting of the pipe bag until he was satisfied that all was in order. Standing on a hillock to one side of the house he started to play launching into a well known pipe tune, 'The Battle of the Somme'. Denzil was intrigued until Dominic explained to him that this was some sort of ritual. The music could clearly be heard over the crofting community and was one way of telling neighbours that a McCulloch ceilidh was in progress.

Sure enough within a few minutes three figures came down the hillside to join them. Rod and Rose MacRae were immediate neighbours along with their daughter Rona and Rod wore his accordion strapped to his chest. They were warmly greeted in Gaelic at first and drinks poured as they exchanged gossip for a while. In the space of half an hour no less than ten neighbours joined the ceildh and the accordion provided background music. Rose MacRae was the first to sing backed by her husband on the accordion, a lovely haunting Gaelic song, the words of which seemed to hang in the air. Rose was an acknowledged singer locally who performed in concerts throughout the area. Duncy had welcomed Denzil to the group saying that this would be all very new to him as it was the first ceilidh he had attended. The ceilidh warmed up with several people taking part in singing mainly Gaelic songs while in between the accordion answered several requests.

To Denzil it was an unforgettable experience. The group of people singing outside the house looking down on the sea loch and the hill beyond while a slowly setting sun lit up the distant ocean in a rosy glow that defied description. He had his own surprise to reveal. In an intermission he moved over to Rod who was downing a stiff dram after a long session on the accordion. He whispered to him and Rod's eyebrows shot up as a result. Denzil resumed his seat as Rod broke into a well know Gaelic song, 'Cailean Mo Runsa 's Mo Gliaidh'

Denzil started to sing and the ceilidh group were stunned into silence as he performed. When he finished there was an outburst of clapping. He had to explain that it was the only Gaelic song he knew and he did not even know what the words meant! His headmaster in school had been a Mod Gold medallist and used to put on end of year concerts. He had taught Denzil this particular song hence it had become his party piece. Rose MaCrae complimented him on his voice and assured him that she would teach him some more Gaelic songs to add to his depleted repertoire.

The ceilidh broke up later as people started to wind their way home in the gathering darkness. That night Denzil, what with his long day out in the boat coupled with the late night ceilidh, slept like a log until he was awoken next morning with sunlight streaming in through the open window. As it was Sunday everybody enjoyed rising late. Breakfast over, the family set out for church service and already many of their neighbours were on their way. The church service too was a new experience for Denzil as his foster parents were not church goers. The service seemed to be a good excuse for a community gathering as people met and exchanged gossip both before and after the service. The men talked on fishing and crofting matters while the women had their own gatherings and subjects to discuss. After the service a slow walk along the sea front back to the croft with a slight shower of rain doing its best to dampen proceedings. A light lunch of lobster salad and new potatoes followed by homemade bannocks and some of Rory's mothers goats cheese was enjoyed. In the afternoon Rory took Dominic and Denzil on a walk exploring the village showing them his former school and other places of interest. Denzil was interested in the huge war memorial set back in a small garden area at the entrance to the village and told them about his foster father being killed in the war.

Dominic,who had been at the memorial before, said to Denzil that he would show him something of interest. On the plaque detailing the names of those who had fallen he pointed out four names all with the surname MacKenzie. They were four brothers - two had fallen in the Somme in the first week in 1916 while two others were killed in the following year 1917 in different actions. Dominic said, "Can you imagine the effect on those poor parents as the telegrams arrived from the War Office." Apparently he said it was the practise for brothers to join up in the family Regiment in this case the Seaforths so they served in the same battalion. In an action such as the Somme when casualties mounted many families suffered in like manner. In the Second World War the lesson had been learnt and family members tended to be dispersed to avoid such morale shattering happenings. Sunday evening was a quieter affair with another excellent dinner and good conversation. The McCullochs invited Denzil to come back when he could as he was always welcome, while Denzil did his best to thank them for an unforgettable experience. Next day he caught the mail bus back to Inverdeen. Just to keep him company Rory had designed a new box lined with wet seaweed to hold the lobsters that had been hauled out of their temporary bath. They were destined for Chef Bonnacorsi who was finding that lobster was featuring highly on the dishes, selected from his a la carte menu. Denzil left Ullamore but something told him that it would not be the last time he would be in the west.

CHAPTER 13   Promoted to Porter

The ballroom of the Royal Hotel had always been treated as a separate entity from the hotel proper. It has its own ballroom manager, bar attendants, doormen, cashiers, part time waiting staff and cleaners. Its main function was to host the two popular public dances held weekly every Wednesday and Saturday nights. Dancing along with cinema going were still the main pastimes for the general public in the post war years. Over 1,000 dancers would regularly fill the ballroom on a Saturday night to the strains of Harry Beach and his orchestra.

Wedding receptions started to feature quite strongly as normal life resumed after the frantic upheaval of the war years. The ballroom soon found itself booked virtually every Friday for wedding receptions with a dance to follow which was very welcome business. The wedding party and guests arrived at the ballroom entrance so the function had no real impact on the main hotel.

Miss MacLean decided to change all that. She arranged for the bridal party to arrive at the Royal in some style with the bridal pair walking into the hotel entrance on a specially laid red carpet. Naturally this caused quite a stir in the main street with a sizable crowd of onlookers gathering to witness the event. Once inside the hotel family photographs could be taken using the impressive staircase to best advantage.

She shrewdly judged that this colourful event not only gave a real sense of occasion to the newly-weds but also helped to raise the Royal's profile as well.

The hotel worked its way through the summer of 1948 with increasing numbers of visitors ensuring that tourism was very much on track. Many of the guests were American servicemen stationed throughout the U.K. taking the opportunity to visit the Highlands before their war service ended and being posted back home. These American visitors were very popular with the Royal porters as they were very generous tippers with money to burn.

Denzil found that although the porter's working routine followed a set pattern, every day was different and the colourful variety of people who passed through the hotel was never the same. It also had its lighter moments. An elderly local man called Archie used to haunt the foyer area. He would call in at mid-morning, every day, order a whisky and sit quietly in a seat in a corner of the foyer to watch the world go by. Smartly dressed he troubled nobody just quietly consuming his drams until the bar closed at 2 pm.

Whenever he wanted another drink he never demanded table service, he simply rose from his seat, walking to the bar to replenish his glass before resuming his seat. Calum said that he had heard on good authority that old Archie had once been a bank manager, a rising star in the Bank of Scotland. Sadly, he became an alcoholic, using the bank takings to fund his growing weakness before a sharp-eyed auditor ended his career. The porters used to try to keep a tally of the number of drinks Archie would consume at a morning sitting. When the bar closed between 2pm and 5pm he simply took up where he had left off until about 8pm he would call time on his tippling and stagger off into the night.

One day about 6pm Archie was well into his evening session when a tour party of some 20 Swiss guests arrived in a small coach led by a lady guide. She was a stout middle-aged woman with a loud voice, ordering her guests around with a no-nonsense manner. As they were booking in at reception with the guide holding forth in her loud voice old Archie decided to replenish his glass, making for the bar. On the way, passing the Swiss party, he tripped falling heavily onto the carpet knocking a table over. He lay there, outstretched, face down as if unconscious. The Swiss party gathered round the incumbent body with some concern.

Immediately the lady guide took charge. She turned Archie over on his side, slackened his tie, ensuring that his tongue was not blocking his airway. That done she barked at one of her charges to get a brandy from the bar and to make it snappy. When the brandy duly arrived the guide cradled Archie's head in her arm, preparing to get him to sip some of the life saving liquid while her Swiss charges drew close to see what would happen. All of a sudden Archie stirred to life, opening one eye, looking directly at the guide saying, "Brandy? If it's all the same with you Missus, I'd prefer a whisky!".

About this time Denzil suffered his first small business reverse. The Royal signed a contract with a major game dealer in Perthshire to supply venison, hares, rabbits, pheasants, grouse and such like. Part of the deal was that the supplier had sole rights to supply such produce. Thus Denzil's supply of rabbits had to cease.

No sooner had he adjusted to this particular loss of income stream than he gained another window cleaning client. A baker's outlet opened up in a former tweed house shop whose owner had retired. They claimed his services so that he now had five clients on his North Bridge Street patch.

At the same time Hetty prevailed upon him to do a second afternoon shift in her shop. Calum grumbled in a good-natured way when he was obliged to arrange Denzil's shifts so he could fit in his outside interests along with his portering duties. Denzil discovered that a rabbit slipped to the head porter every couple of weeks eased things considerably. The increased tip contribution from the porters' tronc, assisted by the American guest influx. meant that he never banked less that £1 per week.

On one occasion he had some clothes to buy ending up with only four shillings to bank. His first thought was just to miss a week but something drove him to bank that amount as somehow he thought that to miss a week would break up his routine. Every week he would pick up his window cleaning money from Finkelstein as he did with other clients. More often that not Mrs Finkelstein attended to him by paying out of her till. Once or twice Finkelstein would be in front of the shop and chat to him without ever once referring to his banking process or how things were going financially.

Rory came down on his monthly trip in September as usual. The two boys were relaxing over a couple of Vimto drinks in the Merry Thought Café when Denzil suggested to his red haired friend that he might consider approaching the Chef at the Station Hotel to see if he might be interested in a west coast fish supply, Rory, ever the man of action, downed his drink and headed off to see if he could get an interview with the Chef. Denzil had to get back to attend to his window cleaning round so they went their different ways. Some time later when he was hard at work on the fashion shop window a gleeful Rory appeared having secured a deal with the Station Hotel. He had also arranged that a Station Hotel commis would uplift any order from the Depot just as Denzil did. Denzil said to him that at this rate one day Rory might be able to afford him as his business agent.

October dawned with the tourist season dwindling away while stock room activity took off as the shop looked forward to another hopefully busy festive season.

That month also heralded the start of the big five day cattle mart that was one of the highlights of the farming calendar in the Highlands. It also spelt the return of old Abrach MacKay along with his faithful collie dog to sell off his summer stock of cattle. He booked into the Royal as usual with Mrs MacBeth gritting her teeth while the housemaids drew lots as to who would be unlucky enough to attend to his room.

Calum was the first to meet him on his arrival and was immediately struck by how much the old man seemed to have failed. His clothes seemed to hang on his shrunken frame while his face had a gaunt expression. They tried to work out in the lodge as to how old Abrach might be with the general consensus that he was well into his eighties. The old farmer settled right away into his normal pattern, dining and drinking away from the hotel with his usual cronies and his only seeming luxury his suite at the Royal.

His arrival brought home to Denzil that time was passing with the coming month of May marking the end of his second year at the Royal.

His days off spent with Jean back at the croft gave him plenty of time to reflect on just how lucky he had been to secure his present job in the first place. He never mentioned to Jean about his dealings with Finkelstein while for her part she was just happy that he appeared to have settled so well into his working life at the hotel. He did his best to ensure that her log pile was kept topped up, the byre cleaned out and other tasks attended to as well. Strangely, Jean never spoke about Duncan although now a framed photo of him in uniform sat on the mantelpiece.

Jessie MacLeod's house still lay vacant but Jean said that a distant cousin of Duncan, a retired police officer from Glasgow, was toying with the idea of turning it into a holiday home.

On 10th November Denzil celebrated his sixteenth birthday. Celebrated is not quite accurate as he told nobody but was pleasantly surprised when Miss MacLead made a point of looking him out to wish him many happy returns while enquiring as to how he was enjoying his portering role.

The other eventful news at this time was the fact that on the 14th November Princess Elizabeth had given birth to a boy – the future king. It was the subject of much discussion round the staff hall table especially by the female members of staff. Someone asked the question as to why the royal name was Windsor and not Mountbatten which was Prince Philip's surname. At that point Paddy entered looking for a porter to assist him in stocking the bar. He overheard the heated discussion and was able to provide the answer. Some time ago the same discussion had been aired in the cocktail bar when by good fortune enjoying a pre-lunch aperitif along with his agent was Sir Russell James the MP for Inverdeen and area. Sir James declared that the formidable Queen Mary had spoken directly to the Prime Minister to the effect that Windsor it was and Windsor it was going to be! Subject closed.

The festive season broke over the Royal once more. Despite the country still being firmly in the grip of deep-seated austerity people seemed determined to make the most of Christmas and New Year. The hotel was busy with various functions, office parties and family gatherings as a year closed business wise on a high note. The war and its aftermath still cast a long shadow. Old Willie, the hotel handyman, had a son who had been captured at the fall of Singapore, then endured an horrific time as a prisoner of war on the infamous railway building project. With the war ended he returned home a virtual skeleton due to the hardship and starvation diet he had to undergo. His homecoming was not made any easier by the fact that his marriage had foundered in his enforced absence. Unable to cope with things he had committed suicide. Old Willie had kept this news to himself. One lunchtime, round the staff hall table, someone read out from a newspaper that General Tojo, the Japanese war time leader had been hanged by American forces at Sugamo prison in Tokyo for his war crimes.

The news proved too much for the old handyman who broke down in tears at the table. It was as if a dam had burst with all his bottled up grief pouring out. Everybody left the table quietly to return to their duties leaving Willie with his head in his hands while a motherly housemaid put her arm around him while he unburdened himself.

On a lighter note MPs at Westminster passed a bill increasing National Service time from 12 months to 18 months. Monty, who was due to be called up in less that a year, groaned at his bad luck.

Denzil's final banking for the year on 30th December read £98 – 15s – 0d. He had hoped to have broken through the £100 barrier before the year end but nonetheless it was still a milestone reached.

CHAPTER 14   Abrach Mackay

The year 1949 slipped by almost unobserved by the Royal staff as they struggled to cope with the busy festive period. The hotel was fully booked, the restaurant was over booked, Paddy's bar overflowed almost permanently into the foyer area and stress levels abounded. The ballroom entered into the fray holding additional festive dances with a couple of major weddings thrown in for good measure.

Then just as quickly it was all over and the hotel settled back into a more normal routine. Denzil somehow, in addition to doing extra shifts, managed to look after his window cleaning clients and even managed to fit in Hetty's tasks. He could not shake off the feeling that this year was going to be very important for him. This was underlined by the fact that on Friday 7th January he banked £3 – 10s – 0d taking his total through the £100 barrier to read £102 – 5s 0d. This was due to a combination of overtime, additional tips and festive tips from his window cleaning clients.

His room-mate Monty was still struggling with his financial situation scrounging advances and cigarettes where he could.

Denzil did suggest that he find a part time job to ease his financial plight but Monty felt that that this might interfere with his social life so the subject was dropped. In February a pay rise for the porters was welcomed and in Denzil's case it meant a weekly wage now of thirteen shillings.

In late February he paid a return visit to Ullamore at Rory's invitation. It was a different journey from the one he had made in August as the bus wound its way through a snow covered landscape. On the high plateau he saw herds of deer, driven down from the high tops, almost at the roadside as they pawed at the deep snow in search of grazing. As they descended into the low lying land leading to Ullamore the snow petered out and by the time they reached the village there was no snow to be found at all.

A warm welcome as usual from the McCulloch family and soon he was back in the boat as they did an afternoon run to clear the lobster creels. On the way back Rory stopped the boat and drew up a creel he had laid in a special place. As the creel broke the surface Denzil noticed that, instead of a lobster as he expected, it was full of small pink shelled fish that he had never seen before. Rory told him that they were prawns. Fisherman considered them to be of no commercial value and usually threw them back into the sea. Rory had experimented with the lobster creel which had a specially designed "soft eye" that allowed the lobster access to the creel for the bait. He had designed this access route to provide a "hard eye" so that the smaller prawn got access. Rory said that we would take them home and have them tonight for supper, "just to see what you think of them".

"The sea is abounding with them", he declared. And he had a hunch that one day in the future there might be a demand for them.

That night after the prawns had been cooked they tucked into this new dish. Denzil loved the fresh tang of the plump prawns and had to agree with Rory that he might well be on to something. "Why not send a catch back to Chef Bonnacorsi free of charge to see what he would make of them?" he suggested. This tactic was agreed but Denzil would talk to the chef beforehand.

The usual ceilidh was held on Saturday night heralded by Rory on his pipes. This time it was held inside the croft house as a rain-storm lashed the hillside. The peat fire glowed, the candles flickered, the drink circulated and some twenty neighbours and family packed the sitting room. Rose Macrae was in good voice and during the evening she introduced Denzil to two songs that she thought might suit him, even going to the bother of writing out the Gaelic words for him. Denzil had prepared his party piece to surprise them as usual. As the ceilidh was about to wind up he launched into a song from some musical he had heard on the wireless, "We'll meet again". It seemed a very appropriate one to finish the evening with and was met with some acclaim. To his surprise Rose also knew the words of the song and joined in, so they finished in duet.

All too soon his west coast weekend was over and he was heading back to Inverdeen with another box of lobsters in the mail bus hold.

On March 1st Joe Louis, the 35 year old American boxer known as The Brown Bomber, hung up his gloves for good after a career that marked him as one of the boxing greats. Denzil took down Monty's picture from the wall and in a marker pen drew a heavy black line right round it to denote mourning before replacing it. Monty appreciated his efforts. In April the Republic of Ireland was born and Paddy received special permission to hold a party or as he called it a "hooley" to celebrate the event. He hung bunting and flags throughout the bar and special supplies of Guinness were ordered to ensure the party went with a swing.

So many people attended the event that additional staff were drafted in to cater for the thirsty customers who drained the Guinness supplies dry. Jennings, the manager, afterwards complained in a good-natured way to Paddy, that if he had known that so many would attend he should have held it in the ballroom.

Paddy was a very energetic MC, organising a small trio from the ballroom orchestra to provide music for the event. Two excellent singers stood out, Margie Ryan from Armagh married to a local businessman and Johnny Cairney from Donegal, an engineer employed on one of the hydro-electric schemes. Paddy however was very keen to have Royal Hotel influence on proceedings and had heard of Denzil's ability as a singer. Late in the evening he introduced Denzil who launched into a song that Paddy had taught him:

'I'll take you home again Kathleen
Across the ocean wild and wide:
To where your heart has ever been,

Since first you were my bonnie bride.'

This well-known Irish song, purported to have been composed by an Irishman in New York to his young wife dying of tuberculosis, ensured that there was hardly a dry eye in the house when Denzil drew to a close. The bar drawings that night were astronomical and Paddy's poke came to no harm either.

When Paddy had first arrived in Inverdeen with his wife and two children they had rented rooms in the town. In January 1949 the family bought a detached house overlooking the river with a large garden so Paddy's poke was clearly bearing fruit. Miss MacLean noted this with a quiet smile as she went about her duties.

Denzil's regular banking continued apace and on the second anniversary on 11th June his total had reached £135 – 18s – 0d.

International problems still clouded the world but relief was expressed as the Berlin blockade imposed by Russia was finally broken by the Allied Forces. The frigate, Amethyst, trapped in the Yangtse River in China managed to make a daring escape in a 140 mile dash for freedom under cover of darkness. This event that gripped the world's attention was also followed with much interest by the Royal staff. Molly Beck, one of the still room ladies, had a son who was a rating aboard the Amethyst. There was much cheering round the staff hall table at the good news.

In July, as the hotel welcomed the height of the tourist season, rationing again hit the news. Sugar ration was reduced to 8oz per week, sweet rationing back to four ozs per week and tobacco supplies cut.

On Denzil's fish front there was good news. Chef Bonnacorsi had welcomed the free supply of prawns from Rory. He very gingerly put them on his menu as a starter dish and experimented with a sauce marie rose to accompany them and called them "fruites de la mer". They slowly caught on and soon a regular supply of prawns were winging their way to the east coast on the trusty mail bus. Denzil found himself attending the bus depot twice a week to uplift the supplies and his monthly envelope swelled to £4, which was very acceptable. He sometimes met the Station Hotel commis collecting their supplies so adjudged that Rory's business was quietly prospering.

In September a sad event took place. Old Sandy who hailed from Caithness had been a kitchen porter for over 30 years at the Royal Hotel. He had served in the Great War with the Cameron Highlanders and suffered from shell shock that caused him to have violent tremors from time to time. He was a very quiet dignified individual who went about his duties efficiently and was a very dependable pair of hands much appreciated by the Chef. His main occupation was peeling the vast amount of potatoes required by the busy kitchen and, long after lunch was finished and the kitchen staff gone, there would be usually two lone figures still hard at work. Walter in his bare feet and trousers rolled up to the knee swabbing the floor with bucket and mop cursing and shouting away to himself good style while Sandy sat on his stool peeling potatoes and whistling quietly to himself.

One afternoon Walter appeared at the porters' lodge still in his bare feet with mop in hand stating that Sandy had fallen in the kitchen. Calum and Denzil followed him urgently back into the kitchen to be confronted by Sandy lying dead, having fallen from his stool. He was lying in the middle of an upturned pool of peeled potatoes and water with the peeling knife still clutched in his hand.

Calum summoned the hotel doctor and the police, as they were obliged to do in the event of a sudden death. The cause of death was quickly established as a heart attack and George Fraser, the local undertaker, contacted. The hearse drew up in the narrow side street. A problem arose as it was not possible to manoeuvre a coffin up the narrow fire escape staircase that led to the street. The remains were bundled into a blanket and the two porters helped the undertakers transport the body down the staircase where it could be transferred into the coffin before setting off for the funeral home. As they struggled down the narrow staircase Denzil could not help thinking what an undignified way for old Sandy to leave the Royal for the last time.

Several days later Miss MacLean along with Chef Bonnacorsi, Calum, Denzil and a few others provided the sparse congregation at the service in the funeral home. There appeared to be no family members in attendance and a fierce rainstorm soaked them all as they laid him to rest in the town cemetery. His personal belongings were sent to a charity shop and Miss MacLean ensured that the hotel settled the undertaker's bill. In due course a new kitchen porter was installed and life at the Royal continued as normal.

Young Brian MacGlennon, one of the kitchen commis chefs, departed to do his National Service in Mid-September. He was very excited at the prospect and at the staff hall table there was much talk about what exotic part of the world he would see out his two years service.

He was accepted by the RAF and, in view of his catering background, was first sent off to the RAF School of Catering at RAF Halton in Bucks. His catering period safely over he found himself posted to RAF Unst in the Shetland Isles! There, as a member of the catering staff at this Early Warning Station, he served out his time manfully. When he came home on leave and dropped into the Royal he was the subject of much leg pulling. Monty, who was due to go in December, braced himself for the worst.

In October the tourist season dropped off as usual and the Royal faced another few winter months handling an entirely different type of business. The hydro engineers headed for the Royal at weekends to escape the rigours of the camps they occupied during the working week. They patronised Paddy's bar to good effect, dined well under the careful eye of Maitre d' Jack Mitchell and usually ended up at the ballroom dance. The stock rooms came into their own and gradually it seemed that business in general was recovering slowly from the war time years.

The October cattle mart time came round and with it the redoubtable figure of Abrach MacKay in his stained raincoat and large shepherds crook in hand. The porters greeted him as an old friend as he lurched out in the morning heading for the mart and to meet up with his farming cronies. Bert Rattray, the night porter, reported that he could not hold his drink as he usually did and had to help him to his room on a couple of nights. On the morning of his departure he had not vacated his room by midday so a housemaid tried to rouse him to no avail. The housekeeper was summoned and with her master key let herself into the room. Abrach lay on the bed fully dressed with his crook lying on the floor and it was clear to Mrs MacBeth that he had passed away in his drunken sleep.

The hotel doctor confirmed this and the undertaker was contacted along with police

"Bloody hell!" growled George Fraser to the subdued housekeeping staff, "What's up with this hotel, twice in as many months we've been here. Usually these things go in threes, you know."

The old farmer's remains were discreetly removed by means of the service lift to the awaiting hearse in the side street. Mrs MacBeth decided that, as it was October, she would close the six bedrooms in that particular wing for the next month or so. They were due to be refurbished anyway as part of the Royal's programme of updating bedrooms.

The old farmer's passing shocked the hotel staff. It became a subject for much discussion round the staff hall table. Miss MacLean was handling the matter from the hotel's side of things. She had enquired along with the police into Abrach's background. It transpired that he had no direct family, lived very simply and, although a man of considerable means, he had left no will, which surprised nobody.

Calum, who seemed to know about these things, told them that in that event his estate would be claimed by the

128

Government. "Aye and for sure they will fritter it away on some daft scheme or other" he concluded.

Denzil's banking routine was by now a well established part of his weekly routine and even the bank tellers were on first name terms with him. On November 11th his total stood at £169 - 10s – 0d. and he realised that he was closing in on the £200 barrier and perhaps, with a bit of luck, he might breach it by Christmas. His days off back at Cabrach provided a welcome break from his active hotel life and window cleaning activities. Jean had sold Ruby as she no longer felt up to the work involved and that in a way was the end of an era. Her neighbours Jack and Helen Munro provided her with a milk supply along with other needs and in return they used her empty byre for storing hay. Denzil still laid his snares to provide rabbits for Jean and always dropped off a rabbit to grace the Munro table.

Jean assured him that she was fine and well able to look after herself so he had to be satisfied with that. He went for another long weekend to Ullamore in late October and found himself as a willing deckhand on the fishing boat. The usual Saturday night ceilidh took place and this time the musical backing was added to when another neighbour, Roy MacPherson, appeared with his fiddle. Denzil had memorised two of the songs that Rose MaCrae had written out for him. His singing was well received and Duncy McCulloch, nursing his umpteenth dram, paid him a compliment when he declared, "Well done boy, you know you would never think you never had the Gaelic!"

As he rode back on the Monday morning with a box of prawns rattling in the hold of the bus he realised that he had been well and truly accepted into Rory's hospitable family.

Back at the Royal Mrs MacBeth finally decided to tackle the rooms that she had laid off including the one that Abrach had occupied. Her idea was to strip the beds, including mattresses, and move them to an unused part of the corridor thus allowing the painters full access to the bedrooms. She appeared one morning in her usual brisk fashion at the Porters' Lodge and spoke to Calum, "Right, I need two strong young men to move some mattresses for me!" Calum immediately delegated Monty and Denzil for this particular task. They followed the housekeeper up to the bedroom area where she explained just where she wanted the mattresses moved to. The mattresses were bulky as well as being reasonably heavy and required two people to manhandle them. The second room that the boys went into was Abrach's old room.

They were about to lift the mattress when the housekeeper called for one of them to do another task. "Right", said Monty who was nearest the door, "I'll go - hang on and I'll be back in a minute." Denzil, left alone in the bedroom, went to lift the mattress on his own to see just how heavy it was. He lifted one side, exposing the stretched wiring below, when to his astonishment he saw lying there a bulky manilla brown envelope. He picked it up carefully. It was clearly a very much used envelope with dark stains and on the front scrawled in ink was "£400". It was unsealed and he opened the flap and inside saw that it was stacked with banknotes. At that moment he heard Monty returning and, without much thought, stuffed the envelope into his uniform inner pocket.

The boys completed the task and returned to the lodge but Denzil did not inform Monty or anyone about his find. Later he went into the toilet and in the safety of the cubicle he opened the envelope. It contained mainly £20 notes and one five pound note. He counted the money and found it amounted to £385 exactly. Was this old Abrach's money from the cattle sale or had it been left by some other guest? How long had this money lain there? Should he declare his find? These were the many thoughts that crowded in on his mind. He decided to stay quiet for a week or so until he had decided on a course of action. His own opinion was that this find was in all probability the old farmer's money but again, uppermost in his mind, was what Calum had said about the Government falling heir to this money. He reasoned that he might make better use of the find than have it fall into uncaring and undeserving hands. His mind was made up and he resolved to bank the money as his own. He decided not to bank the money all at once as it might raise questions about where it came from so, on Friday 25th November, he attended the bank and lodged £21 - 4s - 0d. The £1 - 4s – 0d. was his own weekly take along with the first £20 from the envelope find. The teller, as usual, simply banked the money, signed his book and chatted away. So far, so good. He proceeded to do this each week until, in late December, he decided to bank the lot at one go. Part of his reason for this was that he was uneasy about this amount of money lying around in his locker.

So on Friday 16th December a rather apprehensive Denzil attended to his weekly banking. This time he queued up to lodge no less than £326 – 7s -0d! The major part was £325 the balance of his envelope. The old envelope he had disposed of by tearing it up into small pieces and flushing it down the hotel toilet. The teller again simply took his book and money as usual and amidst small talk about the holiday period it was all over.

He could hardly wait to get back to his room to look at the new bankbook total. £504 – 13s – 0d!! He stared at this new total for some time. It seemed like only weeks ago that he had hoped to close it on £200 by Christmas with a bit of luck and now here he was with in excess of £500. His only thought was thank goodness he did not require Finkie to countersign his bankbook anymore. In November Miss MacLean, on his birthday, wished him the usual happy returns before reminding him that in a year from now he was due for his National Service call up.

So, as 1949 came to a busy end in the Royal Hotel, Denzil had much to occupy his mind. Here he was financially flush and with National Service beckoning he reckoned 1950 was going to be just as much an interesting year as the one just experienced.

CHAPTER 15   Norma the Receptionist

Miss Maclean had always prided herself on being a good judge of character. She took a keen interest in any applicant for an hotel position making a habit of sitting in on the interview with the appropriate head of department. Her reasoning was that if you selected carefully then it would be in the hotel's best interests, thus saving a lot of heart-ache down the line.

She, however, had to admit that she got it quite wrong with Norma. A vacancy cropped up in the reception and the head receptionist Miss Armitage was looking for a more mature member to add to her staff. She had three young receptionists who all lived out so she was looking for somebody to live in the staff quarters and be on hand if any emergency happened.

Quite a few applicants came forward but Norma Urquhart stood out from the rest.   She was in her thirties, very demure, conservatively dressed, with little or no make-up and well spoken. A divorcee from the north of England with no children she was looking to get back into the working world and had all the necessary typing and reception qualifications. She was welcomed aboard. Miss MacLean was more than satisfied about the choice they had made.

All went well for the first few weeks as Norma settled in to her new job. Then slowly and subtly things began to change. Norma's hairstyle that had been severely pulled back and secured with a large comb became more loose and framed her face in a very seductive manner. Her make-up became more pronounced and she even managed to make her reception uniform emphasise her feminine curves. A button on her blouse never seemed to stay tied and, as she bent to her work at reception over a bill, the guest found himself looking down onto a very generous cleavage. It was, for all the world, like watching a butterfly emerging from its chrysalis. The young receptionists were impressed by their new staff member but Miss Armitage was of the old school and not so easily won over.

Norma was good at her work and very diligent so no fault could be found there.

She soon attracted a lot of male admirers among the guests and it was evident that in her off time she was being wined and dined at the Station Hotel. Bouquets of flowers delivered to the reception desk for her became a normal weekly delivery and was very soon all the talk in the staff hall. Her room in the female staff quarters became the first cause of complaint. Norma, coming in late at night or early morning clicking along the corridor in her high heels and shutting the door of her room, upset some of the other staff. Miss MacLean handled the complaint. She spoke to Norma directly and also to Mr Jennings, the manager, to keep him in the picture. He had an immediate solution to the problem. There were a couple of spare bedrooms never used in the annex housing the stock rooms. Transfer Norma there, he suggested, and the problem would be solved. So Norma moved to the bedroom in the annex and the matter seemed to be put to rest.

In this annexe was a Masonic lodge that was used about once a month. Any correspondence for the lodge that came to the hotel was left outside the door of the lodge for their attention. One day, as Calum was going off shift, he handed Denzil a bunch of letters and circulars and asked him to put them outside the Masonic lodge door when he had a chance. Later that night, when he came back to the hotel after a visit to the cinema, he remembered the Masonic mail lying in the porters' lodge and thought he may as well drop them off before retiring. He climbed the stairs above the stock rooms and headed for the darkened corridor that led to the Masonic lodge. Standing outside her bedroom door was Norma clad in a flimsy negligee smoking a cigarette.

"Hi Denzil", she greeted him in her low throaty voice, "What are you all about?" He explained about the mail for the Masonic lodge and as he passed her he was enveloped in her perfume. He dropped the letters off at the lodge door. On his return Norma was still standing by her bedroom but this time there was no cigarette in her hand. He was on the point of saying goodnight as he passed her but to his surprise she grabbed his arm. "Now then, what's all the big hurry about", she whispered and, wrapping her arms around him, pulled him close and kissed him long and lingeringly on the lips. Denzil was definitely in uncharted territory and his head spun with this new experience and the enticing scent of her perfume. He found himself pressed against the yielding warmth of her body and then her tongue forced its way into his mouth darting and flickering in a way that aroused strange emotions in him. He barely realised that Norma had slowly backed into her bedroom and with a deft flick of her foot closed it behind them. They parted and her negligee floated to the floor so she stood naked before him. Her hands swiftly undressed him and, as if in a dream, he found himself pulled onto her bed as they kissed again. Norma pulled herself away for a moment. She stood up, crossed the room and locked the door. "Can't be too careful" she explained as she slid into bed beside him. Her well-practised hands played over his body until, in a state of arousal, he experienced a certain surge of power and, brushing her hands aside, he lowered himself down and penetrated her. Afterwards, all passion spent, they lay locked in each other's arms. Slowly Norma reached out a hand to the cigarette pack on the bedside table. She flicked open the pack, selected a cigarette, put it in her mouth and expertly flicked the lighter. She lay back exhaling a contented plume of smoke. "Nothing like a fag - after a shag! My old mother used to say!", she declared, followed by her husky laugh. Denzil lay in a very contented state, immersed equally in her strong perfume and fragrant tobacco smoke.

Suddenly a knocking at her bedroom door! They both started apart in the bed and looked at each other as if in disbelief. Then a slightly stronger knocking. "Oh Christ!", whispered Norma in a barely audible voice. She slid out of the bed, stubbed out her cigarette, slipping on her negligee in one quick movement. Another more urgent knocking at the door.

"Yes, yes, I'm coming", said Norma, in a put on sleepy voice. Denzil by this time had slipped his underpants on and was out of the bed gathering his scattered garments. Norma turned to him. "Here, get under the bed", she whispered turning back the coverlet. Denzil, with all his clothes in his hands, slid under the bed as directed. Norma, about to turn to the door, spotted his shoes at the last minute. She kicked them under the bed where Denzil lay, adjusted the coverlet, before turning at last to unlock the door. Denzil lay under the bed with literally a birds-eye view of proceedings. He saw Norma's bare feet with painted toenails go towards the door and open it. He heard her say. "Oh, I didn't expect you!" and a man's voice replied but it was so low pitched he could not make out what he said. Norma's feet backed into the room and a man's black shoes and striped trousers bottoms came into view. More whispered conversation and then the feet closed together as if they were embracing. Denzil lay as quiet as he could wondering just how long he would be trapped under the bed. Then he had a sense of deja-vu as first the negligee fluttered to the floor then a man's discarded clothing began to be strewn about. The man sat on the bed to remove his shoes and spoke for the first time so that Denzil could make out the voice. He was thunderstruck!

The midnight caller was none other than Mr Jennings the manager. He had to stuff his hand into his mouth to stifle an involuntary laugh. Hardly had he achieved this than the bed sagged ominously above him as the two bodies intertwined above him. He moved quietly to one side where there was more space, and not a moment too soon, as a very vigorous coupling took place. After a while the movement above him subsided and then the ritual of cigarette lighting took place. The tobacco smoke drifted down to him cramped in his trapped position. The dreadful thought then struck him, what if Jennings planned to stay the night. After ten minutes or so this prayer was answered. Jennings slipped out of the bed and dressed himself. Once dressed Denzil saw Norma's feet slide out of bed to join the black shoes. The two sets of feet then walked to the bedroom door. They locked once more in a long embrace before whispered voices and the sound of the door being locked. Norma's feet approached the bed, she drew back the coverlet, bent down so that her face looked in on the recumbent Denzil. "Right, come on out of there then, the coast is clear - thank God I locked that door", she laughed. Denzil scrambled out from under the bed to dress himself. Norma sat on the bed lighting another cigarette and laughed to herself, "Blimey - here was I having a boring night up until now. It's a bit like waiting for a bus and then two turn up at the same time."

With Denzil ready to go Norma walked him to the door. She pulled him close to her so as to kiss goodbye murmuring to him, "Denzil, we must do this again sometime, you are one eager beaver!"

He made his way down into the darkened foyer ensuring that Bert the night porter did not detect him as he returned to his room in the staff quarters. Monty was snoring happily so he did not have to explain his late coming. Before he fell asleep he reflected on his new experience determining that in future he would keep Norma at a safe distance.

However, the spirit may have been willing but the flesh was weak. Next day Norma was on duty at the reception desk, glamorous as ever, flirting with any male guest who she had to deal with, in a manner that made Miss Armitage wince. In her infrequent dealings with Denzil in his porter's roles he was perfectly normal showing no hint of their shared intimacy.

Three weeks later she observed Denzil alone in the Porters' Lodge. The foyer was quiet so she crossed over with a letter in her hand as if to give him some instruction. Denzil looked up in some surprise as she walked into the lodge. Norma smiled, "Denzil, I will be alone tonight, look forward to having a visit from you after 11pm - OK", and with that she was gone, leaving a lingering perfume presence in the lodge.

No way thought Denzil to himself, but at 11.15pm he found himself knocking gently on her door to gain admittance.

This way of life went on for some months without any

mishap or Norma getting her bedroom booking diary dates mixed up.

All the porters lusted after Norma in their own way. Calum once watched her wiggle her way across the foyer in her high heels and remarked to Denzil, "I wouldn't half mind throwing a lawless leg across that, Denzil my boy, but she wouldn't go for the likes of us.". Denzil quietly smiled his agreement.

But like all good things it had to come to an end. Apparently Jennings' wife had become suspicious of his wandering eye and somehow found out about his regular trips to Norma's room. She appeared at the reception one morning, accusing Norma in a high-powered shouting match so that it became common knowledge throughout the hotel. Miss Armitage summoned Miss MacLean and it was all over bar the shouting.

Next day Mrs Jennings' parents turned up to collect their daughter, grandchildren and personal effects to drive south, leaving one humiliated and deserted manager in their wake. At about the same time Norma appeared with her bulky suitcase and fur coat ready for her departure. As she struggled with her case Denzil said to Calum that he should help her to the station and that was agreed.

Denzil took hold of her case and Norma smiled her thanks. They made their way down the crowded street to the railway station with Denzil trying to express his sympathy at the outcome of events. Norma seemed totally unconcerned and simply talked about fresh pastures. He waited while she bought her ticket before walking to the train together. She kissed him goodbye at the barrier before turning to pick up her case to make the short journey to the carriage door. A smartly dressed businessman observed her doing this and, lifting up his hat, he offered to take her case and was rewarded with a dazzling smile. Denzil waited to see if she would wave to him but it was not to be. Seated in her train compartment Norma was already busy talking animatedly to her new travelling companion.

The staff hall was rife with all the news for a day or so and the stories grew with the telling. Over one lunch somebody tried to close the subject by saying, "Farewell to Norma the nymphomaniac!" Somebody asked what a nymphomaniac was and Monty, as always, had the last word. "I once met a nymphomaniac in a train coming back from Glasgow. She was a right cracker, blond, with a pair of knockers to die for. She had this tight red sweater with the letters N A N embroidered on it. We were alone in the compartment so I asked her if that was her name. "Oh no", she said to me, "that stands for National Association of Nymphomaniacs! My own name is Gladys, I am a district representative of this movement and I have been attending an international conference in Paris. Very interesting conference it was too, and we voted as to which country or race was the most sexy. You'll never guess, the first was American Indians and the runner-up was Scotsmen. I forgot to ask you, what's your name?"

I thought for a minute before replying, "Running Bear MacPhee!" The staff hall dissolved into general laughter. The post-script was Jennings tendered his resignation, which was accepted, drawing a line under the matter, and once more the Royal was looking for a new figure at the helm.

CHAPTER 16   Hetty's Shop

Hardly had the Royal settled down to a normal routine after the busy festive time than Jennings departure in late January together with a reception job vacancy rocked the boat.

Miss MacLean once more held the fort as temporary manager until a new appointment could be made. This was duly made in late February when a certain Mr Frank D. Cochrane, a retired naval officer, was appointed. As he settled in to his new post Miss MacLean braced herself so as to break in a new pair of hands into her way of running the hotel. She joined forces with Miss Armitage once more in interviewing the reception position applicants. After much thought they went for a safe pair of hands in selecting a local 50 year old housewife who was looking to get back to work after her children were off her hands. So by early March she was quite confident that everything was back on an even keel.

Denzil was just getting used to having a room on his own as Monty departed in mid February. Called up for National Service he decided to sign on instead for a 12 year stint in the Merchant Navy as the thought of struggling on meagre National Service pay for two years did not appeal to him.

The bedroom and the staff hall table were much quieter places after he left. A new porter, Bert Reid who lived out, was appointed in his place. Denzil was quite glad that Fritzi had not been promoted as had proved to be a very dependable stand-in on the window -cleaning front when he took a long weekend break in Ullamore.

One afternoon in March, as he went to clean the Building Society windows, he saw that it was covered in scaffolding. Two builders were at work pointing the worn sandstone walls and one turned out to be his former school mate Ally Gordon. Ally promptly slid down the scaffolding with his trowel in hand for a chat.

"Hi Dezzy, is this what you are doing now?" was his greeting. "Whatever happened to the hotel job you had?"

Denzil explained that this was his afternoon side-line job that he inherited.

Ally went on, "We're just patching up these old walls once more. Don't know for how much longer as there is word that this area is ripe for a property development. We are kept busy with different jobs and somehow we now have six men on our books."

After Ally clambered back on the scaffold Denzil wondered to himself if Finkelstein knew about this proposed development and what it might mean to him and his other clients.

About that time, during an afternoon working in Hetty's shop, she expressed her concern about the fact that her landlord had just died. She had got a good deal from Johnny Cameron who owned the premises as he had been in school with her mother. A widower, he had two sons who lived and worked in England, so Hetty was naturally concerned about what would be the outcome when the estate came to be settled. It was to be a dark cloud that was destined to hang over her for several months.

On 5th May Denzil noted as he banked his weekly total of £1 – 5s – 0d that, by coincidence, it was exactly three years to the day since he had started to work in the Royal. Three years! It did not seem possible, as time passed so quickly. One month later, on roughly the third anniversary of his lodging his very first payment into the bank, he noted with some satisfaction that the total now stood at £548 – 5s – 0d.

He wondered idly that if he kept up his saving routine what the total would be in another three year's time. Looking ahead he knew that if he had to do his National Service he would be on a very reduced income and perhaps that would spell the end of his banking routine. If the worst came to the worst then, thanks to his savings, he would have something to fall back on. National Service was also causing Rory MacCulloch to look ahead at the problems it might present. He was fortunate in a way that his medical condition ruled him out of military service. As he laughingly told Denzil he had inherited his father's flat feet along with an asthmatic condition. Denzil's way forward was quite another matter as he would have to rearrange with Chef Bonnacorsi about uplifting orders from the bus depot. His long-term aim was to pass his driving test and get a van to give him more independence and perhaps open up more outlets for his supplies. To this end he duly sat and passed his test in June and so his forward planning was paying off.

In late June Communist North Korea invaded independent South Korea and immediately the storm clouds of war swirled again on the international scene. President Truman ordered American air and naval forces to go to the aid of the invaded state immediately. In Parliament Churchill declared, "Once again America and Britain find themselves associated in a noble cause".

British ships in the far-east were placed under the command of US General Douglas MacArthur to aid the United Nations in South Korea following the crossing of the 38th parallel by North Korean forces. A war weary Britain braced itself for yet another conflict.

One bit of news came at the end of May when petrol rationing was ended after ten long years. It was reported that at some garages motorists tore up their coupons and danced round their vehicles. The Royal like many other hotels looked forward to an increase in trade from the car driving public.

In late June Denzil went for another long weekend to Ullamore only to find a rather subdued Rory. Rory, with his driving licence under his belt, decided to go and get a bank loan to buy a van but ran into a real problem. "I went to see Mr McBride the banker", he told Denzil, "first time I had ever been into a bank. My folks never had any need of a bank as they only ever dealt in cash like most people. Even the second boat we bought, Dad shook hands on the deal with Willie MacRae and agreed to pay him so much every month until the boat was paid. When I asked the banker about a loan he politely informed me that they did not give a loan to just anybody who walked in off the street. Any worthwhile business should have a bank account so that the bank could gauge their credit worthiness before agreeing to a loan. He also spoke about the bank needing a security on a loan whatever that was. The upshot was that I opened up an account for the business for future use but it means that I will have to wait a year or so to show accounts before a loan can be considered."

Denzil thought carefully as Rory detailed his problem. "How much does a van cost?" He enquired. Rory replied that he had a good second hand van in his sights with low mileage that was on sale for £90.

"Right" said Denzil, "How about if I loan you the money. You can expand your business, keeping the bank happy and in a couple of years when you have the bank on your side you can take a loan and then repay me."

Rory was almost lost for words, "£90 quid. How the hell can you manage that kind of money?"

"Never you mind that", Denzil retorted. "I wouldn't offer it to you if I couldn't manage it. So how about it, and the only thing I ask is that this deal is strictly between the two of us."

Rory took a bit of persuading that Denzil was not pulling his leg before the two boys shook hands on the deal. A week later Rory caught the bus to Inverdeen along with a fish supply. The two boys met up and Denzil took him to his bank where he withdrew £90 and handed the cash to a still disbelieving Rory. He left Rory to go off to Cameron's garage to purchase the van on his own. Some time later an exuberant Rory pulled into the Royal car park in his new white van to show Denzil his new proud possession.

"No more picking up supplies from the bus depot for you Dezzy" he laughed as he pulled away heading for the west.

He was as good as his word and soon the van was doing twice weekly trips to Inverdeen and picking up fresh orders from other hotels en route. Denzil still got his £4 weekly envelope although he no longer had to collect supplies and Rory said to consider it as interest on the loan. Chef Bonnacorsi was delighted with the service Rory was supplying and mussels along with lobsters and prawns now featured on his menu.

In August as the summer tourist season reached its peak the Korean situation worsened. British troops arrived in Korea to bolster the American presence in the war torn country. The 1st Battalion the Argyle and Sutherland Highlanders sailed from Hong Kong to get involved and this caused some concern for two mothers on the Royal staff whose sons were doing their National Service in that regiment. Denzil wondered if he had picked the wrong time as his National Service time drew near.

September saw Hetty"s worst fears realised as her former landlord's estate was settled. The two sons decided to sell the property but first of all giving Hetty the first opportunity to purchase before putting it on the open market.

"Where on earth is the likes of me going to get their hands on £400?" wailed Hetty to Denzil one afternoon as she studied the open letter on her counter. "I was hoping to get another eight years out of this business before I got my old age pension and retired, now this has really scuppered my plans."

Denzil felt a lot of sympathy for unfortunate Hetty as her landlord's passing had caused her so much concern at the end of her working life.

He lay in bed that night and turned things over in his mind. He often found that this was the best time to reflect on matters and in the still of the night he could usually come to a decision. He woke in the middle of the night with a start. An idea had come to him and, after some more thought, he went back to sleep and slept soundly.

His morning portering finished he made his way to the Finkelstein's shop in North Bridge Street. He entered the shop and Mrs Finkelstein dealing with a customer gave him a welcoming smile and called out to her husband. He came through, in response, from the workshop area, glassses in hand rubbing his eyes. "Well, well, Denzil, this is just like old times, come away through."

Once in the workshop area they chatted for a while until the old jeweller gave him a long shrewd look. "Right my boy, what exactly is on your mind?"

Denzil opened up. "Well, you know how you said that if ever I needed advice your door was always open? I would like to know what you think of this idea and if it is workable?" Finkelstein replied, "Well tell me all about it then."

Denzil explained about Hetty's problem and the £400 required by her to purchase the shop in her own name. How about if he advanced the money to Hetty and she paid him back just like paying her rent on a weekly or monthly basis? This would mean she could continue working until her pension age came about.

Finkelstein frowned before replying, "Well Denzil your intentions are very laudable but I would advise you to proceed with caution. This figure of £400, I take it you are going to pay a substantial amount down and borrow the rest from the bank?"

"Oh no" Denzil countered "I've got more than £400 in my account so I will have no need to borrow from the bank."

Finkelstein nearly fell out of his chair. "You've got more than £400 in the bank. Goodness gracious! How on earth did you manage that? Perhaps I shouldn't ask. Look, come back tomorrow after I have given it some thought. Also bring your bankbook so I can confirm your financial position."

The next day Denzil reported back as requested and handed over his bankbook. Finkelstein checked it and raised his eyebrows as he confirmed the amount lodged.

He put the bank book down and looked hard at Denzil through his gold rimmed glasses, "May I ask how you managed to reach this astonishing total, Denzil?"

Denzil then made a clean breast of things telling how it came mainly from the discovered money under the mattress. He felt an immediate wave of relief as it troubled him for some time whether he had done the right thing.

Finkelstein fell silent for a moment before speaking as if he had made up his mind on a course of action.

"I am glad you told me Denzil. I feel that in helping out Hetty from her predicament that you are already putting the money to good use. Maybe that is what the old cattleman himself would have approved of. Well, you are certainly in funds alright."

Finkelstein continued, "Now I would advise against lending the money to Hetty and depending on her to pay you rental. You would have to get her to sign a contract giving you security over the property involving lawyers and additional expense. What I suggest is that you buy the property for £400 so you own the property and Hetty pays you rental just as she did for her former landlord. That is a more clean cut way of doing things. Now, you will have a problem if you go ahead and you are still not eighteen years of age and your owning of the property becomes public knowledge. So what I advise is that I buy the property in my name using your funds so that the deal is kept under wraps. I will give you a legal letter detailing your ownership and ensuring the rental payments are channelled to your account. In due course, when you say you are twenty-one, we can put the property back into your name. I will use my lawyer in Edinburgh to handle things. Once the sale is concluded there will be some additional expense as the title of the property is conveyed to my name. That expense you can repay me at a later date once the property reverts back to you. Now how does that appeal to you?" Denzil nodded his head thanking him for this sound advice.

Finkelstein concluded, "When Hetty tells you that I have purchased her property and she has been informed that she can continue trading at the usual rent you can take it as news."

On that note Denzil left the shop with a spring in his step knowing that he had solved Hetty's problem. That week as he worked in her shop he found it hard to resist telling her that her worries were more or less over. Two weeks later he found himself withdrawing £400 from his account and handing it over to Finkelstein as Hetty's shop sale went ahead. The outgoing along with the £90 advanced to Rory left his account somewhat depleted with a meagre total that now read £87 – 5s – 0d.

He consoled himself with the fact that he had put the money into doing some good and in a sense was just farmed out for a time. A month later he was once again comfortably over the £100 barrier.

On 10th November he attained his eighteenth birthday and, as always, Miss MacLean wished him all the best while the government played its part as well by sending him his calling papers for National Service!

At about this time Hetty told him how relieved she was that things had worked out so well. Whoever would have thought that old Finkelstein would have bought the property but I suppose he must be looking on it as part of his pension arrangements. Denzil expressed his delight that her problems seemed to have been resolved and took the opportunity of telling her about his imminent call up. Hetty told him that she had been anticipating that event and had arranged for somebody to take his place.

This was the start of his arranging his affairs. The window cleaning round was next on his agenda. He spoke to Chalmers who had taken on the bulk of old Bob Wright's round when he died and he agreed to take on North Bridge Street clients.

He had a farewell trip to Ullamore in late November. Working on the boat this time on rough sea and squally weather proved quite testing but the ceilidh on the Saturday night was the highlight of his trip. The cottage was packed with family and neighbours and Denzil was asked to sing a rather emotional war-time song to close the evening. "We'll meet again".

Rory was happy with the way the van had opened up the family business and he made sure that the money was put through the bank account he had opened to build up a credit status for future use. He was keen to repay Denzil for the bank loan on a monthly basis but Denzil assured him to keep it on ice until he returned from his army service.

Denzil attended his medical held in the Ballroom and was informed that due to his hotel background he would be enlisted in the Army Catering Corps. A letter would be sent in due course to inform him of where to report.

The sale of Hetty's shop must have gone through as the weekly rent of £2 started to appear in his bank account. This was well timed as very shortly his income streams from window cleaning and Hetty's shop would cease.

The army letter arrived in due course advising him to report to Ramillies Barracks in Aldershot on Monday 11th December. Now that he had a date he could finalise things with the Royal and finish up on Friday 8th December as this would allow him the best part of a week to spend with Jean before heading south.

On Friday he said goodbye to his fellow workers in the Royal and Miss MacLean made a point of looking him out. She wished him all the best, to be sure and keep in touch and hopefully that he would return to his old job when he had completed his army service. His last task was to visit the Finkelstein's and thank them for all that had been done for him over the past few years. Finkelstein was quite moved by Denzil's thanks and tried to brush it aside, "Nonsense my boy, the credit is all yours. You deserve everything you have got as it could not have been easy at times keeping to that strict discipline. Take good care of yourself and always remember, never let anyone know your financial position. I think you have learned that anyway. Keep in touch with us and let us know how you get on in the army. Hetty's shop purchase has now been concluded and here is the letter that I promised detailing your ownership."

Denzil left the shop clutching the letter and it was still in his hand as he said goodbye to Hetty. If Hetty only knew what the letter in my hand detailed she would have had a pink fit, he thought, and almost laughed out at the prospect.

He spent the week with Jean felling birch trees and ensuring that her log pile would see her through the winter and various other chores. Jean had one request. Please do not ever come home in uniform and no photographs of him in uniform. Denzil quite understood that this would only serve to remind her of her great loss when Duncan failed to return from the ill-fated Arnhem invasion.

So on a snowy Saturday morning Denzil took his case and walked down the path, turning to give Jean a last wave as she stood in the doorway of the croft house. Long after he had disappeared from view Jean stood there thinking of the day some four years earlier that he had set off for his first hotel job. She dried her eyes on her apron and walked back into the house.

CHAPTER 17   Back from National Service

"You alright son?"

Denzil looked up through tear blurred eyes to see the ticket collector looking down anxiously at him. He had been so deep in thought that he had not heard him enter the railway compartment.

"Yes – I'm OK" he responded "Just suffering from a heavy head cold, that's all". He wiped his eyes with his handkerchief and blew his nose as if to emphasise the fact.

"Aye this mild winter weather seems to bring on all manner of things. There's no doubt a good hard frost kills off a lot of these bugs", responded the ticket collector.

He was clearly in the mood for a chat and Denzil was quite happy to entertain him. Early December was usually a quiet time for train passengers but soon as the festive season approached that would change dramatically he informed Denzil.

"Your face is familiar," he said, looking hard at Denzil, "did you used to work in the Royal Hotel?" When Denzil confirmed this the ticket collector looked pleased with himself. "Aye I used to see you and the other porters collecting stuff off the train and the hotel barrow. What are you up to these days?"

Denzil replied, "Oh I've just finished my National Service after two years and I am heading home."

"Well, I'm sure you will be glad to put that behind you and no mistake. I remember well when I got demobbed in 1946 and the great feeling to know that it was all over. I'm sure your folks will be as relieved as mine were at the time. Well, I'd better be on my rounds, all the best for getting back to civvy street and mind, a good whisky toddy will soon shift that cold of yours."

With that rejoinder he was gone closing the compartment door leaving Denzil on his own. Denzil turned his attention back to the large brown manilla envelope that he had been looking at before the ticket collector had disturbed him.

He slowly drew out the letter and read it for the hundredth time as if he still had not taken in its content.

Croft 3.

Cabrach

November 5th 1952

My dear Denzil,

This is without doubt the most difficult letter I have ever had to write in my life , and I am not sure even where to start. The whole of Cabrach was stunned with the events of last month and the tragic loss of Jean in the house fire. I enclose cuttings from the local paper that tells its own story.

It happened in the early hours of Saturday morning. Moss, our collie, started howling and Jack got up to see what was bothering her. He could see the flames almost immediately and dashed in to put on his clothes. Fortunately somebody over the marshes at the factor's house saw the flames and, having a telephone, alerted the Inverdeen fire brigade. By the time they arrived there was very little they could do as the fire had gutted the house. Jack showed them where they could get a water supply from the burn back on the hillside. However, all they could do was put out the dying embers.

The police asked if there was any relatives and somebody gave your name and said that you were doing your military service. It was at Jean's funeral service when I noticed that you were not there and I was so bothered that I decided to follow things up. Apparently the police were looking for a Denzil MacGillivray and had drawn a blank, naturally. When I explained that your surname was Morrison we were able to trace your unit and address in Aldershot. I said to the police that I would take it on myself as a neighbour to inform you of what had happened and they were quite happy for me to do this.

I realize that this letter will come as a complete shock and you have our every sympathy. Please confirm that you have received my letter and remember when you come home you will be very welcome to stay with us.

Yours very sincerely,
Helen Munro (Mrs)

The newspaper cuttings spilled out of the envelope. They made stark reading. One headline read "TRAGIC CROFT FIRE CLAIMS ELDERLY WIDOW'S LIFE!" Another said "CROFT FIRE TRAGEDY IN HIGHLANDS". A photograph showed the croft house with just the walls remaining as the roof had fallen in and scorch marks were clearly seen on the stonework by the door and the windows.

Denzil remembered the total shock when the letter reached him. He had opened it in the corridor of the barracks office and reeled against the wall when he first read its contents. He had last seen Jean in mid summer when he had come home on leave and she was looking forward to having him home again in December when he was due for demob. He had written to her only last week telling her of his demob date. He had replied to Mrs Munro as requested thanking her for contacting him and promising to visit them on his return in December.

On the train heading north his sense of loss had struck him forcibly. A feeling of desolation crept over him as he realized that now he was very much alone in the world. He had no home to return to and was not even sure if his hotel job would be available. During his two years military service he had not visited the Royal or Ullamore. He had dropped the odd postcard to Calum, Rory and the Finkelsteins but left it at that and been quite content to spend his leave with Jean at the croft.

The train was now skirting the waters of the Firth and Denzil could see the outskirts of Inverdeen in the distance. He put the letter and cuttings carefully back in the envelope before stowing it into his suitcase. His first task when he alighted from the train was to secure his suitcase in the Left Luggage department. He had decided first of all to visit Mr Finkelstein just to let him know he was back in town.

The jewelers shop bell tinkled with the old familiar sound as he entered. Mrs Finkelstein was busy with some clients but she greeted Denzil with a smile and gestured for him to go into the workshop at the back. Finkelstein was busy with a watch clearly under repair and turned at his entrance. "Denzil my boy, how good to see you!" He greeted him, rising to his feet, with some difficulty. "Calum told me about your sad loss. How tragic and just before you were due home too. You have our every sympathy and if there is anything we can do, please just ask." They shook hands and Denzil sat down on a seat that Finkelstein pulled out for him.

"I can hardly believe that two years have slipped past since we last saw you. We got your postcards so we knew that you were in Aldershot and seemed to be enjoying life. But tell me, what are your plans now?" Denzil shrugged his shoulders as he replied, "I am not sure. I'll go and see Calum at the Royal to see if my job is still available and, I suppose, just take it from there".

Mrs Finkelstein came in at that point and after expressing her sympathy declared that a cup of tea would go down well. As she busied herself doing just that, Finkelstein asked Denzil about his army service.

"Well it was uneventful" Denzil informed him "I did my eight weeks square bashing at Ramillies Barracks before going off on a ten week cooking course to a place in Woolwich. When we returned from that everybody was posted off to do the catering at various units, everybody except two of us. A fellow Scot, Alastair Sutherland, and myself were selected to stay at the Officers Mess at Ramillies. I became batman to three officers: a major and two captains. It was very undemanding and most weekends we were free of any duty and avoided any parades that others had to do.

One of the other staff played in a small band that operated at weekends in the large NAAFI Club down in the centre of the town. I went with him on a couple of occasions until I found myself roped in when the guy who fronted their band as the singer got demobbed. It was a great experience for me and taught me a lot, playing with a group of very talented musicians. It was well paid into the bargain and certainly put my army pay in the shade."

Finkelstein laughed remarking, "I wondered how you would survive on your army pay but I should have realized that you would find a way! Your property deal is going well and Hetty seems to have a weight off her shoulders. I'll wait until you have settled down before I transfer the paperwork over to you. There's no rush. By the way, there is a strong rumour that our side of North Bridge Street has been eyed up by a developer from down south, nothing concrete quite yet but I will keep you posted if things kick off." Denzil left the jeweller's shop in a better frame of mind and headed for the Royal.

He entered the front door to be greeted by Calum at the Lodge desk.

"Well, well! Look what the cat's dragged in!" came the warm welcome from Calum. "We thought you had joined the Foreign Legion."

Denzil had to laugh. He soon found himself in the Porters' Lodge recounting his army experiences to Calum and the two other porters. There were two new faces among the porters that made Denzil realize, of course, that two years had elapsed since he was last in the Royal.

Calum took him through the hotel into the staff hall where he quickly organized a cup of tea. Over the tea he told Denzil about the various changes that had taken place during his absence. Cochrane was still the General Manager but Miss MacLean, at long last, had been promoted to Manager. The other heads of department were still in place.

Eventually the talk came round to Denzil's situation and Calum had to confess that, just at this moment, there was no porter vacancy. Denzil had half expected this but nonetheless it presented him with a very real problem. Not only would he have to go looking for a job but also a place to live in as well.

Calum had an idea that the Station Hotel might have a staff vacancy and it was worth a try to go and enquire there. Calum made no reference to Jean's tragic death and Denzil was quite glad not to have to deal with that as well.

They returned to the front hall and Denzil was on the point of saying goodbye to Calum when a familiar voice was heard. "A little bird told me that the prodigal son had returned!" Denzil turned round to find Miss MacLean bearing down upon them with a smile on her face.

"Well, it's been quite a while since we clapped eyes on you, although Calum here kept me informed when he got an occasional postcard from you. By the way, I heard about the loss of your mother a couple of months ago and you have my deepest sympathy. It must have been a very difficult time for you. What are your plans now?"

Calum spoke up, "As we are fully staffed, Miss MacLean, I was suggesting to Denzil that he might try the Station Hotel to see if they might have a vacancy."

"Nonsense" responded Miss MacLean in her brisk manner, "we've never lost valuable members of staff to a rival hotel, and I can assure you we are not going to start now. Denzil please follow me." She strode off and Denzil, before following her, raised his eyebrows at Calum. They ended up in the office that she had interviewed him in some four years earlier.

"Now Denzil, I am assuming that you are looking both for a job and accommodation", she started. Denzil confirmed that that indeed was his present position. "Well, as you now know, we are fully staffed with porters but I have always felt that you were equipped to be more than a porter. We have a vacancy in the dining room and I was just discussing it with Mr Mitchell the other day. How does that appeal to you? It will mean starting off as a commis but I have no doubt that our Maitre d' will soon fast track you to a station waiter's position."

Denzil readily agreed to this course of action.

"Excellent" declared Miss MacLean with some satisfaction, "I will get Calum to show you an empty room in the staff quarters and tomorrow you can meet up with Mr Mitchell. One thing I can tell you, he will ensure that you get an excellent training as he is one of the old school. It is good to have you back on board again."

They went back to the front hall where Miss MacLean instructed Calum to take Denzil to his room. As they walked down the corridor a slightly astonished Calum remarked, "Denzil, as Paddy would say, you must have the luck of the Irish and no mistake. Anyway, it's good to have you back with us!"

All that was left was to collect his suitcase from the Left Luggage at the station and wondering just what tomorrow would bring.

CHAPTER 18   Royal Waiter

Next morning Denzil presented himself at ten o clock sharp to be interviewed by the Maitre D' Jack Mitchell. They sat down at a corner table well away from where the other waiters were preparing the tables for lunch service. Jack Mitchell explained that four or five part time waitresses covered the breakfast service supervised by his deputy or a senior station waiter. He himself appeared about 9 o'clock to start his working day and also be on hand to say goodbye to any distinguished or regular guests.

The station waiters and commis waiters commenced their work after breakfast service had been concluded. He remembered Denzil from his earlier work as a porter and expressed his pleasure that he was now considering training as a waiter.

"Young man, you are about to enter into the most important department in any hotel. Anybody can carry a case, book someone in or pour a drink and even make a bed, but the restaurant is the beating heart! Certainly the kitchen require staff to be highly trained but no matter how good the food is that they produce, if it is not served properly then it is all to no avail. Never forget that!"

He asked about his Catering Corps experience and declared that it was all good experience to enable him to go far in the hotel industry.

Denzil would first work as a commis to one of the established station waiters. This would take about six months before he could be considered for a position as a station waiter in his own right. His work shift would include covering six lunch services and five dinner services with one day off per week. His pay would be fifteen shillings per week with a share of the tips from the tronc. His uniform would be supplied as a commis but when he reached station waiter status then he would be obliged to supply his own.

He called over one of the older station waiters, Marcus Stratton, and introduced Denzil to him as his commis. Jack Mitchell then left to have his usual morning meeting with Chef Bonnacorsi to discuss the day's menus. This meeting was important as it ensured that both departments were fully informed and any special clients' requests were known in advance. If the Chef had any particular dish that he wanted pushed then this was the time to get the information out. The Maitre d' on his return would meet with his station waiters to pass on the necessary information to ensure the smooth running between both departments.

Left in the capable hands of Marcus, Denzil was issued with his commis uniform. His black trousers and shoes met with approval and a white jacket with black tie completed his dress code. His fingernails and hands were examined to ensure that they were clean and he was told that he could expect this treatment daily. Marcus himself was dressed in the normal station waiter uniform or, as he referred to himself, as a chef de rang. This consisted of black tailcoat and waistcoat with wing collar and white bow tie.

His next task was to show Denzil just exactly how a table was laid up for service even down to placing the linen table napkins. For lunch service it was a Royal tradition to have them in a fan shape but for dinner service a more formal cocked hat design.

That done, he explained that Denzil would be his assistant during his training period and he would do his best to ensure that this training would be as thorough as possible. Denzil was then free to go and report the next day after breakfast service to commence his first shift.

Denzil returned to his room well satisfied with the way that things had turned out: he had a roof over his head and was back at work in familiar surroundings.

Chef Bonnacorsi had informed him that he had to contact Rory for a supply of lobsters and told him that his partner in crime was back from his Army service to work again in the

Royal. Rory had asked the Chef to let Denzil know he would be down late morning and would like to see him.

Sure enough, about eleven o'clock Rory pulled into the hotel car park. Denzil had expected to see the usual white van but this time it was a larger white van with the words "ULLAMORE SEA FARE" blazoned on the side in blue wording with a couple of sea gulls flying above.

Rory popped out with a welcoming smile and hearty handshake. "Well Dezzy - good to see you again! Here, give me a hand with these lobsters to keep Chef happy and then we can have a chat." He opened the van door and together they manhandled the crates of lobsters into the kitchen. Denzil observed that the van was laden with quite clearly a number of other orders. Once this was over Rory locked the van and together they strolled down to the Merrythought Café to have a longer chat over a couple of expresso coffees.

Rory was keen to know how his army service had gone and was intrigued to learn that Denzil had been lead singer with a band for most of his time. He laughed when Denzil told him about the contrast between his miserable army pay of £1 - Is - Od for working in the officers mess and the relative wealth of £5 tax free for singing two nights a week with the band. He was also keen to bring Denzil up to date with his progress. He produced from his pocket a cheque for £90 payable to Denzil.

"Here we go Dez - loan repaid with many thanks for being around at the time when the bank turned me down. As you know I opened up an account at that time with the bank and ensured that most of the business money went through it so I had one happy banker. I traded up the original van as the orders grew. The van made all the difference to the business. I could deliver orders in person without delay and also cover a wider area. The other orders that you saw in the van are deliveries to make down the coast before I head home. One strange thing happened to really move the business into a different league. Many of the local fishermen in the west coast were hampered by having to fish and then face the problem of selling their catch. Well, I took on buying their catches at an agreed price so that took that problem off their hands. It also meant that I no longer had the time to go fishing myself. So I leased out our boat to two of my cousins and also agreed to sell their catch. The old man runs the other boat on a seasonal basis taking tourists out, and that is a growing side of the business. He still ends up in the bar drinking part of the profits as you can guess but still it all adds to the old bank balance. So all in all things are going well on my front."

They chatted for some time on other matters until Denzil made a request.

"Rory - will you do me a favour? See next week when you come down with a delivery, could you run me over to Cabrach as I have to pay a visit to the Munro family?"

Rory agreed and a date was settled before they parted company.

After Rory's van had left the car park Denzil took a walk to the bank to deposit the cheque. During his time in Aldershot he had kept up his saving routine as, once again like his hotel job, he had no rent or food to pay for so most of his money was banked. These payments were transferred to his account in the Inverdeen bank. The rental money from Hetty's shop was also paid in on a monthly basis. After banking the cheque he was quietly satisfied that his account now stood at £721 - 10s - Od. With his investment of £400 in Hetty's shop he was comfortably through the thousand pound barrier. It seemed a long way from the day he had lodged his first payment some five years ago. The next morning he reported for his first day in the hotel restaurant. He assisted Marcus with preparing his tables for lunch service. First of all the restaurant was hoovered so that all trace of breakfast service was removed before the tables were covered with freshly starched white tablecloths. The tablecloths were checked for any stains or wear and tear and the slightest blemish meant that they were discarded. The cutlery then had to be polished and the glassware checked to make sure there could be no complaint before the napkins completed the setting. Even the chairs were checked and dusted to complete the attention to detail. The dumbwaiter, the large sideboard allocated to each station, was then carefully checked to once again ensure that everything was ready for service. Once this was over the maitre d' held a fifteen minute briefing on what was on that day's menu, what dishes the Chef wanted pushed and other details so that everybody was quite conversant with what was on offer. Lunch service started at 12 noon prompt and soon the restaurant began to fill up. Marcus had six tables in his station and soon three of them were occupied. Denzil observed as Marcus greeted his customers. One table consisted of four local businessmen who apparently dined there weekly and insisted on having Marcus to look after them. Once the order was taken Marcus took Denzil with him to the kitchen to place the order and show him the procedure. When they returned to the restaurant Denzil saw that the wine waiter had moved in and taken the drinks and wine order. The other two tables' orders were then taken and placed with the kitchen.

Denzil's first task was to take the bread basket with rolls to each table and offer it to the diners. When they had made their choice he then, using his fork and spoon, placed the roll on the side plate before ensuring a plate of butter pats was on the table. This simple task was to get him used to approaching diners and gaining confidence with performing French service with spoon and fork.

Denzil did not come as a raw beginner to this form of service as his experience in the Officers Mess had made him quite proficient in this respect so it was really just a case of getting used to his new environment. After a day or so even Marcus had to admit that there was not much that he had to learn. As a result he quickly took over much of the station waiter's role still under Marcus's watchful eye. Jack Mitchell even went so far as to praise him and declare that he had a natural ability that would stand him in good stead. He took a personal interest in Denzil's development.

"A good waiter", he passed on to Denzil, "is one who carries out his duties so that the diner is scarcely aware of his presence. Body language is so important and something you have to learn. Observe, and a diners body language will tell you if he is settled or something is bothering him, then you can move in and quickly sort out the situation."

Within a week Denzil was settled in his new role at the Royal and enjoying his work. The following week on his day off Rory arrived at the usual time with a supply of smoked salmon for the kitchen. Denzil met him in the car park and soon they were on their way to Cabrach. It was a moment that Denzil was not looking forward to but he steeled himself with the fact that it was something he had to do. They turned off at the hump-backed bridge to go along the side road that he knew so well. Eventually they reached the track that led up to the Cabrach crofts. Jessie MacLeod's old croft had clearly been taken over and some work carried out to it by the new owner. The sight of his old home struck him like a punch in the solar plexus. The roof had gone completely and the stone walls were scorched black where the windows had been, bearing evidence of the destructive power of the fire that had consumed the building. Denzil fell quiet as so many memories came flooding back of the happy times he had experienced there with his foster parents. It was difficult to realise that those days would never come again.

They pulled up outside the Munro croft. Mrs Munro emerged wiping her hands dry on her apron to see who had arrived at her door. She greeted Denzil with a hug and was quickly introduced to Rory. Once inside she made tea and indulged in small talk with her unexpected guests. When she sat down with them and talk got round to the tragic event of the fire she became quite emotional. Denzil found himself comforting her as she tried to explain the deep shock the fire had had on the crafting community. She was concerned about what would happen to Denzil but was somehow reassured that he had got back to his old job in the hotel. The fire damaged croft house would revert back to the estate and no doubt would be turned into a holiday home just as Jessie MacLeod's house had been.

Before the two boys rose to go she said that she had something for Denzil. She came back with a metal box clearly bearing evidence of scorch marks by the fire. Denzil recognized it immediately. It was a box that Jean had kept in a recess in the wall by the fireside and used to keep ration books, and other paper work. Mrs Munro said, "Jack was down shortly after the fire and everything was gutted until he spotted this box in the recess that the fire had missed. There did not appear to be a key for it and in any event the brass lock had melted with the heat. It will probably take a locksmith Jack thinks to open it. Anyway we have no idea what it holds if anything but we feel that you should have it." She handed the box to Denzil. He took it gingerly thinking to himself that this was all that had survived the inferno.

They took their leave of Mrs Munro with Denzil thanking her for getting in touch with him. On the way down the rough track, Denzil clutching the metal box, deliberately refused to look at the ruined house, making himself a mental promise never to return to the area. He would be content with the happy memories of growing up there that no tragic fire would ever erase. Rory dropped him off at the Royal before going on to complete his deliveries. He shrugged off Denzil's thanks saying it was the least he could do before getting Denzil to agree to coming over to Ullamore when the busy festive season was over. Back in his room Denzil stuck the metal box below his bed out of sight as he would be in no hurry to uncover its contents. The next few weeks were a blur of activity as the festive season took hold. The restaurant was busy as were the two small function rooms on the first floor where small private parties could be held. Jack Mitchell paid Denzil a huge compliment when he left him in charge of one of the small rooms where a private family party numbering twelve people had booked. Denzil with the aid of a commis relished the challenge. Jack Mitchell came in at the conclusion of the dinner to speak to the guests. They were more than satisfied and showed their appreciation with a sizeable tip for the dining room tronc.

One of the older waiters developed a sore hip during the festive rush and had to go off duty for a hip replacement that would inevitably lead to him looking for a job that would not entail so much walking about. Jack Mitchell had no doubts as to who his replacement should be and Denzil found himself elevated to the position of station waiter.

Marcus was delighted for him, saying that promotion within three weeks was setting a new benchmark for any future commis. He also commented that this was in fact due to his thorough training methods. Miss MacLean who missed very little congratulated him on settling so well into his new position remarking that perhaps one day he could be the next Royal Maitre d'!

So as the festive season gave way to January, Denzil was happy with the way that things had turned out. The only cloud on his horizon was on his day off when it struck him that he had nowhere to go and the sadness at the loss of Jean and his old home struck hard. But life had to go on and 1953 lay ahead of him full of promise.

Chapter 19   M S Properties Windfall

The year turned out to be for Denzil a year of consolidation. He settled back into life at the Royal, taking up more or less where he had left off. He absorbed everything he could from Jack Mitchell who in turn relished having an able pupil in his charge keen to master all the skills required of a waiter.

His only breaks were visits to Ullamore where Rory's business was growing apace. Several white vans with the company logo were out daily servicing the many hotels and other businesses throughout the Highlands.

The highlight of Rory's year was to purchase, with the aid of a modest bank loan, the run down property on the pier head as this was to be the future headquarters of his operation.

However it was not a case of all work and no play as several memorable ceilidh nights took place. It may have been a mundane year for Denzil but not so for the country at large.

On June 2nd the young Queen Elizabeth 11 was crowned with due ceremony at Westminster Abbey. The whole country celebrated feeling that the war weary years were safely behind them and a new promising Elizabethan era lay before them. As if to underwrite the momentous event word came through that a British expedition led by Edmund Hillary and Sherpa Tensing had at last conquered Everest. Little wonder that the celebrating crowds in London felt too that they were on top of the world!

Back at the Royal a certain visitor began to become a fairly regular guest. Mike Smith was the developer linked to the proposed North Bridge development as negotiations and planning progressed slowly. Mike Smith was a large domineering individual who had made his fortune after the war as construction work boomed as war-torn London slowly came back to normal life.

As development business in London became increasingly competitive shrinking profit margins, developers like Mike

Smith looked for promising development situations in other areas. This is what had attracted him to the North Bridge project.

The year 1954 dawned and little did Denzil realise that for him it was destined to be a memorable one.

Dominic contacted Denzil in February to inform him that he had received an offer from MS Properties to purchase Hetty's shop for £3,000 pounds, which he had initially refused to see their reaction. About this time he had received notification from Hetty that she would not be renewing her lease which fell due in the coming June as she intended to retire. After the initial offer from MS Properties there was nothing further for two months. Finkelstein kept Denzil informed as one by one the various shops accepted the offers given to them as MS properties cleared the area ready for the major development works to take place. A fresh offer came in from MS Properties for £4000 pounds but Denzil, after a discussion with Dominic, decided to refuse once more. The summer dragged on and in August Mike Smith once again appeared at the Royal. Matters were clearly coming to a head and this was underlined by the fact that he booked a private dining room to meet up with his Inverdeen based advisors. Denzil, sensing that this was not to be missed, spoke to Jack Mitchell and arranged that he along with another waiter would look after this particular booking.

The party gathered in the private dining room for drinks before dinner. There were ten guests, lawyers, accountant, architect and other professionals hosted by Mike Smith. Denzil and the other waiter served the dinner and eventually the party settled down to discuss business as the port decanter was passed around. Denzil remained in the room looking after the coffee service and any other drinks that might be called for,

Mike Smith started the proceedings and the initial talk was about minor planning proposals along with detailed discussions with the architect team. Then the talk turned to a subject that made Dominic very attentive. Mike Smith cleared his throat and stabbed a finger at the scale drawings in front of him, "What's all this about Unit 2? Every other bloody unit has accepted our offer after negotiation, why is this the nigger in the wood pile?" Denzil realised with a slight thrill that Unit 2 on the drawing was in fact Hetty' shop. One of the lawyers spoke up slightly nervously, "We are dealing with a legal firm in Edinburgh who own the property. We have made several offers to date but they have not been accepted." Mike Smith queried, "What was the last offer made to them?" The lawyer consulted his letter file before responding. "The last offer was £5,000 1 believe."

"£5 thousand quid!" Mike Smith exploded, "Who the bloody hell do they think they are, that's good money for a unit of that size. Here we are poised to go and some small time bastard gets big time ideas. Can we freeze them out? In other words, bypass them without a major effect on the development. The architect then spoke up, "I am afraid not, if you look at the plans that unit is smack bang in the entrance to the development. The building is such that we have no other alternative. In short, that unit is key to the whole set-up." This revelation was accepted in silence as the group took it on board. Mike Smith lit up another cigar and called over his shoulder. "Hey waiter, how about some fresh coffee!"

"Certainly, sir" responded Denzil and proceed to replenish the cups.

A heated discussion then took place as Mike Smith examined every angle to get round this sticking point. Eventually it was accepted that Unit 2 was ultra important and had to be purchased at any cost to avoid holding up the development. Mike Smith came to a decision and addressed his legal team. "Time is of the essence and I don't have to remind you of that fact. Make them an offer of £10K and go up to £12K if you have to but get that unit by the end of this week. I don't believe I am saying this, £12K for this tin pot unit but we can't afford to hold up things on that score, so go to it!"

One of the advisors spoke. "£12K seems an incredible amount to be offering for such a unit", Mike Smith exploded, "God dammit to hell! Don't think I don't know it, but there is too much else riding on this timetable so if we have to pay over the odds then so be it. You can look at ways to claw back this over spend once everything is rolling, that's, after all, what I pay you lot for! Hey waiter fetch me a large brandy!"

"Certainly, sir", said Denzil as he appeared at the chairman's shoulder. He left for the drink order well pleased with what he had gleaned over the dinner table discussion.

Two days later Dominic contacted him to inform him that he had a final offer of £10K for his shop unit. "Denzil" he commented, "It's a bloody amazing offer, I take it is in order for me to accept on your behalf?" Denzil had a quiet smile to himself before replying, "No Dominic, 1 think it is time for a final thrust of the sword, so as to speak. Could you reply to them along the lines that I would only accept an offer of £12K to finalise the deal?" Dominic fell silent for a while before replying, "Well I can do if that is what you wish but you might be pushing the boat out too far. They might turn their attentions to other alternatives. The worst scenario could be that they could redesign their development so as not to include your shop and you could be left with a dead space. Remember also that you will have no tenant income after Hetty retires shortly. Do you want to think it over before advising me on what action to take?"

"I appreciate what you say", responded Denzil", But I would really like to ask them for the £12K deal and see how things pan out after that."

"OK", said Dominic with a certain reluctance in his voice. "I will do as you wish, 1 will tell them to cut to the chase and that an offer of £12K would be acceptable. Keep your fingers crossed that they find your arm-twisting acceptable as well. I'll keep you advised."

Four days later Denzil was surprised when Dominic appeared for lunch at the Royal breaking his journey on his way up for a weekend break at Ullamore. He asked to be seated at Denzil's station. Denzil took his order and Dominic requested that they got together after lunch to discuss some matters. In between serving other customers they made some small talk and Dominic said that his weekend to Ullamore was to discuss business with Rory as he had some interesting information for him regarding expanding his operation. Denzil saw him settled in the lounge after lunch with his coffee with Mr Finkelstein already enjoying his post lunch siesta in his usual chair by the fireside. Lunch service over he requested a break from the Maitre d' so as not to detain Dominic from his journey north.

"Well young man", said Dominic as he joined him in the lounge, "I come bearing good news! Yesterday I accepted, on your behalf, a final offer from MS Properties for £12K. Did you know something that I did not know?" He looked shrewdly at Denzil. Denzil laughed. "That's great news, Dominic! No I just had a feeling in my water that they might stretch themselves to that figure." "Aye, just so", returned Dominic, "I'll believe you, though thousands wouldn't! Anyway it is an incredible amount for that size of shop and good on you!"

Shortly after, they parted with Dominc remarking that he was on his way to see his next important client in Ullamore.

This deal had a marked effect on his financial position! He reviewed his situation sitting on his bed in the staff quarters. He had been banking his weekly pay every week while living on his tips, which to his surprise were quite substantial, and his bank account now recorded £1,532 - 10s – 4d or, if you took his shop deal into account, it now stood at £13, 532 - 10s – 4d! He looked back at the original bankbook with its first entry on 11th June 1947 of £1 and reflected on how far he had come in a few short years. He made a decision not to tell anybody, not even Mr Finkelstein, and just carry on as normal. In the event it did not matter as in small towns news travels fast. One of the lawyers, a Mr Graham Douglas, who was part of Mike Smith's local advisory team happened to be in the jeweller's shop arranging for a repair job to be done on his wife's expensive wrist watch. He remarked that he decided to get it done before the shops North Bridge Street closed for business.

At this point Finkelstein realised that he had been closely involved in the project on behalf of the developer. He enquired if all the properties had now been sold and when the development was likely to commence. "Oh yes" supplied the lawyer "All the units have now been purchased, and not without the usual problems. Do you know that the worst unit of the lot was the smallest, that general supply shop called Hettys? We never realised that it was in the hands of an Edinburgh legal firm. Well it dragged on and on and, as bad luck would have it, it was in a vital part of the development. They must have known what they were on about when they acquired the property."

"Oh I see", remarked Finkelstein casually, "I wonder what figure they got for it in the end?" The lawyer bent towards him, "Well, between you and me it was well in excess of £10K!"

After imparting this news he was more than surprised when the old jeweller burst in to laughter, taking off his gold rimmed spectacles and rubbing his eyes while his shoulders shook. Two weeks after the conclusion of the property deal Denzil was with the other waiters clearing up after what had been a relatively quiet lunch service. As was normal among the waiters, as they worked in the now deserted restaurant clearing the dumb waiters and setting up for dinner service, there was a certain amount of banter. A cornmis waiter due to go for his National Service was being teased about how he would be able to survive on the miserable Army pay that they received. Marcus turned to Denzil and asked him how he had fared during his military service. Denzil told them that he had been lucky to have been based in Aldershot for his entire service time and had been able to earn extra money by singing in a band at weekends in the large NAAFI Club. Peter, the other station waiter, then chipped in "What, you sang in a band? I don't believe it."

"Well I did" responded Denzil" I was dead lucky because one of the guys based in the Officers' Mess with me played in the band. It was called The Mellowtones. I went along at first to keep him company and one thing led to another and I found myself fronting the band. It was a great learning experience I can tell you." Peter was still not convinced. "Right Denzil - there's a piano over there, lets see what you can do" "

Well, for a start I don't play the piano, I just sing", replied Denzil. Peter was delighted. "See, I told you he was pulling my leg."

Denzil was stung into action. In the top end of the room was a slightly raised platform on which sat a gleaming Steinway piano. The platform was designed to hold some four musicians at most and Denzil had never seen it used during his time in the Royal and, in fact, there was a permanent floral display of fresh flowers always atop the piano. Denzil sprang up onto the stage and the waiters all stopped working to see what was to happen. He launched into a recent hit recorded by the American singer Perry Como, 'Magic Moments'. As he sang he was pleasantly surprised to realise that the restaurant had excellent acoustics. He finished to a round of applause from his fellow workers and even Peter had to admit he was wrong. Just by chance Harry Beach, whose orchestra was the resident ballroom band, was at that very moment putting his usual band wages breakdown into reception. He heard the singing, then the sound of applause and misled him to the restaurant entrance to see what was going on. He was just in time to see Denzil jump off the small stage. Harry entered and beckoned to Denzil to come over to him. "That sounded real good to me son. What's your background?" Denzil sat down with him at a table and explained at length finishing up with his recent experience of lead singer with the band in England. Harry got more interested as the talk went on.

"Listen, I have been thinking about somebody fronting the band for some time. You sound ideal. I have been singing the odd song from time to time but I really think the punters would relate to somebody younger. What I have in mind is somebody coming on for say a half hour spot to sing any recent hits or golden oldies. It would give the band a fresh feel. How about it? We should be able to work it round your restaurant work shifts. Come down this Saturday evening about 7pm as we usually have a band call then and we can discuss it further".

Denzil, slightly staggered by the speed of events, found himself agreeing in principle to what was outlined. He shook hands with Harry and they parted on that note. The other waiters were eager to know what had been discussed and crowded round him. "Well", Denzil informed them, "Looks like I could be back fronting a band again". The waiters expressed their delight and Peter asked him if he could now be regarded as his agent as it was due to him that he had been discovered!

CHAPTER 20   Singing with the Band

Denzil's first task was to approach Jack Mitchell to see if he could organise his restaurant shifts round his new band duties. To his surprise he was quite enthusiastic about Denzil taking on this new role and that organising the rota to accommodate this would present little problem. That side of things tied up, Denzil presented himself on the Saturday evening for band call as had been agreed. Harry Beach started by introducing him to a somewhat surprised bunch of musicians, stressing that Denzil had considerable experience in fronting a band from his days in Aldershot. He had very definite ideas, "I don't want any formal announcement about a lead singer or anything like that. We will do a medley of songs without any break in between. Denzil, the mike will be centre stage, and at the given moment you just come on and give forth. Okay? The surprise factor could be quite big. We will sort out a number of songs and do a quick run through just now so we are all singing from the same hymn sheet, so as to speak" He already had a selection of songs to go through. "Lets kick off with 'You are my Sunshine' and then some western ones as they are currently very popular." After some discussion they picked a range of songs including 'On top of Old Smokey'; 'Mocking Bird Hill'; 'Blueberry Hill' ending up with current hits like 'Magic Moments' and ' Stranger in Paradise'. A quick run through with the band and all was set for Denzil's introduction later in the evening. Harry told him to report about 9.30pm when the dance, in his words, should be in full swing.

At 8pm the doors opened and the queue of dancers at the pay desk started to be attended to. The Ballroom was licensed to hold some one thousand dancers but a Saturday night crowd usually nudged the eleven hundred figure. As it came close to his appointed hour Denzil waited in the band room right behind the bandstand. He looked out on quite daunting scene. The lights were dimmed and the vast room was crowded with couples as they shuffled round to the dance music. A huge ball composed of small mirrors hung over the floor and a spotlight played on it so that pinpoints of light danced over the darkened hall creating a lively sense of movement. All too soon it was his cue to go on. As the band played the intro he quietly stepped onto the lighted stage, took hold off the mike, glanced sideways until he got the nod from Harry and opened up with 'You are my sunshine, my only sunshine, you make me happy....' He was away. The first song ended with a ripple of applause that was quickly drowned as the band moved into the next number.

Denzil soon relaxed as the songs progressed finding the band right behind him with smooth transition from one song to the next. So absorbed was he in getting the various songs right and remembering the lyrics that he failed to observe that by his third number the dancers had given up any pretence of dancing and instead were crowded round facing the band. Denzil had learned one lesson early on in his career with the Mellowtones. When you sing the hearing of an audience is involved but can be easily distracted. If the singer moves on stage then two senses are involved both hearing and vision. The movement can be quite slight, body movement, a couple of steps to one side or another, hand movement or suchlike: it all helps to transfix the audience attention, especially if it is done in harmony with the song.

When he finished with his final song he felt a huge sense of relief knowing that it had gone quite well. The applause from the dancers was totally unexpected and hit the bandstand like a minor shock wave. He stood for a moment not sure what to do. He glanced sideways to see Harry with a broad smile on his face and jerked his head as if to indicate that it was time for him to exit. Denzil gave a slight bow towards the dancers and left the stage with the applause still ringing out. He sipped a very welcome glass of water in the band room as the band moved onto their next number and the dancing recommenced.

When the band came off for their break the musicians crowded round him with complimentary remarks. Harry

173

grumbled. "Ballroom dancing indeed? It was more like a bloody concert in there!" But Denzil could see that he was delighted that his experiment had gone so well. Before Denzil left Harry told him that his pay would be weekly, £6 for a Saturday gig as he called it and £4 for a Wednesday. His other good news was that he could pay this tax-free as he had a small petty cash fund that he could dip into and this would cover this particular expense. Denzil went to bed that night highly relieved that it had gone so well. He really enjoyed being back in the music scene and also that it would be making a significant contribution to his bank account.

Word of his success quickly spread throughout the Royal and even Mr Finkelstein looked him out in the restaurant one lunch-time to say that some of his customers were speaking in his shop about the new band set-up. He talked about his imminent retirement at the end of the year when his shop would close for good to make way for the redevelopment. Most of the shops were closing or relocating to other parts of the town. The only shop that would feature in the new development was Morgan Charles fashion shop. Apparently he had done a smart bit of business and secured a prime location in the new set-up. Finkelstein did not enquire about what Denzil had done with his unit so Denzil decided not to volunteer any information. His fellow waiters were highly amused that they now had a minor local celebrity in their midst and this involved a fair amount of teasing. Peter even took to referring to him as the Royal Canary!

A few weeks into his new way of life Denzil was preparing one Wednesday a couple of new numbers for his show that night. After the dining room had set up for lunch he sat alone at a table going over the lyrics of his new numbers. He was so engrossed in his work that Miss MacLean was standing by his table when he at last sensed someone was there. She stood erect as usual, immaculate in her business suit, although Denzil noticed that her hair was slightly greying. She smiled down at him, "Far be it for me to disturb a professional musician at his work. Just like to congratulate you on your new enterprise - makes a difference from all that window cleaning and rabbit trapping I can imagine! There seems to be no end to your talents!" They spoke at some length about how he was enjoying working in the restaurant and other matters. Eventually, as she turned to go she remarked, "Oh, by the way - many happy returns!" Denzil was mildly shocked, as with everything, he had completely forgotten that this Wednesday 10th November was his 22nd birthday.

Left alone on his own he could not help thinking how much he would have liked to share these moments with Jean, knowing how much pride she would have taken in his success. One week later he received a phone call from Dominic in Edinburgh. He was coming up to Inverdeen to meet up with Rory to discuss some business later that week and wondered if Denzil could book a private meeting room and lay on a working buffet lunch. His legal work in Edinburgh was so busy he had decided to meet up with Rory halfway and his last request was that if possible could Denzil attend the meeting.

He did just that and Jack Mitchell had no objection to his looking after the private party and attending same as part of his working shift. Rory was first to arrive in his white van stacked with orders including one for Chef Bonnacorsi. They waited in the private room for Dominic to arrive. He appeared slightly late, apologising but blaming the heavy traffic on the road north, and carrying a heavy leather brief case. They first of all tackled the buffet lunch before settling down to business. Dominic took a sheaf of papers out of the briefcase and laid it in front of him before opening the discussion. He started. "Look, I have asked you both to attend this meeting because I feel that Rory's fish business stands at what can be best described as a crossroads. Although it is essentially Rory's business I hope he won't mind if I bring you, Denzil, into the discussion."

"Why would I", queried Rory", Dez is very welcome, after all if he had not loaned me the money for my first van we would not even be at this stage?"

"Excellent", responded Dominic, "I sort of knew that is how you would feel. Right, lets get started. A month ago an invitation came into our office to attend an international conference in Paris to do with the future planning for the farming and fishing industries. I collared the invite and attended. What caught my attention was this expert talking about the current fishing industry and how it affected Europe, where it stood now and perhaps, more importantly, how it could develop in the future.

It was fascinating stuff. He talked about how for centuries an industry like fishing had changed very little and people got into the mindset that that is how it would always be. In fact, when change came along they were suspicious and quite often held out against it. He made out the case that in many instances the industry was located in remote areas far from their markets and how this presented a real challenge. He quoted examples like Scandanavia and Scotland so, as you can imagine, I was all ears!

He quoted the example of cattle ranching in America. In the 17th and early 18th centuries a great part of America was still waiting to be explored and settled. In Texas and New Mexico, for instance, there existed vast areas of grasslands that, apart from some Indian tribes, were untouched. Gradually, and initially led by the Spanish, bands of colonists went out into this unknown territory and set up small missions Now these missions took with them a herd of cattle. This herd of cattle was vital to them as it provided them with milk, meat and leather for boots, clothing and saddles. These missions, largely unfenced, lost cattle that simply strayed or were not found when rounding up a herd that had stampeded after a violent thunderstorm. You can imagine this happening to missions all over the new territory through the decades. The result was that by the mid eighteenth century huge herds of wild cattle numbering millions of beasts were to be found grazing over the lush grasslands. About this time European immigrants were pouring into the New World and industries of all kinds kicked off in areas like New York, Chicago and Philadelphia. These huge concentrations of workers needed food and lots of it.

Enterprising cowboys took to carving out small herds from the Texas grasslands and driving them up the Old Chisholm Trail to the slaughterhouses in Chicago to satisfy this demand. It was hard work driving Longhorn cattle in this way but it was extremely lucrative. It became a way of life for these hardy cowmen and perhaps they thought this was always the way it was going to be. Then along came the railroad and this whole world changed. Cattle could be trucked straight to Chicago quicker and arrive in better condition instead of undergoing the arduous drive up the Old Chisholm Trail. The cowmen got better prices, more cattle could be shipped and so forth.

The expert was really trying to underline that no industry ever stands still. If challenges arise then they are there to be met and overcome. He returned then to the European fishing industry. OK, in many cases suppliers could be a long way from their biggest markets but surely that in time could be overcome. Refrigeration would come to play a major role, he maintained. American homes now had an icebox or refrigerator as an essential part of their domestic kitchen. This would in turn spread into the European market. Some suppliers in America mounted an ice-box unit on a truck and could ship perishable food long distances and, as a consequence, were able to tap in to distant markets. He also put forward the idea that in time perhaps fish could be farmed and that the sheltered sea lochs of Scandinavia and Scotland would be ideal for this purpose. This suggestion drew loud laughter from his audience but he countered by saying that it was a possibility however remote. He said that some people were convinced that one day we would land a man on the moon! This got even bigger laughter. Denzil and Rory found themselves laughing at this way out idea.

Dominic returned to his theme, "Sorry to be so long winded but I wanted to give the full picture. It certainly opened my mind to Rory's situation. Here you are on the remote west coast of Scotland with a mere small local market. Rory struck out by carting salmon on the mail bus to Inverdeen to find a bigger market. Motor transport then made this task not only easier and more efficient but secured more clients. It got to the point that Rory no longer fished but concentrated on selling fish on behalf of a lot of local fishermen. For the local fishermen it was a godsend because, instead of trying to find a market for their individual catch, Rory did it on their behalf allowing them even more time to concentrate on fishing. Now that Rory has secured the purchase of the property at the pier head he is ready to expand. There has been a new Government department set up to help promote the Highlands and Islands with a combination of grants and loans. I have been keeping in close touch with what has been happening on this front. Very shortly it will be announced no doubt with a fanfare of publicity by the politicians. If we are at the door when it opens with our begging bowl and a viable business ripe for expansion and able to create local employment we will be welcomed with open arms. With luck a business will be set up as a leader in its field ready to take advantage of any breakthrough in taking the industry forward.

That, gentlemen, is the opportunity that lies ahead and, as far as I can see, there is little or no risk or downside. Let's look at the financial picture. Rory has built up not only a thriving business but a good relationship with his bank at a local level supported by first class annual accounts. I estimate that the business should aim for a £90K start up capital, bearing in mind the sheds have to be demolished and a state of the art fishing headquarters built. How do we attain this? Well, for a start Rory can come up with £10K without bank borrowing. 1 have persuaded my parents to join with me in putting up a family bloc of £10K - to put our money where my mouth is and that leaves us looking for a third partner in the enterprise whether it is an individual or a pension fund matters little."

He paused and shuffled his papers in front of him allowing them time to digest what he had just outlined. There was a silence before Denzil spoke, "Well, why not keep it among ourselves. 1 think that I would like to be involved."

Rory, slightly embarrassed, responded, "OK Dez but as Dominic has said we are looking for one full partner to put up the remaining £10K."

Denzil countered immediately, "That should be no real problem." He took a secret delight in seeing the bewildered expression on Rory's face who looked at Dominic for some sort of explanation. "Denzil is a client of mine and I have recently concluded some business on his behalf. I can confirm that he is in a position to make such an investment." Dominic confirmed. Rory burst out laughing, "Well I'll be blowed, Dez you never cease to amaze me!" Dominic returned their attention to the business in hand.

"Now that the directors £30K investment is more or less in place, I know that subject to our business plan the government agency will give a matching grant of £30K. Once that is in place the Bank will be easily persuaded to come up with a business loan of the final £30K and the £90K initial capital will be realised. I have a fair amount of work to do in setting up the new Company but I think we should aim for a start up date of 1st January 1955. Any questions?"

Denzil raised his hand, "Just one, can my involvement be kept to a minimum as it might complicate my current working situation?"

Dominic replied, "I can see no problem as you are effectively a sleeping partner in the business. I will look after your affairs in this respect based in my Edinburgh office so you can continue your present way of life up here as normal. Just one other thing for you both to consider, it will not have escaped your notice that in July just past the end of meat rationing spelled the end of wartime rationing. It took eight years of real austerity to throw off the effects of that war. All economic pointers indicate that better times lie ahead. The west coast, if you like, can be compared to a very generous food larder and with any luck our company will be ideally placed to bring it a wider and expanding market"

After some more conversation the meeting drew to a close with them exchanging formal handshakes. Rory remarked as they prepared to go their separate ways, "Well Dez, 1 find it hard to believe that my trip to Inverdeen with a bag of salmon would ever lead to this." Denzil could only agree with this sentiment. Dominic with bulky briefcase in hand turned to Denzil, "I will need a cheque from you in due course, but I'll keep you posted on progress."

After they had departed Denzil returned to work clearing up the remains of the buffet lunch reflecting on just what had taken place. His ill-gotten gains from the sale of Unit 2 had not lain long in his coffers but he knew deep within himself that this was certainly a step in the right direction.

CHAPTER 21 Company Director

In mid December Denzil took a walk along to see the redevelopment process taking place in North Bridge Street. Hetty's shop was boarded up waiting for the attention of the demolishing squad. Work had already started on the properties at the south side of the street with heavy machinery engaged tearing down the sandstone walls and fleets of lorries taking, turns to clear the rubble away. Finkelstein's shop had already gone. He stood there deep in thought remembering the days when he had operated his window cleaning round quite happy to receive his pay from the various shop-keepers to add to his slowly growing bank account.

"Well Denzil my boy", said a well known voice that jerked him out of his reverie, "So you have come along like me to have a last look at the old premises." Finkelstein stood beside him, dapper as ever, but leaning heavily on his walking stick with the ornate carved horn handle.

They stood for a while watching the demolition work. "This is the first time I have been out of work in my lifetime", mused the old jeweller, "I suspect it will take some getting used to. Anyway we are off tomorrow for our usual festive trip to see friends in London as we do every year. What we will do in the future is anybody's guess but we will cross that bridge when we return?"

They walked back to the Royal together and Denzil realised just how frail the old man had become as they walked slowly along. "My future is uncertain, how about yours, what do you intend to do?" Denzil thought to himself, that was a good question, before replying, " I am not sure either, 1 really enjoy my job in the restaurant so I suppose I will just hang on and see what life throws at me and take it from there."

Finkelstein stopped and touched him on the arm, "Well Denzil, I have no doubts that you will be able to handle whatever you have to face. You have some good qualities that will stand you in good stead. In case I don't see you before we leave, my wife and I wish you all the best for 1955!"

By this point they were outside the lift in the Royal hotel foyer, Finkelstein limped into the open lift and, as the doors closed, he lifted his hand in a farewell salute. Back in his room in the staff quarters Denzil lay on his bed and gave thought to his current position. His financial position was more than secure. His investment in Rory's business was sound and gave him no cause for concern while his income from his waiting job and band work ensured that a healthy contribution was made each week to his personal account.

The fact that his hotel job incurred no outlay for rent or food helped enormously. He really enjoyed his restaurant work. It gave him considerable satisfaction to operate a busy run of some eight tables in his station aided by a couple of commis waiters. The fact that Jack Mitchell more or less regarded him as his unofficial deputy underlined things. He had learned so much from the expertise of this most professional of maitre d's. Jack had taught him how to watch the body language of clients unobtrusively so you almost anticipated their demands before they were even aware of it themselves. He had taught himself to be an expert on flambé work so that other station waiters would call upon him if they had a problem. Any important diners Jack always ensured that he steered them to Denzils station for him to attend to them. His band work was really the icing on the cake. He was immediately accepted by the band as a fellow professional and his spot during the evening became a very popular part of the night's entertainment. The local paper even took his photograph and wrote an article headed, 'The Singing Waiter', and he took a lot of leg-pulling over that. He took a weekend off to go to Ullamore in early December for yet another ceilidh weekend and so missed his usual Saturday night spot. Back on the Wednesday as he met up with the others in the band room, Harry announced in an aggrieved voice, "Nearly a bloody riot here on Saturday night Dez, your fans were revolting because you were missing, some chancers were even asking for refunds!

The festive season broke upon the Royal once more as hectic a time as ever. Between the restaurant shifts and band work he found very little time on his hands. On Boxing Day on his way to the restaurant Calum collared him to break the bad news that Finkelstein had suffered a stroke in London and was currently in intensive care in a hospital. Later that day Miss MacLean appeared to say she had been in touch with Mrs Finkelstein and the news was not very heartening. She had a large Get Well card for all the staff to sign that she would send to the hospital on behalf of the Hotel.

Over the next few days various bulletins were passed around among the staff concerning the health of the old jeweller. It seemed that although still on the danger list he seemed to be holding his own. However, on Hogmanay Denzil was preparing his station for a busy lunch period when Mrs MacBeth, the Housekeeper, appeared at the restaurant door with a rather sombre expression. She beckoned to Denzil to come to her.

"Denzil, very bad news I am afraid, Mrs Finkelstein has just been on the phone to say that her husband passed away peacefully last night in hospital. Can you let the rest of the staff know what has happened?"

Denzil had been fearing the worst and now it had come to pass. He felt a real sense of loss. It was hard to take that in Jean and the old jeweller he had lost, in such a short space of time, the two people who had done most to shape his life. This sense of the loss of their long time resident was evident as well among most of the hotel staff. It was as if they had lost a family member. The next day Denzil was talking with Calum at the porter's desk who summed it up in his own way, "Dez, you know I just can't believe the old bugger will never again walk down those stairs, smart as a pin, collect his morning paper and then set off for work out that very door!"

That morning a memo for all Departments was circulated by Miss MacLean expressing sympathy and informing everybody that the funeral would take place in London later that week. She had arranged that a wreath on behalf of the Royal hotel would be sent. Mrs Finkelstein had arranged to stay in London for most of January before returning to Inverdeen to settle affairs. It certainly cast a cloud over the New Year celebrations but the Royal, like a theatre, had to see that the show carried on. Mrs Finkelstein came back to the hotel in early February with her sister and spent the best part of a week clearing their suite and attending to other matters. Denzil met her one day as they came in for lunch and went forward to express his sympathy. She introduced him to her sister before remarking, "This young man used to clean our shop windows, you know. My husband had a lot of time for him, I used to think he sometimes looked upon him, in a way, as the son we never had." On her final day, the General Manager and Miss MacLean entertained the two ladies to lunch before they departed south by train. With the loss of their last long time resident it was in a sense the end of an era.

In February Denzil sat and passed his driving test as he had been taking lessons for some weeks. He decided to hire a car from Cameron's Garage on his day off and approached the owner Donnie Cameron. Donnie was a regular diner in the hotel and always insisted on being put on Denzil's station.

When they came to discuss the hire payment Donnie had a surprise for him. "Listen Denzil, instead of paying cash, how about this for an idea? You meet visitors face to face in the hotel so how about if I give you a stack of business cards and you put business my way. Just put your name on the back of the business card so I will know it is you and any calls from the Royal I will take it as coming from you. In my experience it is better than chucking money away on general advertising. The deal will be that once a week you can have the free use of a car." Denzil was only too happy with this arrangement as in the past he had sent several clients to Donnie who were looking for car hire. Donnie however was not in the habit of being overgenerous. "You can have the car but pay for your own bloody petrol. You know what our fucking Government has just done, put petrol up by 5d so that a gallon now costs four and bloody sixpence! I ask you, where is it all going to end!"

In April two events of importance took place. Sir Winston Churchill, the Prime Minister, now frail at eighty years of age, resigned to make way for Sir Anthony Eden. This sparked off a lively debate in the staff hall table and Denzil happened to stumble in on it. A large section of the staff were adamant that no man of that age, no matter what his past service was, should be entrusted with running the country while the Cold War was complicating the international scene. Others were saying that he was an exceptional human being and, after all, he deserved to be there after the way the country turfed him out of office once the war was safely won. There were no winners as usual in this argument.

The other event was Rory called in one day to inform him that he had an architectural firm hard at work on the plans for the new office block at the pier head. He hoped that by late May or early June the drawings would be finalised so that both Dominic and Denzil could cast an eye upon them.

Things were organised on his financial front as well. The £12K cheque from M S Properties had been paid into a deposit account opened up by Dominic for him with a bank branch in Princes Street. It had not lain for long before a cheque for £10K representing his investment in the new Company to be called Ullamore Country Fare was extracted leaving £2000 in the account. By coincidence, when he banked his band money on Friday 10th June as usual, his Inverdeen account stood at a healthy £2109 - 12s - 4d. This was almost exactly the eighth anniversary of the date in 1947 when he had first banked that very first £1. He had certainly come a long way in a short time. I only hope, he smiled to himself, that old Abrach is approving of how I put his money to good use!

It was not all work, however, as a certain incident in June would show. On a Monday evening a party of three Americans hotel guests arrived at the restaurant door for dinner. Jack Mitchell greeted them warmly and led them down the room to Denzil's station. As they approached Denzil quickly summed them up. Clearly two parents with a daughter of about his own age in tow. The daughter was stunning and heads turned as they approached. The father was tall with a weather beaten face and his whole body language and loud voice conveyed the confidence of a self made man. His wife, who was clearly of Spanish or Mexican extraction, was beautifully dressed and carried herself with a certain natural elegance. Her good looks had certainly been inherited by her daughter. She was a brunette, casually dressed in expensive clothes that showed off her curvaceous figure to maximum effect, lending her an almost film star like quality.

As they arrived at their table Jack Mitchell handed the menus to Denzil with a flourish remarking, "Right I am going to leave you in Denzil's excellent care. He was voted Scotland's best Waiter of the Year last year so you could not be better looked after!" Together Denzil and himself seated the party and he left Denzil to hand out the menus.

The daughter smiled up at Denzil as she accepted the menu, "Tell me, were you really Waiter of the Year?" Denzil smiled back, "Not really, trouble with our Maitre d' he suffers from certain fantasies! But, as he is an old man, we have to humour him!"

The party dissolved in laughter and the ice was well and truly broken. Denzil left them to study the menus in peace until the father beckoned him over. "Say, it is Denzil isn't it. Look, what would you suggest we have. Remember, we are from New York and keen to sample some real Highland cuisine?" Denzil decided to enter into the spirit of things. He suggested a starter of haggis flamed in Drambuie served with a portion of creamed turnip as a starter, followed by one of Bonnacorsi's celebrated salmon dishes as a main course. A reasonably expensive bottle of Piesporter was selected to accompany the meal. The starter dish of haggis gave him an opportunity to prepare the dish in front of the guests. As he worked and they watched him, fascinated with the process, they were able to converse. He learned that Sam Milton had made his money in construction and this was the first real holiday abroad that both he and his wife Maria. who was of Spanish descent, had taken.

Their daughter Natalie had just graduated as a teacher from college, so they had decided to take a trip with her to visit Scotland and then go on to Paris. They were here for three days leaving by train on the Thursday morning. They were a bit travel worn and tomorrow, Tuesday, was going to be a relaxing day. Sam declared that in the morning as the girls went shopping he was going to have a lie-in. Perhaps in the afternoon they might hire a car and visit some local places of interest. Denzil quickly informed that he could hire a car on their behalf and advised them not only on where to shop but also on local places worth visiting by car. As they left to go Sam clapped him on the shoulder, "I would certainly vote for you for Waiter of any Year! We come in for dinner and leave with everything organised. How about that girls?"

As they departed Natalie flashed him a dazzling smile. Later Denzil went to Reception to ensure that a Donnie Cameron hire car would be at the hotel front door for 2pm next day.

Next night they appeared for dinner well satisfied with their day and grateful for all that he had done. They again left the selection for dinner in his hands and he took great care in selecting dishes they were not likely to have encountered before. Dinner over, Sam sat back, nursing a generous vintage port with cigar in hand, and clearly in the mood for a chat. He enquired from Denzil about the hotel business and local construction until he turned to his job as a waiter. He was interested in what hotel pay was like, what hours staff worked and the seasonal nature of the business. Denzil was just telling him that he worked six days a week with one day off and in point of fact he was off on Wednesday, the very next day, and as a result would not have the pleasure of looking after them at dinner on their final night in the Royal.

Sam sat bolt upright at this, "Day off tomorrow you say! Well how about doing us a last favour? It can't be much fun for Natalie here stuck on holiday all the time with a couple of old fogeys like us so why don't you two get together and show her round the town, seems like a good plan"

At this point Maria interrupted him reaching out a restraining arm, "Sam, honey, you can't go around organising Denzil's time off, I'm pretty sure he has his own plans."

Denzil thought quickly before replying, "That's Okay, in fact tomorrow I was going to hire a car and go over to Ullamore in the west coast to see some friends of mine. Your daughter is more than welcome to come along with me."

Sam gave a broad, satisfied smile, "Well that's all organised then. Now Denzil, you be sure to put that car hire on my bill and arrange a pack lunch or whatever you need."

Natalie clapped her hands in delight, "Wonderful I would just love to see a bit more of the Highlands and that sounds great. What time are we leaving in the morning?"

"If we can leave at eight thirty sharp just after breakfast would be ideal. I will pick you up at the reception desk at that time."

That course of action agreed the family left the restaurant. Denzil now had to do some smart thinking as he really had nothing planed for the Wednesday, but the thought of a day in Natalie's company was not to be dismissed lightly by any red blooded man!

He phoned Donnie Cameron at his home number apologising for the late call. Donnie had both his hire cars out for the next day so that seemed at first to present a real problem. After some persuasion Donnie agreed, somewhat reluctantly, to give Denzil the use of his own pride and joy, a gleaming red Morgan sports car that he normally kept for his own personal use. His next move was to get the night porter to prepare an upmarket pack lunch box complete with bottle of white wine ready for the next morning. All that done, he retired and slept soundly.

Next morning he collected the Morgan, stowed away the pack lunch in the generous boot of the car, and went to reception to collect Natalie. The sight of her waiting with a welcoming smile made him catch his breath. She was dressed in smartly tailored tan slacks, topped with a lemon coloured blouse that not only emphasised her figure but set off her tanned skin and dark hair to perfection. A necklace of coloured stones round her neck completed the picture. For all the world she looked like a model just stepped out of a fashion magazine. Standing there she seemed quite oblivious to the number of heads turned in her direction as guests headed for breakfast.

"Ready to go then? said Denzil for the want of something to say.

"And how!" Natalie enthused and taking his hand they walked to the door. On the way across the foyer Denzil was only too aware of Calum and several porters standing at the porter's lodge desk in unabashed admiration. Calum simply raised his eyebrows while another porter gave out with an audible wolf whistle at which Natalie gave a delicious giggle and clutched Denzil's hand even tighter.

Once outside, when she saw the gleaming red Morgan, she laughed in delight and her eyes sparkled as he showed her into the passenger seat. As they prepared to depart Miss MacLean came down Hunter Street ready to start her day's work. She spotted the car as it left the hotel car park and stood amazed as Denzil leaned across his glamorous companion to give her a wave of recognition.

CHAPTER 22   Ullamore and Natalie

The day could not have been better with bright sunshine and an almost cloudless sky. It was so warm that the slipstream of the moving open top car came as a cooling and refreshing breeze. They motored out of Inverdeen and as they passed Cabrach he pointed out to her his former home and found himself telling her about his foster parents and what had befallen them. It was really the first time he had spoken to anybody at length about these things and found in Natalie a quiet and sympathetic audience. He even confessed to her that his friends in Ullamore were not expecting him, nor had he hired a car but the chance to spend some time in her company was too good to pass up. She found this hilarious and promised not to tell her father.

Denzil had never driven a car quite like the Morgan and soon found out what an exhilarating vehicle it was to drive. Natalie was thrilled with the countryside they were passing through before they hit the high ground. The towering majesty of the bare hills and the single track road with passing places was all new to her. There had been heavy rain in the previous week and now at regular intervals streams carrying this water cascaded down the hillside by the roadside. Motoring along the desolate road that wound through the high ground she kept turning in her seat looking intently up at the hills. So much so that Denzil asked her what she was looking for. "I am hoping to see some stags so as to complete this Brigadoon landscape that we are passing through," she replied. Denzil laughed at the mental picture that conveyed but explained that in this good weather the deer kept to the very high tops and in summer were a rare sight. He told her that in winter it was a different matter and how he used to travel by mail bus through the snow cleared roads and hundreds of deer could be seen pawing the deep snow looking for grazing close to the roadside like a herd of cattle.

They passed through the barren high ground and started the slow descent down to lower levels that led to Ullamore. The road led through the area of forestry intermingled with white washed croft houses before travelling along the banks of the Inverdeen river as it led to the open sea at the head of the sea loch. Natalie spotted the blue waters of the sea loch and clutched Denzil's arm. Denzil thought to himself if she is impressed with that, wait until I round the bend and Ullamore comes into view. He would never forget his first sight of the village sheltering in the bay when he first came with Rory in the mail bus so many years ago. First of all Natalie spotted something and asked him to stop the car.

Down by the waterside perched on a rock covered in sea weed stood a large grey bird. Denzil explained that it was a heron and its habit was to perch motionless by the waterside as if on sentry duty waiting for small fish to swim close by. It would then spring into sudden action, plunging its sharp beak and impaling a fish. They basked in the warm sunshine leaning on the Morgan watching the bird and talking quietly. After some ten minutes or so the heron plunged its head into the water and watching its neck movement after it had straightened up they guessed it had been successful. Shortly after the heron launched itself slowly into lumbered flight and with heavy flapping of its large wings headed for the opposite side of the sea loch. Denzil could not help but smile as Natalie clapped her hands as if this had been some floor show put on specially for her. Back in the car, Denzil waited with some anticipation for her reaction when they rounded the bend and viewed Ullamore for the first time. He was not disappointed. Natalie uttered a squeal of delight. The village bathed in sunshine shimmered like an oasis in the desert. Boats littered the bay, the white washed houses reflected the bright sunshine and the back drop of high mountains and blue sea water presented an unforgettable sight. "My God," breathed Natalie almost to herself, "I've never seen anything so beautiful." Denzil although used by now after so many visits had to agree.

The red Morgan turned a few heads as they motored down the shore street now busy with tourists and headed for the pier head. Denzil saw that most of the old sheds had been demolished and workmen were at work on the foundations of the 'new' fishing centre. One old shed remained and clearly Rory was operating from there while work continued on the new development. As he pulled to a stop in the car park behind the remaining shed he spotted Rory in his working clothes and sea boots helping one of his staff load up a white van with orders. Rory turned at the sight of the new arrivals and Denzil took considerable delight at the amazed look on his face as they emerged from the Morgan.

Denzil introduced Natalie to his dumb founded friend. "Pleased to meet you," Rory mumbled, fast recovering his composure. "I won't shake hands otherwise you will be smelling of fish for the rest of the day."

Natalie smiled her understanding but looking around at the building work going on around her expressed curiosity.

"I am surprised your chauffeur didn't tell you all about it," complained Rory. "He's only supposed to be my business partner after all!"

Denzil explained that his visit to Ullamore was a last minute decision and that he didn't have time to advise Rory of their coming. Natalie spoke up asking where she could in her words, 'powder her nose' to freshen up after their car journey. Rory apologised for the lack of a toilet but suggested that she go into the Victoria Arms pub next door and use the facilities there. The two men sat in the sunbathed yard after she left.

"Dez, you never seem to amaze me," declared Rory. "Where on earth did you pull that beauty from, not to mention the transport?

By the time Denzil had explained the situation Natalie had rejoined them.

"Now that you are here," Rory said, "Come up to the office and I'll show you where we are up to on the plans."

Once in the office on a desk covered in drawings, Rory opened out the main plan and started to explain at what stage they were at. Natalie was engrossed in the detail and remarked to them that it was just as well that her father had not come with them as this construction work was just up his street. She was quite intrigued to learn that Denzil was one of the directors in the company as well. "Right oh," declared Rory putting the plan away finally. "Mid morning and all that, let's go and have a coffee with my old lady."

"He means his mother," Denzil informed Natalie seeing a puzzled look on her face.

They walked along Shore Street and then rounded the point where the hillside, dotted with crofts, faced the open sea.

Natalie turned to Rory. "Do you realise how lucky you are to live in a place like this?"

"Oh aye," returned Rory. "It's not always like this let me tell you. You should see it in winter when a Force 8 is blowing and you can't stand up!"

"Don't listen to him, Natalie," Denzil chipped in. " He is a born pessimist!"

As they approached the door of the croft Mrs McCulloch emerged fresh from baking, wiping her hands on her apron.

"Look what the wind blew in!" said Rory by way of introduction.

Mrs McCulloch smiled a welcome. "Dez, it's so nice to see you again. Is this your girl friend?"

Denzil gave her a welcoming hug before saying gravely, "Only for the day I am afraid."

That set them all off laughing. Later they all sat out in front of the croft, in the strong sunlight, drinking coffee and tucking into freshly baked pancakes while in front of them lay the vast panorama of sea and mountains. Natalie regaled Rory's mother with life in New York while Rory brought Denzil up to speed with how things were going in the business and the hopeful finish date of the development. He had changed the name of the company to Countryfare at the last minute because he had been approached by various estate owners who were keen to know if he could handle their venison and game products. This would hopefully open up a huge new potential market base for the business.

Mrs McCulloch wanted them to stay on for lunch but Denzil explained that they had taken a packed lunch and in any event he had to get back to town as he was due to be singing that night with the band.

"How is your band work going? I remember last time we met you mentioned you were due to get started. I have no doubt, knowing you, that you won't be doing it for free!"queried Rory.

Denzil assured him that it was turning out to be a very enjoyable experience and yes, he was being suitably reimbursed. Natalie was suitably intrigued.

"Singing with a band? You never spoke about that."

Rory laughed, "He is a bit of a dark horse, if you'll forgive the expression, with Dez you find out as you go along."

Once back in the yard as they prepared to leave, Rory went into the office and emerged announcing, " Right, just got a message from the Royal for four sides of smoked salmon, so you might as well earn your keep in the business for once and take it back with you, old boy!" The order, duly wrapped up, was placed in the boot of the Morgan by one of the girls on the staff and at last they were ready to go.

The car climbed out of the village and as they neared the bend in the road Natalie asked him to stop for a last lingering look at Ullamore bathed in the afternoon sunshine. As they got back in the car she gave a deep sigh before leaning over and kissing him, " Thanks so much for a wonderful day, Denzil. What a magical experience!"

"Where would Madam care to partake of lunch?" Denzil quipped in his best restaurant voice.

Natalie shrugged her shoulders. "I don't mind. How about heading for the high ground and finding a quiet spot where we can look over the hills as we dine."

"Your every wish is my command," replied Denzil as he gunned the Morgan into action.

When they reached the high ground they pulled the car up at a lengthy passing place. From this point a faint track led up the hillside barely discernible through the heather. They set off hand in hand, Natalie carrying a tartan rug from the car and Denzil the lunch basket with the bottle of wine in a plastic carrier bag. It was reasonably hard going with Natalie remarking that her designer ankle boots with medium high heels were not exactly the terrain the designer had in mind for them. They crested a rise and walked on until they were in small dip in the hillside unable to see their abandoned car or even the road for that matter but the views before them were staggering. While Natalie laid out the rug Denzil spotted a small stream some fifty yards away and declared that he would put the white wine into the cold mountain water to chill for a while. When he returned Natalie was standing admiring the view before her with the slight wind ruffling her hair. Denzil reached her and put his hand round her slim waist, she turned instinctively and they kissed.

Afterwards Denzil could not remember how long they stayed locked in this passionate embrace before they sank down on to the outspread tartan rug. She looked up at him with half closed eyes as he gently eased her blouse out of the waist band of her slacks and slowly and deliberately unbuttoned the garment. As the last button became undone her shapely breasts tumbled into view released from the rather tight confines of the blouse. He lowered his head and gently kissed her breast. He was aware of her cool fingers caressing the nape, of his neck before her hands tightened and drew him down on top of her as her slim demanding body arched into his.

Some considerable time later they lay side by side on their backs on the rumpled rug holding hands letting the warm afternoon shine play on their naked bodies. Words seemed unnecessary as they lay there with a cloudless canopy of blue sky above them. Suddenly Natalie stirred and raising a tanned arm pointed dramatically skywards exclaimed, "Denzil, what on earth is that?"

Denzil shaded his eyes from the bright sunlight and squinted at the sky until he saw a black dot far up in the sky circling and swooping in slow motion.

"That is a golden eagle my lovely, possibly scouring the heather below looking for his lunch."

Natalie excitedly raised herself on one arm with her dark eyes dancing. " A golden eagle eh? Well I may not have seen a stag but I'll willingly settle for your golden eagle. What a day I've had!"

Denzil smiled back. "Talking about lunch - when do we intend to dine?"

Natalie snuggled back into his arms remarking, "Plenty of time for that..".

Sometime later she released herself from his embrace and gave a short laugh as if to herself. Denzil stirred himself and looked down on her. "Penny for your thoughts."

Natalie looked up at him with her startling eyes, "Penny indeed! Worth a lot more than that I can tell you. Do you realise Denzil that in years to come when I am a little old lady in New York on my verandah in my rocking chair I am going to look back on this special memory, a memory of being made love to on a remote Scottish hillside on a sunny day with a bloody golden eagle playing peeping tom!" They laughed in unison at the thought and kissed again as a slight wind rustled the heather and in the distance came the muted piping sound of a nesting bird.

The wind developed a sharp edge as the afternoon wore on and reluctantly they rose to go, deciding to eat the lunch in the car on the way home. Once they were dressed Natalie shivered in her sheer blouse so Denzil wrapped the tartan rug around her and with the untouched lunch basket in hand they descended the hillside hand in hand. Once back in the Morgan they set off for home. Natalie opened the lunch basket and they enjoyed a mobile lunch as they sped along and she handed Denzil portions of food from time to time.

A sudden thought struck Denzil, "Hey Natalie, guess what? We've only left that bottle of wine cooling in that burn. What a waste!"

"Let's come back one day in the future and claim it. Make sure you remember the spot!" was her suggestion.

There was little need for talk on the return journey, they were just comfortable in each other's company. Natalie at one point rested her head on his shoulder until she dozed off. Denzil experienced a surge of real happiness as he drove eastwards with Natalie asleep resting on his shoulder and the faint fragrance from her hair teasing his nostrils. He drew the car up and at that Natalie stirred, sitting upright in the passenger seat.

Denzil turned to her, "I thought we would have supper here. You see tonight I have to do a stint with the band, so I won't have much chance to grab a bite to eat. How about it?"

Natalie brightened up at the suggestion in eager agreement. She looked round and saw that Denzil had parked outside a fish and chip restaurant called 'Ma Kennedy's Chipper.' Denzil explained that he would get two fish suppers which they could consume in the car in a quiet corner of the car park. He soon returned with two wrapped suppers. Natalie was impressed with this new to her dining experience. Denzil remarked as they ate that it was also good for business as Ma Kennedy's establishment was one of Rory's best customers.

As they finished their supper Natalie spoke up, "This stint you are doing with the band tonight, can I come along to watch?"

"Ok," Denzil responded. "But best to clear it with your parents in case they have other plans for the evening."

Once he had returned Natalie to the hotel, Denzil returned the Morgan to the garage. Back in his room he rested for a while before showering and dressing ready for his band performance. He met with Natalie and her parents in the hotel lounge enjoying a pre-dinner Martini.

"Hi there young man," boomed her father by way of greeting. "I understand you young guys had a great day over in the west and now Natalie is keen to see you exercise your vocal chords. Seems like a good idea to me!"

Denzil, making small talk in return, could not take his eyes off Natalie. She looked radiant in a lemon yellow dress set off with a matching yellow type bandana in her hair. As they said goodnight to her parents and moved towards the stairs which led to the ballroom, Denzil stopped in his tracks as if he had come to a decision.

"Look Natalie, you can't come into the ballroom dressed like a million dollars. I won't be with you so you will be pestered by every two bit Romeo wanting to dance with you. I'll get a walking stick from Lost Property department and you can make out you have a bad limp. That should solve this particular problem.

They both laughed as he put the plan into operation. The ballroom was packed as usual with a heaving mass of humanity, with the orchestra in good form. Natalie sat in the back of the raised area off the ballroom with a good view of the bandstand clutching her walking stick as Denzil had directed her. Then it was time for Denzil to take to the stage following Harry's introduction and build up. There was an almighty cheer to greet him and without much ado he launched into his opening number. By the time he was into his third song the dancers had stopped dancing and were simply massed in front of the bandstand like a theatre audience.

For his final song Denzil took the microphone thanking the dancers for being such a great audience. He continued,"I would now like to dedicate my final song to somebody very special and who is present here tonight." He turned to the band and signalled with his hand as the music started up. He sang a Billy Eckstine number that he had been keeping for a special occasion.

'We meet like passing strangers now,
How can you hurry by?
There was never two who loved,
Half as much as you and I.'

As he sang he was dimly aware of Natalie standing at the back with one hand raised clutching her throat still holding her walking stick in the other hand. He finished to a deafening applause from the assembled dancers. When he walked offstage the full orchestra swung into action as the dancing recommenced. He joined Natalie at the rear of the darkened ballroom when he could but both sensed that they were many eyes upon them and they had very little chance of privacy.

Denzil decided that the best way to get out of the public eye was to join the crowded dancers on the floor. Natalie was strangely subdued as they danced slowly before Denzil detected that she had tears in her eyes.

"Let's go somewhere we can talk," he said and led her off the dance floor and out of the ballroom.

Once in the car park with a cooling breeze coming as a relief after the heat of the ballroom they talked. Denzil held her in his arms as she dried her eyes with a tissue and he enquired gently, "What's up?"

Natalie smiled and gave him a playful punch to the body. "It's you!" she declared.

"What have I done?" protested an astonished Denzil.

Natalie answered, "Do you realise that in future every time I hear that song it's going to have a special meaning for me. Another thing you know I am leaving in the morning but do we have to part this way?"

"Well then, what do you suggest?" countered Denzil.

Natalie thought for a moment before replying, "How about if I go back to the hotel, check with my parents so they think that I am heading for bed and that will keep them happy. I know that they will be retiring early ready for our morning departure. Say about 11pm when everything is settled down you take a trip along to my room and we can spend a few more hours together?"

Denzil agreed eagerly to this course of action.

Natalie brightened up at this point, "My room number is 217. Don't forget it and keep quiet as my parents are in 216, so be sure and don't go tapping on the wrong room door!"

They both clung together and laughed at that prospect before Natalie slipped away into the hotel. Denzil, with time to kill, took a walk in the moonlight along the riverside giving the adrenalin rush that his singing always gave him time to subside. He then returned to his room bidding goodnight to Bert the night porter on his way.

At 11pm he took the lift ensuring that Bert was not about and headed down the carpeted corridor towards Room 217. Once there he tapped very gently on the door. Natalie must have been waiting by the door because the door suddenly opened her hand shot out grabbed his shirt collar and dragged him into the bedroom. He stumbled into the room and Natalie doubled up with laughter raised a finger to her mouth to stress silence. The room was in semi darkness lit by a small bedside lamp that had a small towel draped over it to dim the lighting even further. Denzil noticed over her shoulder as they kissed that the bed was invitingly turned down.

He said approvingly, "You seem to have thought of everything."

"I do my best," laughed Natalie in reply.

She moved towards the bed, slipping off the negligee that she had been wearing and naked, slipped into the bed. Denzil took his clothes off and joined her. Later locked in each other's arms they talked in whispers. She disclosed that she was due to go home not only to take up her first teaching post but to have her engagement announced. She had been going with Jerry, whom she had met in college, for some years. It wasn't exactly an arranged marriage but the two families moved in the same circles and somehow they had drifted into this situation. Jerry was steady and dependable if a bit boring, coming out as an accountant, and would give her a life style comparable to her parents so her future was pretty well set out before her. She asked Denzil what lay ahead for him. Denzil had never really thought that far ahead, saying that he would take whatever came his way and he was quite happy so far with what had befallen him.

They were talking in this manner when, all of a sudden, came a quiet knocking at the bedroom door. They both started up. They waited and then the knocking came again and Maria's unmistakable voice calling Natalie's name. Denzil was first out of the bed gathered his strewn clothes and slid under the bed. Natalie in a sleepy voice called out, "Coming" and after first ensuring that Denzil was out of sight headed over to open the door. Denzil lay there trying to suppress a laugh thinking back to when he had hidden under Norma's bed.

He heard Maria standing in the doorway speak to her daughter. "Natalie honey, sorry to disturb you but I left my blood pressure pills in your handbag the other day. I need them or else I'll never get to sleep and we have a long day ahead of us tomorrow."

Natalie rummaged in her handbag to find the pills. Slightly relieved Denzil relaxed and then it hit him. In his haste he had gathered his clothes before sliding under the bed but he was only clutching one shoe! He turned and saw the rogue shoe lying very visibly on the carpet well away from the bed. Hopefully Maria would not see it.

He heard Natalie pass over the pills to her mother and the two women bid each other an affectionate goodnight before the door was closed and locked again. Natalie slipped back into bed remarking that it had been a close call.

About 6am Denzil prepared to leave. They kissed for a final time with Natalie remarking, "I suppose this time it really is goodbye. Will you come and see us off in the morning? I promise to play it pretty cool."

"I'll be there," Denzil confirmed. "After all I did promise your parents I would be there."

Once more he tiptoed down the corridor and made for his own room. A couple of hours sleep and he was up and about ready to see the family on their way. The family having breakfasted and settled their account, met up with Denzil in the foyer. One of the porters had already left with their cases for the station ahead of them. They set off for the relatively short walk to the station. Natalie linked arms with Denzil and her mother and chattered away brightly as they walked down Hunter Street with Sam striding ahead of them. Once in the station it was time for farewell. Sam shook his hand thanking him yet again for having made their stay in Inverdeen so memorable before climbing aboard. Natalie gave him a quick peck on the cheek and squeezed his hand tightly before following her father. Maria was the last to say goodbye. She kissed Denzil on the cheek expressing her thanks as well. She turned to go away, then stopped for a moment before looking direct at Denzil once again. There was a moment's silence before she glanced down at his feet before remarking, "Oh Denzil, I am so glad you managed to find your other shoe!"

Denzil felt himself flush but Maria's face broke into a smile that creased the fine lines of experience around her eyes. He helped her aboard the train and the carriage door slammed. The shrill whistle blew and the train slowly edged out of the platform gaining speed. His last sight was of Natalie leaning out of the window waving furiously and blowing a kiss.

Chapter 23   The legacy

As he turned to leave the station platform Denzil experienced a strange sense of desolation. He shrugged it off and tried to reflect on just what a marvellous few days he had had in the company of this American family. He returned to the Royal and threw himself back into his work and learning some new numbers to run over with the band. Still this flat feeling persisted and in the end it began to prey on his mind.

It was not made any better a few weeks later on an overnight trip to Ullamore to see just how things were progressing on the business front when Rory's mother remarked to him over supper, 'Denzil, are you still in touch with that beautiful girl that you brought over to us, what was her name again?'

'Oh her, Natalie,' said Denzil. 'No, she was just a hotel guest who wanted a day out and anyway she was engaged to some guy back home.'

'Great pity,' remarked Mrs MacCulloch, 'The two of you went so well together.'

Denzil kept his head down making no reply.

He experienced a mild sense of anger when he thought that for Natalie it had obviously been just a holiday romance; something she could simply dismiss before returning to her American boyfriend and her old way of life.

They had left for three days in Paris before returning home and who was to say she would not have a similar fling there just to round off her European holiday. It left him so unsettled that one morning he woke and decided that he would dig out their New York address from reception records and drop her a line. He did that but when he went back to his room to compose a letter to her he ended up by tearing up the half completed letter. If she had wanted to keep contact she would have said so and any letter that he sent might be ignored particularly as she had been honest enough to tell him about her impending engagement. He realised that somehow this beautiful American girl with her quirky sense of humour had affected him deeply, perhaps more than he cared to admit to himself.

His singing spot with the band brought him several female admirers and he decided to take full advantage of this position. An ideal way he thought to put Natalie once and forever out of mind.

Martha was a cosmetic company representative who stayed in the Royal about three times a year in the course of her work. An attractive divorcee in her early thirties she ended up for dinner at his station. A mild flirtation seemed harmless at first but on her third visit she ended up attending the ballroom public dance on a Wednesday night. Denzil had just come off stage after his session when she accosted him in the dimly lit dance hall. They ended up dancing a slow number with her pressing herself close to him. One thing led to another and that night they slept together in her room.

In all he slept with Martha twice but something was missing, something he could not quite define. On her third visit he told her that he had become engaged to a local girl as an excuse and so the relationship foundered. Gradually he was able to get his life back on an even keel as time, as someone once said, is the great eraser. He resolved never again to let a girl affect him in the way that Natalie had done.

Perhaps, he thought to himself, the death of the old jeweller may have had a delayed effect on him as well. He had been such a long term resident in the Royal that many of the older staff regarded it almost as a family bereavement.

In October, as he crossed the foyer, Miss Armitage hailed him. 'Denzil, mail for you!' she said brandishing a long white envelope. It was unusual for any of his mail to go direct to reception. His first wild reaction was that perhaps Natalie had written to him. This was quickly dismissed when he saw that it was a very official looking letter that had been sent recorded delivery. He placed it in his inner pocket to look at later.

After lunch service as he dined in the now deserted restaurant with the other waiters he thumbed open the letter. To his surprise it was from a London firm of solicitors, Mayberry and Barrett. He read on. The legal firm were handling the winding up of the estate of one recently deceased Isaac Finkelstein. One of the partners, a Mr Dundas, was coming to Inverdeen in a week's time in order to deal with some outstanding matters. They requested that he make himself available, stating time and date, to see Mr Dundas and to bring some formal evidence of identification. Slightly puzzled he replaced the letter in his pocket.

The following day he wrote back confirming that he would make himself available as requested. Perhaps it might have something to do with the original purchase of Hetty's shop that had been done on his behalf.

Mr Dundas had booked the private use of a meeting room on the first floor. So that was there where he presented himself on the appointed day. Some chairs had been placed in the corridor outside the meeting room and sitting there was Mrs MacBeth, the hotel housekeeper.

'Well, Denzil, have you been summoned as well? Best take a chair as he is dealing with Mr Ron Murray who was Mr Finkelstein's local accountant. They should not be long I don't think.'

Denzil sat down beside her.

'I wonder what all this is about?' he said to her.

'Not too sure, but we'll will soon find out,' she replied.

They chatted for about a further ten minutes before the door opened. The two men came out still talking and shook hands before parting. Mr Dundas was a tall, thin individual in a dark business suit set off by a Lords cricket tie. He smiled and gestured for Mrs MacBeth to join him and the door was closed once again.

Left on his own Denzil waited patiently for his turn. It was not long before the door opened once more with the Housekeeper emerging looking slightly flushed and carrying an envelope in her hand. They had no opportunity to speak to each other as Dundas appeared with her and with a wave of his hand invited Denzil into the room.

He took a seat in front of the desk which was littered with documents. Dundas seated at the desk took a few minutes to tidy up some paperwork before addressing him.

'It is Mr Morrison I believe, Mr Denzil Morrison? Can we start off by you showing me some form of identification?'

Denzil reached into his pocket and produced his driving license and bank book. Dundas studied them carefully and noted on a pad details of the driving license. Seemingly satisfied he leaned back in his chair.

'As you no doubt know my firm is dealing with the estate of the late Mr Isaac Finkelstein. He was a relatively wealthy man and apart from making ample provision for his widow and a few personal bequests he left the bulk of his estate to Zionist causes in the new state of Israel. It was a cause very dear to him and I believe he was making enquiries about retiring to Tel Aviv at the time of his death. So that accounts for the disposal of his estate.'

He paused and Denzil moved in his chair thinking to himself well that's very interesting but what am I doing here. Dundas reached out and picked up a small folder and looked directly at Denzil. "Now we come to the legacy," he said. "I have to confess that I find this fascinating and one of the more unusual things to crop up in what is usually fairly straight forward probate work. Let me give you the background to the legacy as it will help you to understand the overall picture. It started way back in the mid nineteenth century in Russia. It was unsettled times and pogroms, that is organised massacres of the Jews were breaking out on a large scale. A young boy called Moshe Rachmann returned from school one day to find his family home burned to the ground and his parents and baby sister killed. An elderly bed ridden distant relative took the distraught youngster into his home. The situation did not improve so the elderly relative called Moshe to his bedside and presented him with virtually his life savings and begged him to leave the area and make a life for himself. Moshe took this advice and the money and ended up an immigrant in the Whitechapel area of London. It was a part of London where many such immigrants took refuge.

Moshe was fortunate to find work in a watch making firm run by a Jewish family. He worked hard and prospered, eventually taking over the business and adding jewellery to the business. He never forgot how lucky he had been to receive the elderly relative's life savings that had transformed his life. His resolve was that he would put that original windfall to good use. He struck upon the idea of forming a legacy that would in effect carry on the good work on a permanent basis. At the end of his working life he would pass on this legacy to someone deserving with the only proviso that they in turn would do the same. On his staff as an apprentice was Isaac Finkelstein who proved himself to be an excellent and trustworthy employee.

The business remained and is still to this day in the hands of the original family. So when the time came the legacy was passed to Isaac. This allowed him to look around for a suitable location to set up his own business and that is how he came to settle in Inverdeen. So that, Mr Morrison, brings you up to date. The legacy now passes to you – and has grown with inflation taken into account to a fairly substantial sum. £25,000 in fact!   Quite a fascinating story I am sure you will agree. Now I have here a cheque for that amount made out in your name and merely require your signature to acknowledge receipt of same.   There is also a sealed letter made out to you. Congratulations and I hope the legacy serves you well." Denzil with his mind in a daze scrawled his signature on the form and gathered up the two envelopes. He stood up, shook hands with Dundas across the desk and left the meeting room.

Once back in his room he opened the envelope and drew out the £25,000 Lloyds Bank cheque still disbelieving what had just taken place.   For sure it would take some time for the staggering amount of money to sink home.   He turned his attention finally to the sealed letter and broke it open. He noted that it was in Finkelstein's neat handwriting:

My dear Denzil,

I trust that this will come as a pleasant surprise to you. It has given me considerable pleasure to be able to pass on the legacy to you as I can think of nobody more deserving. Little did I think when I first saw you as a shy young boy of fourteen starting up on your first job that I would be writing to you along these lines. However you surprised me in the way that you matured into a fine young man well able to cope with whatever life throws at you.

There are no conditions attached to the legacy. All I ask is that you accept the legacy in the spirit intended and in due course pass it on to some deserving person who in turn will carry it on. I know you will do this. I hope you have a happy and healthy life and put the legacy to good use.

Very sincerely,

Your old friend

Isaac Finkelstein

Denzil read it through twice allowing the contents to sink home. He lay back in his bed, his mind full of mixed emotions. How he wished he had been able to talk with Jean about his good fortune. Eventually he got up, carefully putting the documents into his locker. The mental decision was made. This decision was to sleep on the matter and then, in the cold light of day, when the initial excitement had passed, to decide what exactly to do.

Two days later he turned his attention with his mind more or less made up. His first intention had been to post the cheque to Dominic to bank in his Edinburgh account but he had second thoughts. He would open up a Deposit account in his Inverdeen bank. It would remain there until he decided how to use it. He no longer banked on a weekly basis. Instead he still lived quite frugally, allowed his wages, tips and band income to accumulate before banking a fairly substantial sum at the end of each month. In mid October Jack Mitchell took ill with angina and was hospitalised for a week or so and Denzil took over as temporary Maitre d'. The upshot was that once he had emerged from hospital Jack listened to the entreaties of his family to take well earned retirement,

His leaving was a major event after his long and valued service to the Royal. Hotel guests, along with the owners and staff of the Royal contributed to his parting gift of a Mediterranean cruise for both himself and his wife. Denzil was asked to continue holding the fort until the position was advertised for a new Maitre d'. Naturally for the next couple of weeks the restaurant staff could talk of little else other than who the next person would be to fill this important post. One morning in early November as the restaurant staff were preparing for lunch service Peter Smart informed everybody that he had heard Miss Armitage talk that an appointment had been settled. Calum the head porter suddenly appeared to ask Denzil to report to the General Manager's office. The waiters naturally were in a high state of excitement.

"Hey Dez "- said Marcus "On you go and see who they have selected."

Denzil ended up in the office where both the General Manager and Miss Maclean confronted him. Mr Cochrane opened up proceedings – "Denzil- we would like to thank you for holding the fort during Mr Mitchell's time in hospital and also since his unexpected retirement. It was much appreciated and we both feel more than comfident in the manner that you handled it." Denzil noted that Miss Maclean sitting beside Mr Cochrane had a quiet smile on her face.

Cochrane continued, "I think that what impressed us both was not only the way you ran things but also the way in which the rest of the waiters accepted you. You are young in years but have a natural leadership quality. My service career, if it did little else, taught me to recognise this quality. After some considerable thought we have decided to promote you to the position of Maitre D' of the Royal Hotel. Congratulations. I have to leave now for another engagement so Miss Maclean will go over the fine points of your promotion. Once again, congratulations and I have every confidence in you."

Once they were on their own Miss Maclean spoke, "Denzil, I would like to add my congratulations on your appointment. As the General Manager was talking just now, my mind flitted back to the morning so many years ago when I first interviewed you for the boots job. Just where do the years go? It was quite a thought to give this senior position to one so young, but I have to say, you deserve it. Times are changing and as a young man you will hopefully bring your own stamp to the post. Now there are some practical aspects to be put into action. You will take up my old room in the main hotel as we cannot have a Head of Department living in the general staff quarters. That has been arranged. Your new post will mean you can no longer continue singing with the ballroom band. How do you feel about that?"

Denzil felt in much the same dazed way as when he learned of the legacy but managed to respond, "I can quite appreciate that as it would affect my restaurant duties. Can I also say that I feel very honoured to be selected and will do my very best to maintain Mr Mitchell's high standards."

"Excellent, that's the reaction I expected from you," said Miss Maclean. "However I have not quite finished on the musical front. You will know that in the restaurant we have a small inbuilt stage where the grand piano sits. Now Mr Mitchell was very much of the old school preferring a quiet restaurant. Times however are changing. We had decided some time ago that whenever Mr Mitchell retired we would take a fresh look at that situation. That time is now in my opinion. We intend to hire a trio to play for a couple of hours each evening in the Restaurant, mainly soft background music to give it a sort of night club effect. We feel that if you use your vocal talents from time to time, it would enhance the reputation of the restaurant. After all you established your reputation in the ballroom as the singing waiter I believe, so this will be taking that to a different level. I can imagine a couple coming for say a wedding anniversary and the husband requests you sing her special song to surprise her. We can talk further on this in the week ahead."

They moved on to other matters before Denzil, with his head in the clouds, returned to the restaurant.

The waiters were waiting expectantly while even Paddy, knowing something was afoot, found an excuse to be there as well.

Denzil went straight to the head waiter's desk to look at some papers without engaging with them deliberately.

"Dez, what happened? Who have we got? Did they tell you? asked Marcus.

Denzil faced them, "Oh yes, they have certainly picked somebody alright."

He gave a stiff formal bow in their direction.

"A most deserving person in my humble opinion – yours truly!"

There was a moment of silence as they digested this news, then whoops of excitement as they crowded around him with their congratulations while Paddy shook his hand warmly before shooting off to set the hotel grapevine into action.

Peter Smart was one of the last to shake his hand saying, "Well, better the devil you know. What do we call you now you are in your elevated position? We can't call you Dez; it wouldn't be right."

"How about Mr Dez?" suggested another waiter and that was agreed upon.

Denzil spent the rest of the day receiving congratulations from other departments. Clearly his promotion to this senior position had brought a breath of fresh air and interest into the hotel operation.

That afternoon, as he moved his belongings into the more luxurious surroundings of the first floor bedroom with its en suite bathroom, he had time to reflect on fast moving events.

The legacy nestling in his new account quickly followed by his promotion would take some getting used to, but one thing he thought grimly it might dispel once and forever the memory of Natalie.

Two days later Rory rang him to say that work on the fishing HQ was over and Dominic was arranging for a formal opening early in January. On all fronts things were happening!

CHAPTER 24   Royal Maitre D' Hotel

The next day the 10th November, the very first day he assumed his duties as the new Maitre d' of the Royal happened to be his 23rd birthday. He dressed carefully in the relative luxury of his new bedroom. His first port of call was to meet up with Chef Bonnacorsi who greeted him with a firm handshake before they got down to business. Brian MacGlennon who was now his sous chef joined in the welcome. As their meeting broke up Bonnacorsi pointed jokingly at his sous chef remarking "I suppose when my time comes to stand down - he'll take over from me. God help the old Royal when you two will be running things!" On his way to the restaurant to collect the up to date guest list he spotted a young commis loitering at the restaurant door way. He darted back in as Denzil headed in his direction. It was evident that he had been posted as a lookout so Denzil was half prepared for something to happen.

The waiting staff were assembled like a choir on the stage now cleared of the grand piano. Marcus stood in front of the waiting staff like a conductor. As Denzil came into view he raised his arm and the would be choir broke into song. They had adapted a popular song derived from the popular musical "Oklahoma" that was currently taking London by storm.

'Oh what a beautiful morning!
Oh what a beautiful day.
We've got a brand new maitre d'
everything's going our way!'

As the rough and ready chorus ended Denzil spoke, "Thanks for the welcome, but clearly none of you should consider giving up your day job!"

Then it was down to work. The waiting staff were excited about the new musical slant that was shortly going to be introduced into the restaurant operation although one or two of the older waiters had some reservation. Miss MacLean appeared to see him settled into his new post on his first day not forgetting to wish him happy birthday as usual. She was already organising things on the musical side. In fact by the end of the week a trio of experienced musicians had signed a contract to supply music in the restaurant five nights a week. The trio would play each evening Tuesday to Saturday nights inclusive from 8pm to 10pm. The restaurant opened each evening from 6.30pm to 10.00pm. After discussion it was decided that the restaurant would operate as normal until 8.00pm and then at this point the main lights would be dimmed and an attractive lantern containing a candle be placed on each table. This would give a very cosy and intimate ambience for later diners.

Marcus was delighted to be invited by Denzil to be his deputy with the older man providing a good counter balance to the restaurant team. The band soon settled into their new routine. Denzil discussed with them on the importance of playing music at a volume that did not drown out customer conversation. The first week although he practised vocals with them after the restaurant closed he did not sing. His non appearance with the ballroom orchestra did not go unnoticed and Harry Beach was quite put out that something he had put into place with considerable success had been cut off in mid stream. He complained loudly to Miss MacLean but it got him nowhere.

The following week a couple who had dined at his station on many occasions booked a table to celebrate their wedding anniversary. The husband called into see Denzil to ask if he would surprise his wife by singing one of their favourite songs. They had honeymooned many years ago in Italy and had been attracted by an old Italian love song that the hotel band played. This was a new venture for Denzil as he had never sung in Italian before but he rose to the challenge and fortunately one of the trio knew of the song. On the night in question the restaurant was packed so he waited until all the tables were served. He climbed onto the bandstand as the band were coming to the end of a selection from the American songbook He was aware that this was breaking new ground and it was important to pull it off. He nodded to the trio as they started to play. He concentrated on memorising the Italian words of the song and this dispelled any nervousness that he might have felt. After the first two lines he was aware that all conversation in the restaurant had ceased and chairs were being turned round to face the bandstand. He moved from side to side with slow steps he had perfected in the ballroom sessions.

Across the crowded room he concentrated his gaze on the couple who had requested the number. They appeared to be holding hands listening intently to him singing. When he finished there was considerable applause that went on for quite a while with Denzil noticing that even the waiting staff were applauding as well. Satisfied that he had pulled it off he picked up a small bouquet of flowers that he had left on the stage. Winding his way through the tables he made his way to the couple's table to surprise the wife with the bouquet. She jumped to her feet at his arrival and kissed him on both cheeks as she accepted the flowers. There were some quiet calls for an encore from some tables but Denzil smilingly ignored them.

It had clearly gone way beyond his expectations and the compliments he got as guests departed simply underlined this. As the celebrating couple were leaving, the husband pulled Denzil aside, "That was wonderful. To think we are the first guests to be serenaded. Well I'm sure we won't be the last. I think you have started something quite big in Inverdeen. Just can't wait to tell our friends at the Golf Club." He handed Denzil a £5 note by way of thanks.

Later as the staff tidied up the restaurant there was much excited talk about the way the evening had gone. The couple had already left a tip for their station waiter who had put it into the tronc as was the custom. Denzil then produced the £5 note, letting them see him putting the extra money into the tronc as well. The waiting staff realised that not only would the increased business benefit the hotel but it would mean increased earnings for them as well. By early December the trio had become an accepted part of the restaurant service. Table bookings came in with song requests slowly but surely as the word spread and Miss MacLean was delighted with the way everything had gone. It got to the stage that people locally found they had to book a week or so in advance for the most popular Friday and Saturday nights.

On a Tuesday night in early December Denzil was on duty as usual on a rather busy night. He had one song to sing that evening from an elderly local couple who were celebrating their Golden Wedding with a quiet intimate dinner paid for by their son working in Australia. He had left the choice of music to Denzil who decided to sing the Jimmy Young hit song, 'Too Young." It went off perfectly and after he presented the bouquet of flowers to the astonished couple the whole restaurant stood up and applauded. The feel good atmosphere in the restaurant as it settled down after this floor show had to be experienced to understand it.

Denzil went back to his tall desk at the entrance. The tall desk had been in the restaurant probably since the hotel came into operation. It was made of elaborately carved dark wood with a sloping top that held the paper work consisting of that day's hotel guest list and room table chart to allow the maitre d' to operate the room efficiently. Below the ledge was a receptacle that held the supply of leather bound red menus with the Royal Hotel picked out in gold lettering. He was checking the paper work while at the same time saying goodbye to departing guests. The restaurant was ticking over nicely with every station well under control so he had time to relax to a certain extent. A Mr and Mrs Thorpe a wealthy retired couple from Poole in Dorset who frequently stayed at the Royal had finished their dinner and rose up to leave their table. They approached Denzil smiling broadly and Mrs Thorpe caught Denzil by the arm in an affectionate manner. "Denzil" she exclaimed " You have kept your talents well hidden away, that was absolutely marvellous, your singing and the wonderful reaction of that couple!"

They stood talking for a few minutes before Denzil sensed that a party was waiting behind him to come in for dinner. Mr Thorpe seeing that another party was waiting to be attended to, shook hands with him warmly before they departed. Denzil reached out for a couple of menus before turning to greet the party waiting for his attention. He turned and stopped dead in his tracks.

Natalie! Natalie stood before him smiling at his shocked reaction.

Denzil's first thought was that he was dreaming as he shook his head as if to clear it. She stood in a pink cocktail dress styled in such a way that it had an oriental look to it. Her hair was differently styled as well, no longer hanging loose but piled high on her head that only served to convey the eastern effect. He took all this in as he stood speechless before her. Natalie, her dark eyes shining clearly relishing the effect her entrance had made was first to speak-

Is there any chance of a table for a passing stranger?" she said. Denzil still stood transfixed trying to take in the vision of this beautiful woman standing smiling at him. At last he managed to speak, "Natalie. What ... what are you doing here?"

"Well, a table for dinner would be a good start. Perhaps we can have a chat after dinner? He managed at last to regain his composure somewhat, " Yes of course " In an attempt to lighten the moment he adopted an affected voice, "Would Madam care to accompany me?" He led their way down through the restaurant very conscious of the heads turned in their direction openly admiring Natalie as she walked beside him. He took her to Peter's station pulling out her chair so she could be seated. Peter approached smiling remembering her from the original visit earlier in the year. "Good evening Madam - so nice to see you back with us again" was his greeting. Denzil handed the menu to Peter, hearing her reply, "What a lovely welcome. Thank you so much" He left her in

Peter's care as he returned to his desk to gather his thoughts. His mind was in a turmoil. Why was she here? Were her parents with her? Maybe she was here with her fiancé. Perhaps she was even over here on honeymoon?

A sudden thought struck him and he checked the resident's list. In his confusion on seeing her he had forgotten to check her room number but Peter would have made a note of this on her restaurant order. He made for the kitchen and sure enough Peter had spiked her order on the board for the kitchen's attention. Room 217 - well that number certainly rang a bell! Back at his desk he checked the list and against Room 217 it read, Miss Stranger! Her sense of humour brought a wry smile to his face but it did not answer any of the questions running around in his mind. To play it cool he decided to let her have her meal in peace. He moved around the room speaking to several tables as normal but managed to avoid even making eye contact with Natalie.

Paddy was waiting for him at the desk clearly wanting to speak to him. "Dez - Will you do a poor Irishman a big favour? I intended to speak to you earlier but the bar was as busy as a fiddler's fair. You see that table over there? Well my in-laws are over here for the first time from Donegal, so I arranged for my wife to take them out to dinner tonight. Any chance of singing an Irish song for them on my behalf? I would be forever grateful." It struck Denzil that singing might just settle himself down instead of just standing here with his mind full of jumbled thoughts. "Delighted, Paddy" he said "What song do you think might be suitable?" Paddy clutched his arm "Sure I'll leave that up to you Dez, I'm only too grateful my friend and can't wait to see the look on their faces."

"How about' Lake Isle of Innisfree' – I know the words to that one." Paddy replied.

Spot on! Great choice and now I had better get back to the bar." Once on the stage Denzil had a quiet word with the trio. Taking the mike he identified the table occupied by Paddy's wife and her parents. "Ladies and gentlemen" he announced

"Tonight we welcome a party of guests from across the Irish Sea. I have no intention of making you homesick but here is a song that has been requested for you by you know who. Enjoy your stay In Inverdeen and the Royal."

He sang the song to a hushed dining room, making sure he faced well away from Natalie's table. After he had finished he made his way through the applause to talk to the Irish party. By this time he was in charge of his scattered thoughts. He noted that Natalie was just completing her main course so he decided on a course of action. Beckoning to Marcus, they met in the middle of the dining room, "Look Marcus, I am going to go off duty in a few minutes, got a migraine coming on. Can you shut up shop for me tonight?" Marcus gave a laugh "No problem. Just you head off, hope your migraine improves. I have to say it is the most beautiful migraine I have ever seen!" Marcus like any good waiter lets nothing much pass him by. Peter came up to announce that the young lady had declined dessert or coffee and was ready to leave the restaurant. Denzil waited just outside and as she left he fell into step beside her. Natalie smiled at him as they crossed the foyer heading for the lift without speaking,

Once inside the lift her composure crumbled. She suddenly turned towards him, wrapping her arms around him and burying her face in his chest exclaiming "Oh Denzil." Equally taken aback he embraced her in turn sinking his face and inhaling the fresh scented perfume of her hair. They stood locked like this for some time. A discreet cough brought them back to life. The lift had reached the second floor, the door had opened and a middle-aged American husband and wife waiting to enter stood there clearly enjoying the sight of the entwined young couple.

Denzil took Natalie's hand, leaving the lift with an apology to the waiting guests "No problem" drawled the husband "One thing we like about the old Royal is the warm welcome it always extends to its guests!" Alone in the corridor they looked at each other for a moment. Natalie said, "We have so much to talk about. How about my room?"

"OK by me " said Denzil "but look I'd be happier out of this monkey suit, I'd be a bit more relaxed. I have a room now on the first floor so I won't be long."

"So you have a room on the first floor now. My, we have certainly come up in the world!" Natalie commented. She stood on tip toe, giving him a quick kiss before they headed for the respective rooms. It took Denzil about ten minutes to shower and change into his casual clothes before heading for Room 217. The door was slightly ajar so he pushed it open, closing the door behind him. The room was dimly lit with a small bedside lamp providing the only illumination. The room was empty but the en suite bathroom door was half open and he could hear Natalie moving about in there, "Anybody at home?" he called out.

"Well hi there!" Natalie answered "Just cleaning my teeth be with you in a minute. I managed to get Room service to serve up some refreshment." He observed close by the bedside table a wine cooler on a stand with the neck of a champagne bottle protruding and a white napkin draped across it. He picked up the champagne bottle. A bottle of expensive Veuve Cliquot he noted - clearly this girl had been well brought up! He sat on the edge of the bed but did not have long to wait. Natalie dressed in a flimsy negligee emerged. For a moment she stood framed against the bright light of the bathroom with one hand brushing her hair that now cascaded round her shoulders. It was a sight that made Denzil catch his breath. Natalie crossed over and sat beside him on the bed. She nodded in the direction of the wine stand - " Would you like to do the honours?" Denzil picked up the champagne along with the napkin remarking "Certainly Madam - your every wish is my command!" Natalie giggled and nudged him in the side. He expertly used the napkin to stifle removing the cork, pouring out two generous glasses. As he stood up to do this he was aware of Natalie disrobing and slipping her naked body into the bed. She propped a pillow behind her, sitting up with the coverlet pulled and her hand extended to receive her champagne glass. Denzil resumed sitting on the bed. He turned to face her and they formally clinked their glasses before saying almost in unison ,"Here's to passing strangers!" This set them off both laughing so that she spilled some of her drink. They drank some champagne before Denzil grabbed her free hand and said " Now young lady you have a lot of explaining to do."

Natalie pulled a face commenting, " Well it's a bit of a long story but you asked for it! When we left Scotland for our three days in Paris everything seemed to be fine. It was when we got back to New York and things settled down that if hit home. I felt so unsettled and hoped that you would write and make contact." Denzil burst out - "What me make contact? You were the one who told me you were going home to get engaged to Jerry - what's his face. I did try to write to you but felt I had no real right to butt into your life." Natalie laughed "What are we like? Weeks passed and I told Jerry that marriage for us was not an option. Gentleman to the end he said he would give me some space and hoped that I would think again. Mama was pretty cool about that with me for some months, I can tell you. I enjoyed my teaching post but on a personal front I was pretty down not sure what to do. It came to a head just last week. Mama had gone off with some of her girl friends for a health spa weekend. Dad and I were having supper when he mentioned our Scottish holiday. I guess I got a bit emotional, anyway Dad hugged me and comforted me. Unable to get a direct answer from me he eventually said in a quiet voice 'It's Scotland isn't it? Strangely enough he never mentioned your name and I just nodded.

I suppose stupidly I told him I didn't know quite what to do. He then told me to go and follow my heart or I would have to live the rest of my life with regrets. He said that next morning he would get his personal assistant in his office to book a flight and accommodation at the Royal hotel. It will be a return ticket he added but go back and sort things out once and for all. If the situation has changed for whatever reason, then simply pack up and return home and no harm done. Don't worry he assured me I will square things with your mother when she returns. So there and then it was settled. I asked him to bring Room 217 in the name of Stranger as I wanted to take you by surprise - and I sure did! The day after I picked up the airline ticket from his office. He drove me to the airport and his final gesture was to stick 1000 dollars in my handbag. As I kissed him goodbye at the departure desk he joked about looking forward to seeing me in a weeks time. So there you have it, that's my sorry tale."

Denzil sipped his champagne as a sense of general relief flooded over him and all the questions disappeared." We'll talk further tomorrow" he said "I think I've had quite enough tension for one day." He slipped out of his clothes and joined her in the bed." Hey" said Natalie holding out her empty champagne glass "The service is falling down here."

"Later" said Denzil. Natalie half protesting surrendered her glass, "but the champagne will only go flat."

"I am sure we will get used to flat champagne in time" said Denzil gathering her into his arms.

CHAPTER 25   Natalie

Next morning they woke early but lay in bed talking for some time. Their future was clearly going to take some organising. Natalie was going to see her hotel booking out for the week before looking for somewhere to rent, along with looking for a suitable job. Denzil explained that he could not take time off from the hotel as business was stepping up as the festive season drew near. However, this coming Friday was his day off so he proposed a trip to Ullamore and Natalie jumped at the chance.

Denzil was concerned as to how she would pass the time during the day while he was tied up with hotel business. No problem, declared Natalie in her forthright fashion, I will hire a car along with a pack lunch and explore the surrounding area. Next day Denzil contacted Donnie Cameron and managed to wheedle the use of the Morgan out of him for the rest of the week. His other concern was where Natalie would stay after her hotel room booking expired, as the hotel was fully booked for the entire festive season. The gods were smiling on him. He spoke on the subject of letting flats to Paddy who he knew was dabbling in the local property market. Paddy was only too happy to return a favour. He had acquired a run down property on the riverside in a good area and refurbished it into an upmarket two-bedroomed flat. He was only too happy to let Natalie have it free of charge until such time as it took her to find a suitable flat to rent. His intention was to market the flat in the springtime to recoup his outlay.

They both viewed the flat one afternoon with Natalie thrilled with it combined with the superb river view. On their walk back to the hotel she said wistfully that it would have been ideal if they were able to get it for themselves. Denzil was quiet for a moment as they walked hand in hand.

"How about if I see Paddy and strike a deal to buy the property", he suggested. Immediately Natalie was enthusiastic declaring that she would even contemplate getting a loan from her father to fund the project. Denzil told her that there was no need for such extreme action as they could manage it out of their own resources. Natalie drew back for a moment and asked him directly how he could afford it, but Denzil told her just to leave it to him to organise things.

Paddy was delighted, not only to realise such a quick sale but to also help the young couple into their first home. They moved their belongings almost straight away into the flat. In the process Denzil unearthed, from under his bed, the fire scorched locked metal box that Mrs Munro had handed over to him as the only item that had survived the cottage fire that had claimed Jean's life.

"What on earth is that relic?" laughed Natalie when she saw it.

Denzil explained its history and said that somehow he had never wanted to open it and simply put it to one side giving it no more thought.

"One day, Denzil", promised Natalie, "I will get you to find somebody to force it open so you can confront your past".

So on a cold wintry Friday morning they set off for Ullamore. It was quite a change from the beautiful summery day they had experienced earlier in the year. Natalie had bought some suitable outdoor clothing and fashionably styled Wellington boots. On the journey they talked about how amazing that things had seemed to fall into place for them along with plans for the future. When they reached the high ground with its covering of snow Natalie suddenly grasped his hand. "Denzil - let's stop and go up Blueberry Hill once more!" For a moment he was unsure of what she was driving at and then the penny dropped. In the summertime, as they walked through the ankle deep heather, Natalie had stooped to look closely at some dark blue berries growing amidst the purpling heather. She asked what they were. Denzil told her that they were blaeberries that game birds such as grouse fed on. There then followed a lively discussion as to whether they were of the same genus as American blueberries.

This time they stopped the Morgan, donned their winter footwear then trudged hand in hand up and over the rise. Before them soared the snow clad hills in all their majesty. Denzil pointed out a herd of stags on a nearby ridge pawing at the deep snow in an attempt to find some edible grass. "Let's see if our wine is still chilling", he said.

He led the way to the bank of the slow flowing burn now encrusted with ice. No sign of their bottle of Liebfraumilch, no doubt carried away by the force of some autumnal spate. Walking back they stopped once more and embraced at the spot where they had lunched on that eventful summer's day.

Denzil made a quick decision, realising that this place would always hold a special memory for them. It was where they had first declared their love for one another. Looking at Natalie he said, "I guess you must miss your parents, not saying goodbye properly to them and all that. Do you think they might come over to attend a wedding someday?"

"Is that your idea of a subtle proposal?" countered a laughing Natalie.

"I suppose that was my general drift" he responded.

"What a romantic old thing you are turning out to be, and what an ideal place to pick!" Natalie replied closing into his waiting arms. They carried on to Ullamore in high spirits. Soon the village nestling by the sea came into view. Even in its wintry setting it retained a certain charm with boats docked at the pier-head rocking in the choppy waters. A great welcome awaited them as usual at the MacCulloch croft. Rory's mother greeted Natalie with a big hug declaring to one and all that she knew she would be coming back to see them.

Rory had laid on lunch in the local pub and a bottle of Pol Roger champagne draped in a white serviette crowned the table. Denzil said to Rory that he must have the second sight before telling the group about their very recent engagement. The champagne was uncorked and fitting toasts proposed to the young couple. After lunch Rory took them round the impressive new fishing headquarters that was now virtually complete, ready for the official opening in late January. "Not a moment too soon", commented Rory as business was flooding in while a fleet of six vans now radiated out daily to cover the surrounding area, including Inverdeen and other townships further afield. Before long he added, "we will probably outgrow this set-up".

It was then down to the pier and into the trusty 'Sea Mist' before heading out into the sea loch. A sharp wind with flurries of snow was in evidence with Natalie, her cheeks glowing, loving every minute of the trip. On the way down the sea loch Rory and Denzil pointed out the different species of wild life that frequented the waters. They stopped at a cove dotted with another fisherman's buoys explaining to Natalie just how they used to haul aboard the lobster creels.

Later they landed on a small, uninhabited island to stretch their legs until dark. Billowing clouds told Rory that they should head for home. They returned to harbour in late afternoon as darkness was settling in and, all too soon, it was time to head for home. Denzil drove back in the darkness with a contented Natalie, tired after her days outing, sleeping with her head resting on his shoulder. He stopped the car at Inchroy so that they could eat. Natalie had no particular wish to dine alone in the hotel restaurant so Denzil decided on a special treat. He bought two fish and chip suppers so they could pull into a lay-by and enjoy them. So ended a memorable day. Next day, Saturday, Denzil was back on duty, but he had planned a special surprise in the restaurant that night. Natalie had taken the Morgan for a final trip out country so he did not see her until she came down to dine that evening. Once again she was dressed in a simple silver cocktail dress that showed her tanned skin off to perfection. Her hair was elegantly styled with an attractive silver brooch of Mexican design as a finishing touch. As he watched her approach Denzil felt a surge of love and pride that this beautiful girl would one day be his wife. He met her with menu in hand and said unsmilingly, "I am sorry Madam, but you can't come in here!"

"Why ever not?" was her reply.

"Because Madam, you are too beautiful and we fear you will give some of our elderly male guests a heart attack!"

"Drop dead!" Natalie laughed brushing past him.

He had two singing spots that evening. He had completed one just before Natalie appeared while the other one was due in fifteen minutes. It was yet another wedding anniversary celebration, a ruby wedding for a local doctor and his wife. The wife had selected a Frank Sinatra classic, 'Fly Me to the Moon'. Denzil always enjoyed doing a Sinatra number having spent many sessions back in Aldershot with 'The Mellowtones' perfecting Sinatra's highly unique phrasing and delivery of a song.

When he had finished the number there was that wonderful moment of silence as if the audience wanted the magic of the moment not to end. It was broken by an Australian guest calling out, "Good on you mate!" The applause followed like a wave of sound. He did his customary walk through the tables of diners to present the bouquet of flowers to the table that had requested the song. Walking back on to the stage he took hold of the mike:

"Ladies and gentlemen, thank-you for being such a wonderful audience, I have something special to tell you, yesterday I got engaged to a very beautiful girl, well, I think I did, but we are saving up for the ring."

He was forced to stop as the diners burst out laughing and applauding again.

Denzil held his hand up to get some measure of silence before continuing, "So tonight I want to dedicate this song to her, to Natalie, she will know just what it means to us both".

"I found my thrill
On Blaeberry Hill
On Blaeberry Hill
When I found you.
The moon stood still

On Blaeberry Hill
It lingered until
My dreams came true
The wind in the willows played
Love's sweet melody.......

As he sang he observed Peter approach Natalie with a huge bouquet of flowers that he had organized. The song ended with all the diners up on their feet clapping wildly. Natalie stood up clutching her champagne glass in salute.

Later that night as they unwound over a more than welcome refreshing cup of tea, Denzil came to another decision. He told Natalie about his true financial position in every detail. About his early struggles and how he kept to the plan laid by Mr Finklestein, then the lucky breaks that came his way culminating in obtaining the substantial legacy. He was conscious as he unburdened himself that Natalie would be the only person apart from himself who would know the full facts. Dominic of course knew most of it but as a trusted advisor would never disclose the matter. Rory may have guessed at the most part of it but could be depended upon for his discretion.

Denzil finished by saying how important it was to him for his financial position to remain a closed book. Natalie had listened to him curled up on top of the bed with her untouched cup of tea gone cold, quite fascinated as the story unfolded.

Once Denzil had quite finished, she rose up, crossed the floor and kissed him tenderly. "Wow that is quite a tale! I did wonder when you purchased the flat without recourse to a mortgage just what the full picture might be but I figured that you would tell me in your own good time. What are your future plans or should I say, what are our future plans?"

Denzil shrugged his shoulders, "Who knows my darling? But let us go on as we are at the moment and cross that bridge when we come to it." They embraced with Natalie commenting, "Now you have told me all your dark secrets, let me tell you one of mine. In a few years time I come into a substantial Trust Fund set up by my father. I did not tell you before as I suspected you might be some sort of gold digger. "

They laughed in unison. "Gold digger?" mused Denzil, "Whatever gave you that idea?"

Epilogue

Early the next week Sam Hilton, cigar held in his huge fist, was chairing a weekly board meeting in his plush oak-panelled New York head office boardroom

A quiet knock was heard at the door before a secretary glided in across the heavily carpeted floor bearing an airmail letter on a silver salver. The other directors looked on slightly astonished as it was a golden rule that a boardroom meeting in session was never to be disturbed.

Placing the salver before the chairmen the secretary quietly said, "I think sir that this was the letter you were waiting for," before silently retiring.

Sam held his hand up in mute apology to the onlooking directors before thumbing open the letter which read:

Dearest Papa,

This is in some haste. Everything has worked out so well I cannot even begin to tell you. I could not be happier! Thanks to you - will write more fully with all my news when my feet touch the ground. All my love to you both.

Nat XXXX.

Attached to the letter with a paperclip was her return ticket. Sam smiled deeply, folded the letter carefully before placing it in his inside jacket pocket.

He turned his attention to the waiting table saying, "Now Gentlemen, where were we?"

END OF BOOK ONE